作者 Eduwill 語學研究所　　　嘉珮／莊曼淳

NEW TOEIC

實戰新多益
高分必備

狠準五回1000題
黃金試題

MP3

寂天雲 APP

或登入官網下載音檔
www.icosmos.com.tw

試題本

系統化分析出題動向，
掌握新制多益最新趨勢

「中譯＋逐題詳解＋各題核心單字」，
快速理解題目內容，秒懂學習盲點

貼心標示各題答案提示句，
解題線索一看就懂，
迅速理解出題法則

附錄配有各回題庫核心字彙表，
系統性彙整核心字彙，
背誦效率加倍

作者 Eduwill 語學研究所　　譯者 黃詩韻／劉嘉珮／莊曼淳

NEW TOEIC

實戰新多益
高分必備

狠準五回1000題
黃金試題

MP3

寂天雲 APP

或登入官網下載音檔
www.icosmos.com.tw

解析版　　試題本

如何下載 MP3 音檔

❶ 寂天雲 APP 聆聽：掃描書上 QR Code 下載
「寂天雲 – 英日語學習隨身聽」APP。加入會員
後，用 APP 內建掃描器再次掃描書上 QR
Code，即可使用 APP 聆聽音檔。

❷ 官網下載音檔：請上「寂天閱讀網」
（www.icosmos.com.tw），註冊會員／登入後，
搜尋本書，進入本書頁面，點選「MP3 下載」
下載音檔，存於電腦等其他播放器聆聽使用。

實戰新多益高分必備

解析版 | 試題本 + 解析本

狠準五回1000題黃金試題

作　者	Eduwill 語學研究所
譯　者	黃詩韻／劉嘉珮／莊曼淳
編　輯	林明佑
校　對	郭輕安
主　編	丁宥暄
內文排版	林書玉／蔡怡柔
封面設計	林書玉
製程管理	洪巧玲
出 版 者	寂天文化事業股份有限公司
發 行 人	黃朝萍
電　話	+886-(0)2-2365-9739
傳　真	+886-(0)2-2365-9835
網　址	www.icosmos.com.tw
讀者服務	onlineservice@icosmos.com.tw
出版日期	2023 年 11 月 初版一刷

版權所有　請勿翻印

郵撥帳號 1998620-0 寂天文化事業股份有限公司

訂購金額未滿 1000 元，請外加運費 100 元。

〔若有破損，請寄回更換，謝謝。〕

國家圖書館出版品預行編目（CIP）資料

實戰新多益高分必備：狠準五回 1000 題黃金試題
【試題＋解析雙書裝】(寂天雲隨身聽 APP 版)/
Eduwill 語學研究所著；黃詩韻，劉嘉珮，莊曼淳譯 .
--
初版 . -- 臺北市：寂天文化事業股份有限公司，
2023.11
　面；　公分
ISBN 978-626-300-226-5(平裝)

1.CST: 多益測驗

805.1895　　　　　112017864

에듀윌 토익 실전 LC+RC

Copyright © 2022 by Eduwill Language Institute
All rights reserved.
Traditional Chinese Copyright © 2023 by Cosmos Culture Ltd.
This Traditional Chinese edition was published by arrangement with
Eduwill through Agency Liang

目錄

前言

　　多益是結構和類型都很明確的考試，因此只要具備一定的基礎，並且持續練習模擬試題，提高對題目的熟悉感，就能獲得高分。所以，盡可能多練習模擬試題並複習錯誤的題目，藉此補強弱點是相當重要的。

　　然而，在練習模擬試題時，比起題海戰術，更重要的是解決「好的問題」。考生需要**練習難度適中並且和考古題相近的題型**，才能正確診斷自己的程度和弱點，並依此建立學習計畫。

　　本書詳細分析近年考題的出題趨勢，並經過資深多益研究員和母語人士團隊的反覆研究，透過多次審查和各種程度的考生試測後，才研發出此本絕佳的模擬試題。因此，本書值得各位考生信賴，相信使用本書能讓你應考過程事半功倍。

　　本實戰題庫不僅提供良好的練習題，還特別著重於測驗後的檢討與複習。在解題之後，可以對照**聽力內容**和**中譯**，搭配**逐題詳解**，更能加深學習印象。此外，使用附錄中提供的**「核心字彙表」**，確實熟悉重要字彙與常用片語。即使起初測驗分數不如預期，只要充分利用這些內容，逐漸掌握不熟悉的字彙和片語，很快就能成功考取目標分數。

聽力 & 閱讀金選戰略

聽力

第一大題	照片描述 （6 題）	本大題是測驗**看圖作答**的能力，可藉由以下方式來練習：找一些照片來看，並思索針對這些照片，可能會問哪些問題。
第二大題	應答問題 （25 題）	本大題是測驗**對問句的理解**，作答時請特別注意**問句開頭的疑問詞**（Who、What、Where、When、Why、How 為六大疑問詞），可提示需要什麼樣的答案。
第三大題	簡短對話 （39 題）	本大題會先播放簡短的對話，再測驗你對於對話的理解程度。本大題訣竅是**先看問題、答案選項和圖表**，然後**再聽對話內容**，這樣你在聽的時候會比較知道要注意哪方面的資訊。
第四大題	獨白 （30 題）	本大題是聽力測驗中最具挑戰性的部分，平時就需要**多聽英文演講和廣播**等來加強聽力。

Look at the example item below. Now listen to the four statements.

(A) They're pointing at the monitor.
(B) They're looking at the document.
(C) They're talking on the phone.
(D) They're sitting by the table.

Statement (B), "They're looking at the document," is the best description of the picture, so you should select answer (B) and mark it on your answer sheet.

| Photographs I 第一大題：照片描述

第一大題

指示： 本大題的每一小題，在測驗本上都會印有一張圖片，考生會聽到針對照片所做的四段描述，然後選出最符合照片內容的適當描述，接著在答案卡上找到題目編號，將對應的答案選項圓圈塗黑。描述的內容不會印在測驗本上，而且只會播放一次。

（A）他們正指著螢幕。
（B）他們正在看文件。
（C）他們正在講電話。
（D）他們正坐在桌子旁。

描述 (B)「他們正在看文件」是最符合本圖的描述，因此你應該選擇選項 (B)，並在答案卡上劃記。

❶ 如照片以<u>人物</u>為主，人物的<u>動作特徵</u>是答題關鍵。

照片題中有 7–8 成的題目是以**人物**為照片主角，這些照片時常會測驗**人的動作特徵**，因此要先預想相關的動作用語。舉例來說，如照片中有一個人在走路，就要立刻想到和走路有關的動詞，如 walking、strolling 等，聽題目的時候會更容易抓到線索。

❷ 如照片以<u>事物</u>為主，事物的<u>狀態或位置</u>是答題關鍵。

如照片以事物為中心，要特別注意其**狀態或位置**。須預先熟習表示「位置」時常用的介系詞，還有表現「狀態」的片語。舉例來説，如要表達「在……旁邊」時，next to、by、beside、near 等用語可能會出現，最好一起背誦。另外，也須**事先熟悉多益中常出現的事物名稱**。

❸ 出人意料的問題時常出現。

與一般題型不同，題目的考點可能會靈活變化。舉例來説，照片是一個小孩用手指著掛在牆上的畫，按照常理，會想到是要考人物的動作，要回答 pointing 之類的動詞。但有時正確答案會是掛在牆上的畫（The picture has been hung on the wall.）。所以出現人的照片時，除了注意**人的動作**，**周邊事物**也必須稍微觀察。

II **Response** 第二大題：應答問題

第二大題

指示：考生會聽到一個問題句或敘述句，以及三句回應的英語。題目只會播放一次，而且不會印在測驗本上。請選出最符合擺放內容的答案，在答案卡上將 (A)、(B)、(C) 或 (D) 的答案選項塗黑。

高分戰略

❶ 新制加考<u>推測語意</u>的考題。

Part 2 少了五題，但命題方式變得更靈活，難度也隨之提升。新制多了**推測語意**的考題，考生必須根據全文判斷語意才能找出答案。聽完此類題目後，須迅速推敲並挑出正確的答案，才不會錯失下一題的解題機會。請務必勤加練習，熟悉此類題型的模式。

❷ 題目最前面的<u>疑問詞</u>至關重要。

Part 2 經常出現以疑問詞（Who、What、Where、When、Why、How）開頭的疑問句只要聽清楚**句首的疑問詞**，幾乎就能找到這類題型的正確答案，所以平常要培養對疑問詞的敏銳度。

❸ 善用<u>消去法</u>縮小選擇範圍。

Part 2 是最多陷阱的大題，所以事先統整陷阱題可以事半功倍。舉例來説，若疑問句題目以疑問詞開頭，那幾乎可以判斷用 yes 或 no 回答的選項不可選，可以先將其刪除。另外，若題目出現的單字在選項中再次出現，或出現與題目中字彙發音類似的單字，如 copy 與 coffee，也是常見陷阱題。在準備時可**將具代表性的陷阱題整理好**，以提升本大題的答對率。

❹ 常考片語要熟背。

多益中常出現的用語或片語，最好**整組背起來**。舉例來說，疑問句「Why don't you . . . ?」是表達「做……好嗎？」的提議句型，而非詢問原因。

📋 Ⅲ　Conversations 第三大題：簡短對話

第三大題

指示：考生會聽到一些兩個人或多人的對話，並根據對話所聽到的內容，回答三個問題。請選出最符合播放內容的答案，在答案卡上將 (A)、(B)、(C) 或 (D) 的答案選項塗黑。這些對話只會播放一次，而且不會印在測驗本上。

高分戰略

❶ 有策略地聽比全部聽更高效。

Part 3 是兩到三人的對話，本大題作答時並非記下全部內容，而是**事先快速瀏覽題目和圖表**，判斷須注意哪些線索，在聽對話時重點記下與題目對應的資訊。

❷ 聽對話與找答案要同步進行。

光是事先掃過題目，而沒有邊聽邊找答案，仍無法達到高答對率，因為有些細微末節聽過後很容易忘記。**邊聽邊作答**的能力於新制多益中更為重要，因為新增了角色性別及彼此關係更為複雜的三人對話題，所以避免聽完後混淆的方式則是立刻作答，須在平時就不斷積累。

❸ 對話開頭不可漏聽。

詢問職業、場所或主題的問題在 Part 3 中經常出現，這些問題的答案時常會出現在**對話開頭**。不僅如此，掌握對話開頭也可幫助推敲接下來會出現什麼內容，在解其他題目時更為順利。

📋 Ⅳ　Talks 第四大題：簡短獨白

第四大題

指示：考生會聽到好幾段單人獨白，並根據每一段話的內容，回答三個問題。請選出符合播放內容的答案，在答案卡上將 (A)、(B)、(C) 或 (D) 的答案選項塗黑。每一段話只會播放一次，而且不會印在測驗本上。

高分戰略

❶ 要事先整理好常考的詢問內容。

不同於 Part 3，本大題談話種類較固定，像是交通廣播、天氣預報、旅行導覽、電話留言等的題目經常出現，且內容大同小異。所以只需要按這些談話種類，整理出常考的問題類型即可。

❷ 具備背景知識可加快答題速度。

Part 4 的談話種類常依循固定模式。舉例來說，若是機場的情境談話，飛機誤點或取消是最典型的情境，最可能的原因則是天候不佳，這就是多益的背景知識——不一定要全部聽懂，光看題目也能找出最接近正確答案的選項。平時**多累積背景知識**很重要。

❸ 訓練找出重點線索的能力。

Part 4 和 Part 3 一樣，每個題組有三個問題，所以同樣要養成**先掃描過題目和表格**的習慣。由於 Part 4 的談話內容更長，聽完全部內容後再答題很容易會有所遺漏。因此可以**先找出題目的要點**，利用**背景知識**，在試題本上推敲正確答案。不像 Part 3，Part 4 的答案通常會按照題目的順序，一一出現在對話中，**答案逐題出現**的機率很高。

閱讀

第五大題	句子填空 （30 題）	本大題**字彙**和**文法**能力最重要。其所考的字彙大都跟職場或商業有關，平時就要多背誦單字。
第六大題	段落填空 （16 題）	除了單字，也需要將比較長的片語或子句，甚至是一整個句子填入空格中，掌握整篇文章來龍去脈才能找出答案。
第七大題	單篇文章理解 （29 題） 多篇文章理解 （25 題）	本大題比較困難，須熟習經常出現的商業文章，像是公告或備忘錄等。平時就要訓練自己能夠**快速閱讀文章和圖表**，並且能夠找出主要的內容。當然，在本大題**字彙量**越多，越可快速理解文意。

 Incomplete Sentences 第五大題：單句填空

第五大題

指示：本測驗中的每一個句子皆缺少一個單字或詞組，在句子下方會列出四個答案選項，請選出最適合的答案來完成句子，並在答案卡上將 (A)、(B)、(C) 或 (D) 的答案選項塗黑。

高分戰略

❶ 要先看選項。

試題主要考句型、字彙、文法以及慣用語。要先看選項，掌握是上述的哪一個，便能更快速解題。所以要**練習判斷題型**，並正確掌握各題型的解題技巧。

❷ 找出意思最接近的單字。

Part 5 是填空選擇題，若能找出和空格關係最密切的關鍵字彙，便能快速又正確地解題。所以要**練習分析句子的結構**，並找出和空格關係最密切的字彙作為答題線索。一般來說，**空格**

前後的單字就是線索。舉例來説，如果空格後有名詞，此名詞就是空格的線索單字，以此名詞可以猜想出空格可能是個形容詞。

❸ 擴大**片語**量。

多益會拿來出題的字彙，通常以**片語**形式出現。最具代表的是：動詞和受詞、形容詞和名詞、介系詞和名詞、動詞和副詞等。有些詞組中每個單字都懂，但合起來就並非所猜想的中文意思。因此，平日要將這些片語視為一個單位整個背下來。舉例來説，中文説「打電話」，但英文是「make a phone call」；而付錢打電話不能用「pay a phone call」，要用「pay for the phone call」。但是多益中 Part 5 考「pay for the phone call」的可能性很低，因為多益大多出常見用語，而這句不是。所以，常考片語要直接背起來，不要直接用中文去猜想，才能在本大題奪得高分。

Ⅵ Text Completion 第六大題：短文填空

第六大題

指示：閱讀本大題的文章，文章中的某些句子缺少單字、片語或句子，這些句子都會有四個答案選項，請選出最適合的答案來完成文章中的空格，並在答案卡上將 (A)、(B)、(C) 或 (D) 的答案選項塗黑。

高分戰略

❶ 掌握**空格前後**的文意。

Part 5 和 Part 6 不同的地方是，Part 5 只探究一個句子的結構，而 Part 6 要探究句子和句子間的關係，因此要練習**觀察空格前後句子彼此的連結關係**。如果有空格的句子是第一句，要看後一句來解題；如果有空格的句子是第二句，就要看前一句來解題。偶爾，也有要看整篇文章才能作答的題目。PART 6 最難處在於要從選項的四個句子中，選出適當的句子填入空格中。此為新制增加的題型，不僅要多費時解題，平時也得多花功夫訓練掌握上下文意。

❷ 掌握**動詞時態**

Part 5 的動詞時態問題，只要看該句子內的動詞是否符合時態即可，但 Part 6 的動詞時態，要看其他句子才能決定該句空格中的時態。大部分的時態題目都區分為：已發生的事或尚未發生的事。從上下文來看，已發生的事，要用現在完成式或過去式；尚未發生的事，就選包含 will 等與未來式相關的助動詞（will、shall、may 等）選項，或用「be going to . . .」。針對 Part 6 的時態問題，**多練習區分已發生的事和尚未發生的事**便能順利答題。

❸ 掌握連接副詞（**轉折語**）的功用

所謂的連接副詞，是指翻譯時要和前面的內容一起翻譯的副詞。一般來説，這不會出現在只考一句話的 Part 5，而會出現在有多個句子的 Part 6。舉例來説，副詞 therefore 是「因此」的意思，所以若前後句的內容有因果關係，多半會用它。若是轉折語氣，用有「然而」含意的 however。此外，連接副詞還有 otherwise（否則）、consequently（因此）、additionally（此外）、instead（反而）等。另外，連接詞用於連接句子，而連接副詞是單獨使用的，要將它們做清楚區分。

VII Single Passage / Multiple Passage 第七大題：單篇／多篇文章理解

第七大題

指示：這大題中會閱讀到不同種類的文章，如雜誌和新聞文章、電子郵件或通訊軟體的訊息等。每篇或每組文章之後會有數個題目，請選出最適合的答案，並在答案卡上將 (A)、(B)、(C) 或 (D) 的答案選項塗黑。

高分戰略

❶ 字彙量是答題關鍵。

字彙能力是在 Part 7 拿高分最重要的一環，它能幫助你正確且快速地理解整個篇章。平時就要**將意思相似的字彙或用語一起熟記**，以快速增加字彙量。

❷ 要將問題分類。

Part 7 的題目看似無規則可循，事實上可以分作幾種類型，如：

① 細節訊息類型：詢問文章細節。
② 主題類型：詢問文章主題。
③ Not / True 類型：詢問哪個選項是錯誤資訊。
④ 邏輯推演類型：從文章提供的線索推知內容。
⑤ 文意填空類型：將題目中的句子填入文意通順的地方。

在解題前**先將題目分類**，解題會更有頭緒。

❸ 複合式文章題要注意彼此關聯性。

從 176 題開始是複合式文章類型，每題組由兩到三篇文章組成，有許多問題出自多篇文章內容的相關性。解題關鍵在於**找出相關或相同的地方**，並注意篇章之間是以何種方式連接。

❹ 培養耐心。

Part 7 是整個聽力閱讀測驗的尾聲，注意力是否在前面的奮戰後仍高度集中是勝負的關鍵。平常要**訓練至少要持續一個小時不休息地解題**，養成習慣才能在正式考試時不被疲勞影響。

〔寂天編輯群整理製作〕

SELF CHECK 自我檢測表

請以參加實際測驗的心態作答每回試題，並於作答完畢後，記錄測驗結果。此作法將有助於提升學習動力與專注力。

		作答日期	作答時間	答對題數	答對總題數	下個目標
Actual Test 1	聽力					寫完所有題目！
	閱讀					
Actual Test 2	聽力					要有更遠大的夢想！
	閱讀					
Actual Test 3	聽力					我做得很好！
	閱讀					
Actual Test 4	聽力					離目標越來越近了！
	閱讀					
Actual Test 5	聽力					我做得到！
	閱讀					

Actual Test 1

LISTENING TEST

In the Listening test, you will be asked to demonstrate how well you understand spoken English. The entire Listening test will last approximately 45 minutes. There are four parts, and directions are given for each part. You must mark your answers on the separate answer sheet. Do not write your answers in your test book.

PART 1 🎧 01

Directions: For each question in this part, you will hear four statements about a picture in your test book. When you hear the statements, you must select the one statement that best describes what you see in the picture. Then find the number of the question on your answer sheet and mark your answer. The statements will not be printed in your test book and will be spoken only one time.

Statement (C), "They're sitting at the table," is the best description of the picture, so you should select answer (C) and mark it on your answer sheet.

1.

2.

GO ON TO THE NEXT PAGE

3.

4.

5.

6.

PART 2 🎧02

Directions: You will hear a question or statement and three responses spoken in English. They will not be printed in your test book and will be spoken only one time. Select the best response to the question or statement and mark the letter (A), (B), or (C) on your answer sheet.

7.   Mark your answer on your answer sheet.

8.   Mark your answer on your answer sheet.

9.   Mark your answer on your answer sheet.

10. Mark your answer on your answer sheet.

11. Mark your answer on your answer sheet.

12. Mark your answer on your answer sheet.

13. Mark your answer on your answer sheet.

14. Mark your answer on your answer sheet.

15. Mark your answer on your answer sheet.

16. Mark your answer on your answer sheet.

17. Mark your answer on your answer sheet.

18. Mark your answer on your answer sheet.

19. Mark your answer on your answer sheet.

20. Mark your answer on your answer sheet.

21. Mark your answer on your answer sheet.

22. Mark your answer on your answer sheet.

23. Mark your answer on your answer sheet.

24. Mark your answer on your answer sheet.

25. Mark your answer on your answer sheet.

26. Mark your answer on your answer sheet.

27. Mark your answer on your answer sheet.

28. Mark your answer on your answer sheet.

29. Mark your answer on your answer sheet.

30. Mark your answer on your answer sheet.

31. Mark your answer on your answer sheet.

PART 3 🎧03

Directions: You will hear some conversations between two or more people. You will be asked to answer three questions about what the speakers say in each conversation. Select the best response to each question and mark the letter (A), (B), (C), or (D) on your answer sheet. The conversations will not be printed in your test book and will be spoken only one time.

32. Where is the conversation taking place?
(A) At a bookstore
(B) At a dry cleaner's
(C) At a department store
(D) At a post office

33. What does the man check?
(A) The available sizes
(B) The sale price
(C) The delivery fees
(D) The shipment date

34. What does the man recommend doing?
(A) Checking for an item online
(B) Placing a rush order
(C) Visiting another branch
(D) Purchasing a different brand

35. What most likely is the man's job?
(A) Head of marketing
(B) Graphic designer
(C) Repairperson
(D) Personnel manager

36. What has the woman ordered for the man?
(A) A uniform
(B) A desk
(C) A file cabinet
(D) A laptop computer

37. What does the woman remind the man to do?
(A) Sign up for a workshop
(B) Read a user manual
(C) Transport an item carefully
(D) Contact a customer

38. What does the man want his friend's opinion about?
(A) A payment method
(B) A reservation time
(C) A food order
(D) A seating option

39. Why does the man say, "That's more than I expected"?
(A) To make a complaint
(B) To turn down an offer
(C) To give an excuse
(D) To express excitement

40. What does the man inquire about?
(A) A discount offer
(B) A chef's recommendation
(C) The hours of operation
(D) The parking situation

41. Where do the speakers work?
(A) At a business institute
(B) At a library
(C) At a publishing company
(D) At a newspaper office

42. What was Jennifer surprised about?
(A) Attendance at an event
(B) Some negative reviews
(C) A proposed contract
(D) A coworker's transfer

43. What will happen this afternoon?
(A) Some customers will give feedback.
(B) A new shipment will arrive.
(C) The man will conduct an interview.
(D) Photos will be added to a Web site.

44. Where most likely are the speakers?

(A) At a business school

(B) At an accounting firm

(C) At an insurance company

(D) At a government office

45. How did the woman learn about the job opening?

(A) By reading a magazine

(B) By receiving an e-mail

(C) By speaking to a colleague

(D) By attending a career fair

46. What accomplishment does the woman mention?

(A) Training other staff members

(B) Earning the highest employee rating

(C) Developing a new software program

(D) Bringing in the most new customers

47. What is the problem?

(A) Some equipment was damaged.

(B) A company is not reliable.

(C) Some new employees are inexperienced.

(D) A workspace is too small.

48. Why does the man say, "my friend Felix works in real estate"?

(A) To suggest getting a recommendation

(B) To reject a business proposal

(C) To correct a misunderstanding

(D) To explain the reason for a decision

49. What does the woman say she will do?

(A) Visit a neighborhood

(B) Read some reviews

(C) Make a phone call

(D) Prepare some documents

50. Where most likely does the man work?

(A) At a coffee shop

(B) At a bank

(C) At a car rental company

(D) At a shoe store

51. According to the man, what is the problem?

(A) Some products are sold out.

(B) A delivery did not arrive.

(C) Some software is malfunctioning.

(D) An employee has made an error.

52. What does the man offer to do for the woman?

(A) Call her later

(B) Get a supervisor

(C) Provide a refund

(D) Send a catalog

53. Who most likely is the woman?

(A) A travel agent

(B) A delivery driver

(C) A furniture salesperson

(D) A hotel manager

54. What will the man do next month?

(A) He will take a trip out of town.

(B) He will open a new business.

(C) He will give a talk at an event.

(D) He will move to a new home.

55. What does the woman suggest?

(A) Advertising on a Web site

(B) Viewing some images online

(C) Hiring a professional decorator

(D) Downloading a smartphone app

56. In which department do the speakers work?

(A) Human resources
(B) Finance
(C) Marketing
(D) Shipping

57. What does the woman offer to do?

(A) Review a company policy
(B) Call one of Ms. Lee's clients
(C) Organize a work schedule
(D) Make preparations for a meal

58. According to the woman, why should the man talk to Tina?

(A) To contribute to a gift
(B) To collect a prize
(C) To express a preference
(D) To check a report

---

59. What does the man want to talk about at the meeting?

(A) Some customer survey responses
(B) Some employee complaints
(C) A new supplier of ingredients
(D) An upcoming sales promotion

60. What problem does Claire mention?

(A) An ingredient is considered unhealthy.
(B) The product selection is not large enough.
(C) Some business hours are inconvenient.
(D) Some staff members are not fully trained.

61. What are the women asked to do?

(A) Oversee an ad campaign
(B) Work some additional shifts
(C) Create a summary report
(D) Hire a new employee

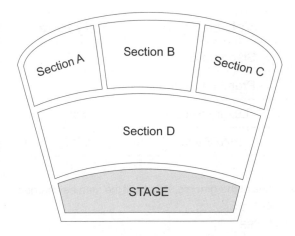

62. Why does the woman express surprise?

(A) The price of some tickets has increased.
(B) Some new performance dates have been added.
(C) A dance group has won an award.
(D) The man is interested in watching ballet.

63. Look at the graphic. For which section are the man's tickets?

(A) Section A
(B) Section B
(C) Section C
(D) Section D

64. What will the man's sister do on Friday?

(A) Go to a party
(B) Move out of town
(C) Attend an interview
(D) Teach a dance class

GO ON TO THE NEXT PAGE

Vehicle Type	Daily Rate
Standard Sedan	$65
Premium Sedan	$70
Luxury Sedan	$85
Elite Sedan	$110

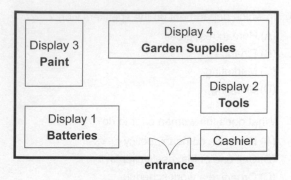

65. Look at the graphic. What will the man be charged per day?
   (A) $65
   (B) $70
   (C) $85
   (D) $110

66. Why is the man visiting Atlanta?
   (A) To sign a contract
   (B) To lead a group discussion
   (C) To attend a conference
   (D) To tour a building

67. What does the woman recommend doing?
   (A) Avoiding a busy road
   (B) Keeping a receipt
   (C) Downloading an app
   (D) Visiting a popular restaurant

68. Where are the speakers?
   (A) At an art institute
   (B) At a repair shop
   (C) At a hardware store
   (D) At a toy store

69. According to the man, what did employees do yesterday?
   (A) Recorded a video
   (B) Completed some training
   (C) Unloaded some new items
   (D) Installed safety equipment

70. Look at the graphic. Where will some paint cans be moved?
   (A) Display 1
   (B) Display 2
   (C) Display 3
   (D) Display 4

PART 4 (04)

Directions: You will hear some talks given by a single speaker. You will be asked to answer three questions about what the speaker says in each talk. Select the best response to each question and mark the letter (A), (B), (C), or (D) on your answer sheet. The talks will not be printed in your test book and will be spoken only one time.

71. How does each workshop tour end?
    (A) An employee answers questions.
    (B) An informative video is shown.
    (C) A group photo is taken.
    (D) A piece of equipment is demonstrated.

72. What does each tour participant receive?
    (A) A piece of jewelry
    (B) A voucher
    (C) A map of the site
    (D) A beverage

73. What do the listeners receive a warning about?
    (A) Which entrance to use
    (B) Where to meet
    (C) What clothing to bring
    (D) How to book in advance

74. Who most likely is giving the speech?
    (A) A factory worker
    (B) A driving instructor
    (C) A gym manager
    (D) A bank employee

75. What have the listeners been given?
    (A) A product sample
    (B) An employee directory
    (C) A daily pass
    (D) A list of classes

76. What does the speaker mean when she says, "You won't see anything like it again"?
    (A) A membership process can be confusing.
    (B) A presentation is worth watching.
    (C) The business is expected to succeed.
    (D) Listeners should take advantage of an offer.

77. What kind of business do the listeners most likely work for?
    (A) A construction company
    (B) An international delivery service
    (C) A newspaper publisher
    (D) A medical facility

78. What does the speaker say she is reassured about?
    (A) A worker's attention to detail
    (B) An investor's future plan
    (C) The responses from a customer survey
    (D) The score on an inspection

79. What are the listeners encouraged to do?
    (A) E-mail Ms. Arnold
    (B) Ask for advice
    (C) Attend a training event
    (D) Sample a new product

80. Why is the bus's departure delayed?
    (A) It is being cleaned.
    (B) It is undergoing repairs.
    (C) There is heavy traffic in the area.
    (D) There was a scheduling error.

81. Why does the speaker say, "We do have some indirect routes"?
    (A) To confirm a new schedule
    (B) To explain a policy
    (C) To suggest an alternative
    (D) To make a complaint

82. What are the listeners asked to do?
    (A) Talk to the speaker
    (B) Show a ticket
    (C) Come back later
    (D) Present a receipt

GO ON TO THE NEXT PAGE

83. Where most likely is the speaker calling from?
    (A) A real estate agency
    (B) A dental clinic
    (C) An architecture firm
    (D) A manufacturing facility

84. What qualification does the speaker mention?
    (A) A flexible schedule
    (B) A university degree
    (C) State certification
    (D) Sales experience

85. What does the speaker say she plans to do?
    (A) Send an employment contract
    (B) Arrange an interview time
    (C) Keep some documents
    (D) Check the listener's references

86. Where most likely does the speaker work?
    (A) At a marketing firm
    (B) At a local newspaper
    (C) At a cosmetics company
    (D) At a fashion magazine

87. Why does the speaker say, "our photographer works full time"?
    (A) To explain a problem
    (B) To reject an offer
    (C) To correct a misunderstanding
    (D) To request some help

88. What does the speaker ask the listener to do?
    (A) Inform him of her availability
    (B) Send him some documents
    (C) Confirm a final payment
    (D) Select some photographs

89. What is the speaker mainly discussing?
    (A) A customer complaint
    (B) A staff promotion
    (C) A payment system
    (D) A company policy

90. What are the listeners asked to do?
    (A) Complete an online form
    (B) Work with a partner
    (C) Read a handout
    (D) Attend a training session

91. According to the speaker, what will Olivia do?
    (A) Return some equipment
    (B) Print some materials
    (C) Answer questions
    (D) Create a schedule

92. What will be discussed during the broadcast?
    (A) Online deliveries
    (B) Fruit picking
    (C) Home gardening
    (D) Farmer's markets

93. According to the speaker, why is an activity popular?
    (A) It keeps people in shape.
    (B) It is fun for all ages.
    (C) It saves participants money.
    (D) It is environmentally friendly.

94. Who is Stephanie Lutz?
    (A) A reporter
    (B) A city official
    (C) A farmer
    (D) A radio host

Room 201	Room 202	Room 204
Elevator		
Staff Room	Room 203	Storage Room

Project A	Corporate Sponsorship
Project B	Video Competition
Project C	Free Webinar
Project D	Annual Trade Expo

95. Who is the speaker addressing?

(A) Potential investors
(B) Company managers
(C) Job applicants
(D) Government inspectors

96. Look at the graphic. Which office will the listeners use for most of the day?

(A) Room 201
(B) Room 202
(C) Room 203
(D) Room 204

97. Where will listeners go at four-thirty?

(A) To a conference room
(B) To a computer lab
(C) To a cafeteria
(D) To a security office

98. Why does the speaker thank the team?

(A) They finished a project on short notice.
(B) They created a popular product.
(C) They found some new clients.
(D) They helped to train new employees.

99. Look at the graphic. Which project will start tomorrow?

(A) Project A
(B) Project B
(C) Project C
(D) Project D

100. What will Patrick do on Thursday?

(A) Receive an award
(B) Give a speech
(C) Visit a client
(D) Finalize a budget

This is the end of the Listening test. Turn to Part 5 in your test book.

GO ON TO THE NEXT PAGE

READING TEST

In the Reading test, you will read a variety of texts and answer several different types of reading comprehension questions. The entire Reading test will last 75 minutes. There are three parts, and directions are given for each part. You are encouraged to answer as many questions as possible within the time allowed.

You must mark your answers on the separate answer sheet. Do not write your answers in your test book.

PART 5

Directions: A word or phrase is missing in each of the sentences below. Four answer choices are given below each sentence. Select the best answer to complete the sentence. Then mark the letter (A), (B), (C), or (D) on your answer sheet.

101. Some officials ------- expressed concerns about the changes to the corporate tax structure.

(A) privacy
(B) privatize
(C) private
(D) privately

102. The new electric car from Baylor Motors is intended for ------- journeys within an urban environment.

(A) shortness
(B) short
(C) shortly
(D) shorten

103. Ames Manufacturing developed a packaging method that ------- much less cardboard.

(A) uses
(B) using
(C) to use
(D) use

104. The building's owner increased the fees ------- parking lot access.

(A) for
(B) about
(C) at
(D) among

105. Few market analysts ------- predicted the industry effects of the factory's closure.

(A) locally
(B) constantly
(C) kindly
(D) correctly

106. Customers who wish to ------- us a review on social media are encouraged to do so.

(A) explain
(B) say
(C) give
(D) have

107. Every weekend ------- the month of August, the hotel's restaurant features live musical performances.

(A) even
(B) during
(C) when
(D) while

108. Portland Insurance's employees should complete a form with ------- desired vacation days.

(A) their
(B) its
(C) themselves
(D) it

109. Many construction businesses are nervous about a new ------- on the importation of building materials.

(A) restrictively
(B) restrict
(C) restrictive
(D) restriction

110. Concert tickets have not been selling well, ------- the event has been advertised heavily for weeks.

(A) because
(B) unless
(C) in addition to
(D) even though

111. Prices were ------- reduced for the store's summer sale.

(A) significantly
(B) significance
(C) significant
(D) signify

112. People who are self-employed should keep ------- records of their business's profits and costs.

(A) accurate
(B) unfair
(C) visual
(D) spacious

113. Attendance at Saturday's community picnic was high ------- the cold weather.

(A) regarding
(B) opposite
(C) despite
(D) across

114. Soil samples were taken to carry out the ------- testing to check for pollution.

(A) narrow
(B) mandatory
(C) perishable
(D) obvious

115. Before ------- the air conditioner, Mr. Perkins ordered some replacement parts for the task.

(A) fixing
(B) fixed
(C) fix
(D) fixes

116. Product sales ------- a setback recently and may not improve without further action.

(A) to suffer
(B) have suffered
(C) suffering
(D) suffer

117. Business travelers tend to ------- hotel rooms with a large desk.

(A) apply
(B) involve
(C) prefer
(D) believe

118. Even though ------- than expected, the delivery service was not worth the high cost.

(A) quick
(B) quicker
(C) quickest
(D) quickly

119. The three tallest ------- in the city, luxury apartment complexes can be seen from most parts of town.

(A) communities
(B) streets
(C) residents
(D) structures

120. The garage was damaged ------- repair in the storm and had to be rebuilt.

(A) of
(B) under
(C) beyond
(D) onto

121. Department managers ------- between June 4 and 8 to formally assess employees' work performance.

(A) will be meeting
(B) meeting
(C) having met
(D) to meet

122. The past few years' favorable market conditions have resulted in more business ------- across most industries.

(A) invested
(B) investment
(C) to invest
(D) investor

123. All meeting rooms at the VC Conference Hall are ------- with built-in speakers and a projector.

(A) conducted
(B) equipped
(C) activated
(D) revealed

124. The new shopping center will have a ------- effect on the local economy.

(A) benefits
(B) beneficially
(C) beneficial
(D) benefit

125. Employees are expected to complete all assigned tasks, ------- difficult they may seem.

(A) however
(B) likewise
(C) indeed
(D) rather

126. How ------- a candidate answers the questions is an important component of being considered for the role.

(A) create
(B) creation
(C) creative
(D) creatively

127. Visitors to the national park must be accompanied by a guide ------- the trails can be dangerous.

(A) than
(B) given that
(C) although
(D) much as

128. The purchase of the restaurant by a corporate chain led to a decline ------- food quality.

(A) below
(B) at
(C) in
(D) as

129. Mr. McCrae explained that ------- between the two companies has created innovative products.

(A) confirmation
(B) consequence
(C) competition
(D) commission

130. Southfield Fitness Center ------- closed its main swimming pool for a week while it was being cleaned.

(A) currently
(B) perfectly
(C) adamantly
(D) temporarily

PART 6

Directions: Read the texts that follow. A word, phrase, or sentence is missing in parts of each text. Four answer choices for each question are given below the text. Select the best answer to complete the text. Then mark the letter (A), (B), (C), or (D) on your answer sheet.

Questions 131-134 refer to the following e-mail.

Georgina Harrison

962 Warner Street

Cape Girardeau, MO 63703

Dear Ms. Harrison,

Thank you for your interest in making a group booking at Westside Hotel. I have attached a comprehensive ------- of our amenities for your convenience. We aim to personalize the guest
131.
experience. We are prepared to meet the needs of most guests on short notice. However, if you

have ------- requests, we may need advance notice in order to fulfill them. Once your booking is
132.
made, you may be charged a fee according to our cancellation policy. -------. Before confirming
133.
your booking, please download a copy of the payment details and ------- them carefully.
134.

Warmest regards,

The Westside Hotel Team

---

131. (A) describe
(B) describes
(C) described
(D) description

132. (A) unusual
(B) absent
(C) plain
(D) flexible

133. (A) The front desk is open twenty-four hours a day.
(B) You should complete the form with honest feedback.
(C) We appreciate your ongoing patronage.
(D) The terms of this are included on our Web site.

134. (A) reviewing
(B) review
(C) to review
(D) reviewed

Environmental Responsibility at the Kimball Museum

"Waves of Wonder" will be on display throughout the summer at the Kimball Museum. This
------- features sculptures made from beach glass. The artwork focuses ------- marine animals
135.   136.
whose populations have been severely hurt due to ocean pollution. Interesting facts about each
animal will be posted next to the work. Visitors ------- advice on reducing their impact on the
137.
oceans, both locally and worldwide. -------. "Waves of Wonder" will be available from June 10
138.
to September 5.

---

135. (A) award
(B) manuscript
(C) exhibit
(D) film

136. (A) before
(B) to
(C) on
(D) by

137. (A) are also getting
(B) can also get
(C) have also gotten
(D) also got

138. (A) See how you can make a positive change.
(B) To become a member, visit our Web site.
(C) Fortunately, the hours have been extended.
(D) The glass can be recycled at most locations.

Questions 139-142 refer to the following advertisement.

Verdant Landscaping, founded by brothers John and Jeremy Robles, ------- top-quality
139.
landscaping services for residential properties. We can plant a garden from scratch, maintain
existing lawns and flowerbeds, trim trees, and remove unwanted garden debris.

------- , your outdoor area will be a beautiful and relaxing place for you to enjoy. -------. We can
140.   141.
send a crew of any size, including just one person. If you're unsure whether hiring professionals
would be within your budget, call us at 555-4433 for a free ------- of the costs. We look forward
142.
to serving you!

139. (A) will provide
(B) provides
(C) had provided
(D) providing

140. (A) For example
(B) On the contrary
(C) As a result
(D) In comparison

141. (A) Other businesses cannot compete with us.
(B) These techniques are environmentally
friendly.
(C) We are willing to offer training.
(D) No job is too big or too small.

142. (A) vacation
(B) estimate
(C) installation
(D) pathway

GO ON TO THE NEXT PAGE

As a small business owner, Kelly Spencer spends a lot of time researching the best way to improve ------- 143. . Her staff was not responding well to her previous methods, but then she found an interesting piece of software, Pause-Pro. "I was hesitant at first due to the high cost. However, the company was offering free use of the software for thirty days, so I thought I'd give ------- 144. a try."

Pause-Pro allows employers to block access to distracting Web sites, such as social media pages, so employees don't waste time. It wasn't ------- 145. what Ms. Spencer was looking for, but she couldn't deny the results. She purchased the full version of the software for all of her employees' computers. ------- 146. . "With Pause-Pro's help," she said, "we can all focus on the most important tasks."

143. (A) wages
(B) efficiency
(C) competition
(D) education

144. (A) mine
(B) everyone
(C) these
(D) it

145. (A) more original
(B) originally
(C) original
(D) originality

146. (A) She also bought the program for her laptop.
(B) She has founded a few different businesses.
(C) She looks forward to meeting them.
(D) She could not understand the features.

PART 7

Directions: In this part you will read a selection of texts, such as magazine and newspaper articles, e-mails, and instant messages. Each text or set of texts is followed by several questions. Select the best answer for each question and mark the letter (A), (B), (C), or (D) on your answer sheet.

Questions 147-148 refer to the following article.

New Library Program Creates "Buzz"

April 30—This summer, Syracuse Library is launching a program to help local bees. The number of local bees has sharply declined, and the library aims to help these creatures. It will have a special section with books about bees and will host lectures about how they benefit the environment. Anyone who attends a lecture will be given a free pack of seeds for flowers that will attract bees.

147. What is the purpose of the program?
(A) To support the bee population
(B) To teach people a new skill
(C) To attract new library members
(D) To raise money for a charity

148. How can participants get a free gift?
(A) By completing a survey
(B) By attending a talk
(C) By making a donation
(D) By showing a library card

GO ON TO THE NEXT PAGE

Questions 149-150 refer to the following invitation.

Please join us for a meet-and-greet session with Adam Jackson, the new Public Relations Director of Watkins Bank.

Monday, December 12, 1 P.M.–2 P.M.
Conference Room A

Adam Jackson handled public relations for CHK Bank for nearly two decades. He will give a brief presentation on his plans for rebranding Watkins Bank and building closer connections with our customers. If you have a question for Mr. Jackson, please send it to the HR team prior to the event.

Coffee and hot tea will be served.

149. What is implied about Mr. Jackson?
(A) He currently works at CHK Bank.
(B) He recently changed his employer.
(C) He will receive an award on December 12.
(D) He founded his own business.

150. What can guests do in advance?
(A) Order hot beverages
(B) View some images
(C) Reserve a seat
(D) Submit their questions

E-Mail	
To:	Tamara Atwood
From:	City Swim Center
Date:	November 14
Subject:	Request

Dear Ms. Atwood,

I am writing to acknowledge receipt of your e-mail. We have processed your request, and your membership will be continued for another year. The new end date of your membership will be November 30 of next year. You are eligible for a free locker upgrade. Please come to the front desk anytime after November 30 to swap your current locker key for the new one.

Thank you for your patronage,

Derek Surette
Customer Services, City Swim Center

151. Why did Mr. Surette send the e-mail?

(A) To apologize for an error
(B) To introduce a new service
(C) To confirm a renewal
(D) To make a job offer

152. What can Ms. Atwood do after November 30?

(A) Contact Mr. Surette
(B) Receive a refund
(C) Attend a class
(D) Exchange a key

Questions 153-154 refer to the following text-message chain.

Monique Ross [9:21 A.M.]	Good morning. I'm Monique from the Outdoor Gear customer service team. How may I help you?
Eric Harper [9:22 A.M.]	Hello. I ordered a dome tent on August 2 that was supposed to arrive yesterday. However, I still don't have it. I'm wondering when it will get here.
Monique Ross [9:23 A.M.]	I can help with that. What is the order number?
Eric Harper [9:24 A.M.]	It's order #034587.
Monique Ross [9:25 A.M.]	Thank you. Please wait a moment.
Monique Ross [9:28 A.M.]	It looks like there was an issue at the warehouse, and the item is now scheduled to be sent tomorrow. So, it will arrive on Thursday, two days later than originally expected.
Eric Harper [9:29 A.M.]	Since I paid for overnight shipping, I think I should be refunded for the shipping fee.
Monique Ross [9:31 A.M.]	Absolutely. I'll take care of that right now, and it should appear on your account within a few hours. Do you need any other help?
Eric Harper [9:32 A.M.]	Not for now. Thanks.

153. Why did Mr. Harper send a message to Outdoor Gear?

(A) To report damage to a tent
(B) To request a product catalog
(C) To exchange an unwanted product
(D) To check when an item will arrive

154. At 9:31 a.m., what does Ms. Ross most likely mean when she writes, "Absolutely"?

(A) She understands the need for a fast service.
(B) She can open a new account for Mr. Harper.
(C) She enjoyed resolving a problem.
(D) She agrees to issue Mr. Harper a refund.

Questions 155-157 refer to the following Web page.

| Home | Photo Gallery | **Events** | Contact Us |

Posted: January 19

Cincinnati Encounter

Saturday, March 12, 9:00 A.M.-11:00 A.M.
Instructor: Diane Robinson

Are you new to Cincinnati? Learn about what the city has to offer, such as:

• Where and how to look for jobs with local businesses
• What bus and streetcar routes are available to commuters
• Volunteer opportunities with charities and how to participate

This class would be especially helpful to those who have moved to Cincinnati from overseas. Registration opens on January 25 and ends on March 5. Spots will be assigned on a first-come, first-served basis. The class is expected to fill up quickly, so early registration is recommended.

Thanks to a government grant, Cincinnati Encounter is provided for free to anyone living in Cincinnati, but registration is required.

155. When will Ms. Robinson teach a class?

(A) On January 19
(B) On January 25
(C) On March 5
(D) On March 12

156. What is NOT indicated as a topic in Cincinnati Encounter?

(A) Using public transportation
(B) Running for local government
(C) Seeking employment in the area
(D) Assisting nonprofit organizations

157. What is stated about Cincinnati Encounter?

(A) It is offered to residents at no cost.
(B) It will last for three hours.
(C) It was developed by a businessperson.
(D) It is part of an ongoing series.

GO ON TO THE NEXT PAGE

E-Mail

To: Angela Klein <kleina@rtinternet.net>
From: José Damico <jose@sapphire-yoga.com>
Date: June 12
Subject: Level 3 Certification

Dear Ms. Klein,

We have received your deposit payment for Sapphire Yoga Studio's upcoming Yoga Teacher Training Course for the Level 3 certification course. —[1]—. This is a full-time intensive course that will last four weeks, beginning on June 29.

—[2]—. Please e-mail Veronica Clark at veronica@sapphire-yoga.com to submit health check records from your doctor showing that you are fit to take on the demands of the course. This is for your safety and is required by our insurance provider.

Yoga mats and blocks are available on site for every class. —[3]—. So, you can use them with confidence. However, we find that most students would rather bring personal items from home. You are free to do so, but please be aware that we cannot store anything for you overnight.

Please let me know if you have any questions about the course. —[4]—.

Warmest regards,

José Damico
Manager, Sapphire Yoga Studio

158. Why should Ms. Klein e-mail Ms. Clark?
(A) To get a doctor recommendation
(B) To sign up for insurance
(C) To confirm her physical health
(D) To get more course information

159. What does Mr. Damico suggest about students?
(A) They prefer to use their own equipment.
(B) They will do part of the course from home.
(C) They can participate in the class for free.
(D) They have the option of different start times.

160. In which of the positions marked [1], [2], [3], and [4] does the following sentence best belong?

"We implement sanitization practices between each use."

(A) [1]
(B) [2]
(C) [3]
(D) [4]

Questions 161-163 refer to the following contract.

Contract Agreement

This contract is entered into by Adrienne Sales and Oscar Rascon, a freelance graphic designer, on April 22. Mr. Rascon agrees to create an original logo for Adrienne Sales. Mr. Rascon will meet with representatives from Adrienne Sales at the company's headquarters to discuss the intended appearance of the logo. Adrienne Sales will reimburse Mr. Rascon for up to £25 in travel-related expenses for the meeting, provided Mr. Rascon presents receipts of the spending. Mr. Rascon will create and submit three versions of the logo by May 20. Adrienne Sales can ask for up to three additional rounds of revisions to the selected logo. Adrienne Sales agrees to pay Mr. Rascon £750 upon completion of the final image.

Agreed by:

Oscar Rascon	_April 22_
Graphic Designer	Date

Elizabeth Norris	_April 22_
Adrienne Sales	Date

161. What does the contract imply about Mr. Rascon?

(A) He will complete a project by April 22.
(B) He used to work with Ms. Norris.
(C) He is a salesperson at Adrienne Sales.
(D) He will be paid to create a design.

162. The word "presents" in paragraph 1, line 5, is closest in meaning to

(A) publishes
(B) submits
(C) gifts
(D) displays

163. According to the agreement, what is Mr. Rascon required to do?

(A) Give a presentation
(B) Research some industry trends
(C) Make some requested adjustments
(D) Provide professional references

GO ON TO THE NEXT PAGE

From:	Nicola Fallaci
To:	All Briarhill Employees
Date:	July 2
Subject:	For your information

Dear Briarhill Employees,

To keep employees better informed, I'll be sending you regular updates about the company's progress. —[1]—. Compared to this quarter last year, our domestic sales have increased by 15%. Though it seems that having some of our goods as part of the *Family Fun* TV show set did not make much difference, it still provided some interesting photos for our Web site.

—[2]—. In Indonesia, we experienced an amazing 63% boost in sales following our participation in the Jakarta Housewares Trade Fair. Sales were steady in Australia, where we saw an increase of just 0.5%. —[3]—. This was not a surprise, as our new line of cotton curtains has been receiving mixed reviews. In Sweden and Norway, sales have been sluggish, down 8% and 6%, respectively. This is due to heavy competition from other businesses.

—[4]—. As you can see, there are some regions that need improvement and others that are doing well. I am sure that the proposal made by Pedro Reid, which targets hotels directly for sales across their entire chain, will yield promising results and grow our sales further.

Sincerely,

Nicola Fallaci

164. What type of company most likely is Briarhill?

(A) A chain of supermarkets
(B) A home furnishings retailer
(C) A book publisher
(D) An electronics manufacturer

165. According to Ms. Fallaci, where did people see Briarhill's merchandise in person?

(A) In Australia
(B) In Indonesia
(C) In Norway
(D) In Sweden

166. What does Ms. Fallaci expect will likely lead to increased business?

(A) A customer loyalty program
(B) Association with a TV show
(C) Contracts with hotel chains
(D) Online advertising campaigns

167. In which of the positions marked [1], [2], [3], and [4] does the following sentence best belong?

"Here is an overview of our international performance."

(A) [1]
(B) [2]
(C) [3]
(D) [4]

Questions 168-171 refer to the following article.

BERLIN (September 7)—The Historical Preservation Foundation (HPF) aims to make historical artifacts available to the public as well as provide support for ongoing research. The HPF plans to work on a collection of objects from a 1940s excavation in Western Asia. Fragments of vases and bowls dating back to the 2nd century were acquired by Aldeen University. These will be restored at HPF's main facility in Berlin. "We are honored to have these items under our care," said director Mathias Vogel. "Our track record for dealing with fragile artifacts is unmatched, and we have the resources to give them the attention they deserve."

HPF's staff members are proficient in working with metal objects such as tools, weapons, and jewelry, but they are somewhat new to working with clay items, especially molded ones. "We are forming a partnership with Aldeen University to ensure the work is carried out properly," Vogel said. "We're excited that Jamila Ahmed will travel to our site in Berlin to oversee operations. This project lines up perfectly with her specialized knowledge and extensive experience."

The artifacts are currently housed at Aldeen University. The university's team is starting to examine them to prepare them to be shipped to Berlin, which they are expecting to do on October 2. A date for a public display of the items has not yet been determined.

168. What is the main topic of the article?

(A) The grand opening of a museum
(B) A fundraiser for an excavation
(C) The new discovery of some artifacts
(D) A pottery restoration project

169. What position does Mr. Vogel have?

(A) Maintenance manager
(B) Assistant researcher
(C) Head of Aldeen University
(D) HPF director

170. What is most likely true about Ms. Ahmed?

(A) She is an expert in pottery.
(B) She graduated from Aldeen University.
(C) She grew up in Berlin.
(D) She plans to publish a book.

171. What is implied about the artifacts?

(A) They have been donated by private collectors.
(B) They will be examined for several weeks before transportation.
(C) They will go on display from October 2.
(D) They sustained some damage while being shipped.

GO ON TO THE NEXT PAGE

Yuhan Gao [9:18 A.M.]	Hi, everyone. Since I canceled yesterday's team meeting, I wanted to check in with how things are going. Lisa, how is your trade show research coming along?
Lisa Timko [9:19 A.M.]	Even better than I expected! I have found one in August, the National Beauty Expo, that I think would be perfect for promoting our natural skincare products. The registration fee is only $1,500.
Yuhan Gao [9:21 A.M.]	Wonderful! Please go forward with that.
George Lainez [9:22 A.M.]	That's great! High-profile events are just what we need.
Ron Fulkerson [9:23 A.M.]	Good job, Lisa! If you send me the details, I can register our company for the event by the end of the day.
Lisa Timko [9:24 A.M.]	I guess we'll be busy preparing for this along with our extensive television campaign on the Mayfair Network.
Yuhan Gao [9:25 A.M.]	Unfortunately, that fell through. We can't afford the prices the station was charging, so we're going to have to promote the new line of lotions in another way.
Lisa Timko [9:27 A.M.]	I see. And I appreciate your dealing with this so quickly, Ron.
Ron Fulkerson [9:28 A.M.]	It's nothing.
Yuhan Gao [9:29 A.M.]	Keep up the good work, everyone!

SEND

172. In what industry do the writers most likely work?

    (A) Travel

    (B) Technology

    (C) Clothing

    (D) Cosmetics

173. What most likely is Ms. Gao's occupation?

    (A) Security advisor

    (B) Human resources director

    (C) Marketing manager

    (D) Research assistant

174. What is true about the Mayfair Network?

    (A) It is hosting an annual event.

    (B) It will form a partnership with the writers' company.

    (C) Its employees have a lot of experience.

    (D) Its fees are too high for the writers' company.

175. At 9:28 A.M., what does Mr. Fulkerson mean when he writes, "It's nothing"?

    (A) He is pleased that Ms. Timko will resolve a problem.

    (B) He is willing to complete a registration process quickly.

    (C) He is surprised about the lack of information available.

    (D) He is happy to have found an event for the team.

★ ★ ★ ★ ★   ★ ★ ★ ★ ★

Make your event magical and memorable with Edsel Gardens!

Edsel Gardens, located near Stockton and comprising 4 acres of botanical gardens, features a truly unique and romantic location. You'll love the peaceful backdrop, gorgeous views, and modern amenities offered at our site. We specialize in weddings and anniversary parties and have recently doubled the size of our parking lot to accommodate larger groups. You can hold your event completely outdoors or use our giant tent, which protects against rain and can be heated in cold weather. Our tent seats up to 180 guests, and we have a Food and Liquor License that permits us to serve food and/or drinks from 11 A.M. to midnight on weekdays and 10 A.M. to 1 A.M. on weekends.

Our team will work with you to make sure everything is exactly what you want. With our Premium Package, you can use our in-house photographer and caterer to make planning easy. If you want live music, we can provide a recommendation for bands or singers.

Call us today at 555-8790 to get started. And if you're not sure what kind of theme you'd like for your event, get inspired by visiting our photo gallery at www.edselgardens.com. We look forward to hosting your event!

★ ★ ★ ★ ★   ★ ★ ★ ★ ★

E-Mail

To: Edsel Gardens <info@edselgardens.com>
From: Ramona Murphy <rmurphy@haven-mail.com>
Date: April 11
Subject: Thank you!

To Whom It May Concern:

I recently held an anniversary party for my parents at your site, and I wanted to thank you for a great experience. I got the Premium Package, which was convenient and affordably priced. I was really impressed with the photos taken by Fred Warren, the professional photographer. I also got a lot of compliments on the band I hired. The beautiful venue was a perfect fit for my parents' style. I plan to highly recommend Edsel Gardens to all my friends and family who are looking for a place to hold an event.

Warmest regards,

Ramona Murphy

176. What is NOT true about Edsel Gardens?

    (A) It is now operating under new ownership.

    (B) It recently expanded its parking area.

    (C) It can provide recommendations for musicians.

    (D) It can accommodate different types of weather.

177. When can food be served at Edsel Gardens?

    (A) Monday at 10 A.M.

    (B) Wednesday at 1 A.M.

    (C) Saturday at 11 A.M.

    (D) Sunday 9 A.M.

178. Why does the advertisement recommend visiting a Web site?

    (A) To view a price list

    (B) To read customer comments

    (C) To get some inspiration

    (D) To make a reservation

179. What is suggested about Fred Warren?

    (A) He only took photos inside a tent.

    (B) He had excellent reviews on a Web site.

    (C) He is a friend of Ms. Murphy's parents.

    (D) He is employed directly by Edsel Gardens.

180. In the e-mail, the word "fit" in paragraph 1, line 4, is closest in meaning to

    (A) position

    (B) match

    (C) development

    (D) adaptation

GO ON TO THE NEXT PAGE

Wanda Milburn
Corbitt Enterprises
4443 Rardin Road
Nashville, TN 37210
January 5

Dear Ms. Milburn,

We are writing to inform you of an increase in the fees for the cleaning services we perform for Corbitt Enterprises at the above address. The current fees you pay will be valid until March 4. As you were one of our customers in the very first month we opened, we have kept the fees at a lower rate for as long as possible.

We are implementing this change to ensure that our workers are compensated fairly, as they always perform a complete and careful cleaning service. This is rare in our industry. Enclosed you will find a breakdown of the new fees.

The change will go into effect on March 5. If you wish to terminate the contract, please inform us of your desired final day of service. We hope to continue serving you for many years to come.

Sincerely,

Grant Berg

Grant Berg
Manager, Shinetime Commercial Cleaning

To:	Grant Berg <grant@shinetimecommcleaning.com>
From:	Wanda Milburn <w.milburn@corbittenterprises.com>
Date:	January 11
Subject:	Cleaning contract

Dear Mr. Berg,

Thanks for informing me about the upcoming changes. We've been satisfied with the level of care provided. I know many business owners have had trouble hiring reliable cleaners, so I feel very lucky. I can't believe it has already been four years since you started working for us. Everyone who has visited us to receive financial advice has been impressed by our office, and your company has played an important role in creating that positive first impression.

In spite of your excellence, we will soon no longer need your services, and we would like the last cleaning day to be February 28. We are moving to a new office building at 579 Ohio Avenue, and the building's maintenance team provides cleaning as part of the monthly fee. I'd be happy to recommend your business to others if the situation arises.

All the best,

Wanda Milburn

181. According to the letter, when will fees for a service increase?

(A) January 5
(B) January 31
(C) March 4
(D) March 5

182. On what point do Mr. Berg and Ms. Milburn agree?

(A) That cleaning should be done regularly
(B) That good cleaners are hard to find
(C) That regulations are becoming tighter
(D) That the cost of cleaning services has risen

183. What type of business does Ms. Milburn most likely work for?

(A) A graphic design firm
(B) A software development company
(C) A commercial construction company
(D) A financial consulting firm

184. What is suggested about Shinetime Commercial Cleaning?

(A) It has been in operation for four years.
(B) It will relocate its head office in March.
(C) It has recently been sold to a competitor.
(D) It plans to recruit more employees.

185. How does Ms. Milburn provide what Mr. Berg has requested?

(A) By giving feedback about a service
(B) By agreeing to some new contract terms
(C) By confirming the desired termination date
(D) By reporting a new business address

Oakdale (April 9)—Preparations are underway for Oakdale's 8th Annual Health and Well-Being Expo, which will take place on Sunday, June 19. The expo will feature businesses offering a variety of health-related goods and services. Additionally, local physicians and nurses will provide free screenings for blood pressure and cholesterol levels as well as a basic eye exam.

After many years at Juniper Hall, the expo has been moved to the Bayridge Convention Center this year. "Due to the growing popularity of the event, Juniper Hall could no longer contain the number of vendors interested in participating in the expo," said Ken Exley, one of the event planners. "Visitors can easily find what they're looking for, with vendors of vitamins and health supplements in the main hall, massage therapists and spa representatives in the east wing, and gym representatives and sports-related businesses in the west wing."

To register, visit www.oakdalehealthexpo.com. Members of the Oakdale Business Association can get a twenty percent discount.

Annual Health and Well-Being Expo
Vendor Feedback Survey

Name: Anna Pierson
Business/Company: Sunrise Spa

I was informed about the event through my membership in the Oakdale Business Association. This was my first time participating as a vendor, and I reached more people than I expected. However, I would have liked a larger booth to provide massages on-site, and I spoke to some other vendors that needed a smaller one. Not everyone has the same needs, so it would be a good idea to address this in the future.

http://www.rtgoakdale.com/reviews

Please let us know about your experience.

Reviewed by (optional):

Sheryl Baum

How did you first find out about RTG Oakdale?

By visiting the Oakdale Health and Well-Being Expo

How satisfied were you with your experience (0=Very Dissatisfied, 5=Very Satisfied)?

5

Comments:

I have recently become more interested in the vegetarian lifestyle due to its beneficial effects on the environment. I decided to transition to a completely vegetarian diet very soon but was concerned about getting enough protein, iron, and anything else that may be lacking. However, I wasn't sure what kind of vitamin supplements I would need. After speaking to Anthony Cress at his business's booth, I felt like I was fully informed. Mr. Cress was knowledgeable and made great recommendations for my specific circumstances. Overall, it was a very positive experience for me.

186. According to the article, why did the event planners use a different site this year?

(A) To ensure more space
(B) To minimize traffic problems
(C) To promote a new building
(D) To reduce travel times

187. What is suggested about Ms. Pierson?

(A) She qualified for early registration.
(B) She recently started her business.
(C) She has participated in past events.
(D) She was eligible for a discount.

188. What does Ms. Pierson recommend for the next expo?

(A) Addressing some noise complaints
(B) Providing more power outlets
(C) Offering booths in various sizes
(D) Advertising the event to more people

189. What is implied about Mr. Cress?

(A) He has lived in Oakdale for a long time.
(B) He worked at a booth in the main hall.
(C) He was an event planner for the expo.
(D) He is considering hiring Ms. Baum.

190. What does Ms. Baum plan to do?

(A) Undertake further research on a topic
(B) Write another online review
(C) Change her daily eating habits
(D) Start a health-related business

GO ON TO THE NEXT PAGE

E-Mail

To: Armina Giordano <a.giordano@conway-co.com>
From: Rashid Fadel <r.fadel@conway-co.com>
Date: August 21
Subject: Submission

Dear Ms. Giordano,

We appreciate your participation in the Conway Future Growth Initiative here at Conway Co. This is the first time we have requested suggestions for expanding the business, and we were pleased to see so many ideas shared by staff throughout the entire company.

Your submission regarding opening a small-scale version of our usual store in the Brighton Shopping Complex is intriguing. The committee members loved the idea of exposing customers to our most popular items, but we feel like we don't have the big picture. For example, we're wondering what kind of foot traffic could be expected at that site. I understand that the monthly lease fee is quite high, so we would have to make sure it's worth it. In addition, what other businesses are in operation there or plan to do business there? I know that Arcadia has advertised a grand opening at the Brighton Shopping Complex for October. This may be a major issue, as it is our main competitor and carries a very similar inventory to ours. We would like to explore this matter further before making a final decision.

Warmest regards,

Rashid Fadel
Committee Head, Conway Future Growth Initiative

LONGVIEW (October 3)—Later this month, Arcadia, the maker of high-end athletic shoes for basketball, running, and more, will hold a grand opening at its newest branch at the Brighton Shopping Complex. Customers who attend the event will have the opportunity to enter a prize drawing for $5,000 in Arcadia merchandise.

The store will be located next to Golden Apparel and is expected to become one of the company's highest-earning branches. With famous athletes such as basketball player Scott Atkinson and marathon runner Caroline Holmes wearing its products, it is no surprise that Arcadia has grown in popularity over the past few years.

http://www.brightonsc.com/floorplan

| HOME | DIRECTORY | **FLOOR PLAN** | CONTACT |

Site Map of Brighton Shopping Complex

Unit 101 (Vacant)	Officeland	Home Designs	Unit 107 (Vacant)
Superb Gifts	Food Court		Golden Apparel
	Unit 104 (Vacant)	Unit 106 (Vacant)	

191. What is suggested about the Conway Future Growth Initiative?

(A) It targets new staff members.
(B) It will last for one month.
(C) It was suggested by Mr. Fadel.
(D) It was open to all employees.

192. Why did Mr. Fadel send the e-mail?

(A) To suggest merging with a competitor
(B) To request further information about a proposal
(C) To explain the rules of a company program
(D) To recommend improvements to a department's operations

193. In what industry does Conway Co. work?

(A) Footwear manufacturing
(B) Property development
(C) Job recruitment
(D) Media services

194. In what unit of the Brighton Shopping Complex will Arcadia be located?

(A) Unit 101
(B) Unit 104
(C) Unit 106
(D) Unit 107

195. What aspect of Arcadia's products is emphasized in the article?

(A) Its wide range of options
(B) Its affordable price
(C) Its use by celebrities
(D) Its environmentally friendly design

GO ON TO THE NEXT PAGE

FOR IMMEDIATE RELEASE

TORONTO (15 March)—A spokesperson for Millerbrook Enterprises has announced that Salvador Tolentino has been promoted to CEO to replace the outgoing CEO, Mary Gilhurst. He was unanimously selected by the Millerbrook Enterprises board and will take on his new role from May 25 after training with Ms. Gilhurst.

Millerbrook Enterprises provides cutting-edge software for artificial intelligence. Its products and research have led the industry for the past decade, and it has plans to open several international branches in the next few years. As Mr. Tolentino was formerly working as the company's CFO, the company is seeking to fill this position quickly. Duties include analyzing financial data and monitoring company expenditures. The role requires the ability to clearly communicate to the board and investors in both written and spoken form. Further details about the position and the hiring process are posted on www.millerbrook.com.

E-Mail

To:	Millerbrook Enterprises Board
From:	Walter Vinson
Date:	April 4
Subject:	CFO Candidate

Dear Fellow Board Members,

I would like to put forth Brianna Chomley as a candidate for the open CFO position. She was a university classmate of mine at Ralston University, and she meets all of the required qualifications for the position. I've spoken to her about applying for the position. However, she is not sure whether it would be right for her. This is because the job description on our Web site only lists the salary and does not include information about the quarterly bonuses, stock options, and housing allowance that we offer. I think we should update this because other candidates probably have the same misconception.

Sincerely,

Walter Vinson,
Vice Chair, Millerbrook Board of Directors

E-Mail

To:	Walter Vinson
From:	Erin Solberg
Date:	April 4
Subject:	Updated job description

Hi Walter,

Thank you for your advice on the job description for the CFO position. I've added the information you suggested. As we voted in the last meeting to add another member to our board, we need to start the search for that person as well. According to the bylaws, the selection process should be carried out by a committee of three people and must be headed by a high-ranking officer on the board—that is, the chair or vice chair. Please let me know what you think.

Sincerely,

Erin Solberg
Secretary, Millerbrook Board of Directors.

---

196. What is indicated about Mr. Tolentino in the press release?

(A) He will be given an award from the company.

(B) He is leaving to start his own business.

(C) He had the support of all board members.

(D) He plans to train his replacement.

197. What is suggested about Ms. Chomley?

(A) She plans to relocate to a new city.

(B) She has strong communication skills.

(C) She is Mr. Vinson's former coworker.

(D) She has designed software programs before.

198. According to Mr. Vinson, why is Ms. Chomley unsure about the position?

(A) The job responsibilities are too specialized.

(B) The expected working hours are too long.

(C) The compensation package is not fully described.

(D) The company has a lengthy interview process.

199. In the second e-mail, what is implied about the Millerbrook board?

(A) It will increase in size.

(B) It will meet more frequently.

(C) It will receive larger payments.

(D) It will update the bylaws.

200. What is suggested about Mr. Vinson?

(A) He is the newest member of the board.

(B) He opposed a proposed change.

(C) He will be supervising his friend.

(D) He is eligible to lead a committee.

Stop! This is the end of the test. If you finish before time is called, you may go back to Parts 5, 6, and 7 and check your work.

LISTENING TEST

In the Listening test, you will be asked to demonstrate how well you understand spoken English. The entire Listening test will last approximately 45 minutes. There are four parts, and directions are given for each part. You must mark your answers on the separate answer sheet. Do not write your answers in your test book.

PART 1 (05)

Directions: For each question in this part, you will hear four statements about a picture in your test book. When you hear the statements, you must select the one statement that best describes what you see in the picture. Then find the number of the question on your answer sheet and mark your answer. The statements will not be printed in your test book and will be spoken only one time.

Statement (C), "They're sitting at the table," is the best description of the picture, so you should select answer (C) and mark it on your answer sheet.

1.

2.

GO ON TO THE NEXT PAGE

3.

4.

5.

6.

GO ON TO THE NEXT PAGE →

PART 2 🎧06

Directions: You will hear a question or statement and three responses spoken in English. They will not be printed in your test book and will be spoken only one time. Select the best response to the question or statement and mark the letter (A), (B), or (C) on your answer sheet.

7. Mark your answer on your answer sheet.

8. Mark your answer on your answer sheet.

9. Mark your answer on your answer sheet.

10. Mark your answer on your answer sheet.

11. Mark your answer on your answer sheet.

12. Mark your answer on your answer sheet.

13. Mark your answer on your answer sheet.

14. Mark your answer on your answer sheet.

15. Mark your answer on your answer sheet.

16. Mark your answer on your answer sheet.

17. Mark your answer on your answer sheet.

18. Mark your answer on your answer sheet.

19. Mark your answer on your answer sheet.

20. Mark your answer on your answer sheet.

21. Mark your answer on your answer sheet.

22. Mark your answer on your answer sheet.

23. Mark your answer on your answer sheet.

24. Mark your answer on your answer sheet.

25. Mark your answer on your answer sheet.

26. Mark your answer on your answer sheet.

27. Mark your answer on your answer sheet.

28. Mark your answer on your answer sheet.

29. Mark your answer on your answer sheet.

30. Mark your answer on your answer sheet.

31. Mark your answer on your answer sheet.

PART 3 🎧07

Directions: You will hear some conversations between two or more people. You will be asked to answer three questions about what the speakers say in each conversation. Select the best response to each question and mark the letter (A), (B), (C), or (D) on your answer sheet. The conversations will not be printed in your test book and will be spoken only one time.

Actual Test 2

32. How did the woman find out about the sale?
    (A) By reading a banner
    (B) By performing an Internet search
    (C) By receiving a flyer in the mail
    (D) By seeing an ad in the newspaper

33. What does the man recommend buying?
    (A) An electronic device
    (B) Some cookware
    (C) A piece of furniture
    (D) Some clothing

34. Why does the woman want to make a phone call?
    (A) To increase a budget
    (B) To get an opinion
    (C) To confirm an address
    (D) To check another store

35. Where most likely are the speakers?
    (A) At a conference hall
    (B) At a vehicle rental agency
    (C) At a computer repair shop
    (D) At an airport

36. What does the man say he did yesterday?
    (A) Traveled by airplane
    (B) Opened a new business
    (C) Ordered some components
    (D) Gave a presentation

37. What does the woman offer to do for the man?
    (A) Show him a catalog
    (B) Provide a refund
    (C) Consult an expert
    (D) Work extra hours

38. What is the purpose of the man's visit?
    (A) To make a delivery
    (B) To inspect a building
    (C) To introduce a company
    (D) To install security equipment

39. What does the woman plan to do?
    (A) Call the man back
    (B) Keep an entrance locked
    (C) Reschedule a visit
    (D) Put up a sign

40. What does the man inquire about?
    (A) A company invoice
    (B) A parking situation
    (C) An hourly fee
    (D) A road closure

41. What are the men encouraged to do?
    (A) Borrow a company car
    (B) Sign up for a workshop
    (C) Share rides to work
    (D) Reserve a parking spot

42. What will the woman do in the afternoon?
    (A) Meet with managers
    (B) E-mail a plan
    (C) Announce a change
    (D) Launch a program

43. Why does the woman thank Aiden?
    (A) He completed a task ahead of schedule.
    (B) He agreed to attend a meeting for her.
    (C) He volunteered to provide suggestions.
    (D) He will help new employees get settled.

GO ON TO THE NEXT PAGE

057

44. What does the man need assistance with?
    (A) A film screening
    (B) A retirement party
    (C) A training session
    (D) A recruiting process

45. Why is the woman unable to help the man?
    (A) She has to meet with a client.
    (B) She has interviews with candidates.
    (C) She has to complete a coworker's tasks.
    (D) She has a doctor's appointment.

46. What will the man probably discuss with Ms. Hendricks?
    (A) Changing a due date
    (B) Transferring to another office
    (C) Hiring a temporary worker
    (D) Updating a company policy

47. What has the man recently done?
    (A) Accepted a promotion to a new position
    (B) Introduced new products to a company
    (C) Received negative feedback from employees
    (D) Encouraged the business owner to buy more vans

48. What does the man mean when he says, "it's a lot to ask"?
    (A) He believes a workload is unreasonable.
    (B) He feels bad for needing a big favor.
    (C) He is unable to meet a deadline.
    (D) He needs some time to think about a decision.

49. What does the woman suggest doing?
    (A) Expanding the hours of operation
    (B) Recruiting some drivers
    (C) Finding a new supplier
    (D) Reducing a service fee

50. What is the conversation mainly about?
    (A) Misprints in a catalog
    (B) Images on a Web site
    (C) A product launch
    (D) A customer complaint

51. What does the woman mention about a project?
    (A) It doesn't have enough workers.
    (B) It has been canceled.
    (C) It needs a budget adjustment.
    (D) It is still in progress.

52. What does the man plan to do next week?
    (A) Assess a service
    (B) Replace some images
    (C) Assign a new task
    (D) Repair some equipment

53. Why is the man visiting the business?
    (A) To have a dental checkup
    (B) To get a receipt
    (C) To pick up an item
    (D) To schedule an appointment

54. What did Ms. Michaels do in the morning?
    (A) Processed a credit card payment
    (B) Noticed a billing error
    (C) Filled out some paperwork
    (D) Left a telephone message

55. What will the man most likely do next?
    (A) Speak to a dentist
    (B) Confirm a schedule
    (C) Show an ID card
    (D) Go to an exam room

56. What is the purpose of the call?
    (A) To complain about a damaged item
    (B) To apologize for a delay
    (C) To check on the status of an order
    (D) To inquire about a discount

57. According to the man, what has caused a problem?
    (A) An engine malfunction
    (B) A computer error
    (C) An employee's absence
    (D) A major storm

58. What does the man recommend doing?
    (A) Checking information online
    (B) Calling back later
    (C) Waiting another day
    (D) Providing a tracking number

---

59. Where most likely are the speakers?
    (A) At an airport
    (B) In a public library
    (C) At a convention center
    (D) In a hotel lobby

60. What does the woman mention about the parking lot?
    (A) It is restricted to guests.
    (B) It is currently full.
    (C) It is under construction.
    (D) It is closed in the evenings.

61. What does the woman imply when she says, "I can't help you"?
    (A) She does not know the directions to a place.
    (B) She is not allowed to make exceptions.
    (C) She has trouble making recommendations.
    (D) She cannot explain the policy's details.

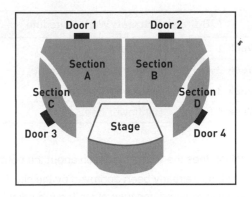

62. Who most likely is the woman?
    (A) A theater employee
    (B) A media critic
    (C) A musical performer
    (D) A stage manager

63. Look at the graphic. In which section will the man probably sit?
    (A) Section A
    (B) Section B
    (C) Section C
    (D) Section D

64. What will the man most likely do next?
    (A) Send a message
    (B) Give the woman his seat
    (C) Exchange a ticket
    (D) Wait for a friend outside

GO ON TO THE NEXT PAGE

778 Crowley Street: Work Schedule	
Week 1	Trim trees
Week 2	Install irrigation system
Week 3	Erect wooden fence
Week 4	Dig flower bed

Market Share

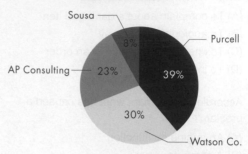

65. What does the woman mention about the permit?
   (A) It has already been approved by the city.
   (B) It is required because of the fence's height.
   (C) It will take several weeks to process.
   (D) It will be valid for eight months.

66. Look at the graphic. What will the speakers do next week?
   (A) Trim trees
   (B) Install an irrigation system
   (C) Erect a wooden fence
   (D) Dig a flower bed

67. What will the woman send to Ms. Kenmore?
   (A) A set of photographs
   (B) An updated schedule
   (C) A final bill
   (D) A list of materials

68. What does the man say happened yesterday?
   (A) A budget proposal was submitted.
   (B) A new branch opened.
   (C) A marketing campaign was launched.
   (D) An award was presented.

69. Look at the graphic. Which company recently changed its CEO?
   (A) Purcell
   (B) Watson Co.
   (C) AP Consulting
   (D) Sousa

70. What is the woman concerned about?
   (A) Losing customers to a competitor
   (B) Spending too much on marketing
   (C) Failing to keep up with demand
   (D) Having dissatisfied staff members

PART 4 🎧08

Directions: You will hear some talks given by a single speaker. You will be asked to answer three questions about what the speaker says in each talk. Select the best response to each question and mark the letter (A), (B), (C), or (D) on your answer sheet. The talks will not be printed in your test book and will be spoken only one time.

71. What is the main topic of the broadcast?
(A) A museum tour
(B) An art contest
(C) A painting lesson
(D) A fundraiser

72. How can participants receive a free gift?
(A) By adding their names to a mailing list
(B) By making a regular donation
(C) By being one of the first fifty people to enroll
(D) By purchasing more than one ticket

73. What does the speaker encourage listeners to do?
(A) Call the radio station
(B) Contact Ms. Coleman
(C) Listen to a program
(D) Visit a Web site

74. Where most likely does the speaker work?
(A) At a taxi company
(B) At an airport
(C) At a train station
(D) At a travel agency

75. What will listeners be asked to do?
(A) Show a receipt
(B) Take their seats
(C) Wait for further instructions
(D) Present their tickets

76. What does the speaker say that employees will do?
(A) Issue new tickets
(B) Help to move luggage
(C) Update safety procedures
(D) Hang up some notices

77. Why is the speaker calling?
(A) To accept a task
(B) To handle a complaint
(C) To show appreciation
(D) To leave early

78. What does the speaker imply when he says, "Tourist season is starting soon"?
(A) He is concerned about being short-staffed.
(B) He doesn't understand why profits are low.
(C) He agrees with the listener's suggestion.
(D) He thinks the store should advertise more frequently.

79. What does the speaker ask for?
(A) An access code
(B) A floor plan
(C) An authorization form
(D) A colleague's phone number

80. Who most likely is the speaker?
(A) A librarian
(B) A personnel manager
(C) A marketer
(D) A teacher

81. Why does the speaker say, "It truly saddens me to say this"?
(A) To express his regret
(B) To emphasize his disagreement
(C) To reject an application
(D) To show his mood change

82. What does the speaker ask the listener to do?
(A) Volunteer for a charity
(B) Provide a document
(C) Recommend a worker
(D) Lead a new program

GO ON TO THE NEXT PAGE

83. What is the purpose of the meeting?

    (A) To report on a competitor's plan
    (B) To announce a leadership change
    (C) To explain a new company policy
    (D) To congratulate the listeners on an award

84. What kind of company do the listeners most likely work for?

    (A) An energy plant
    (B) A vehicle manufacturer
    (C) A communications company
    (D) A construction firm

85. According to the speaker, what has Ms. Melville done?

    (A) Ordered replacement parts
    (B) Received an award
    (C) Analyzed a competitor
    (D) Prepared an employee list

___

86. Where is the introduction taking place?

    (A) At a manufacturing plant
    (B) At an auto repair shop
    (C) At a construction site
    (D) At a convention center

87. Who is Gustav Palmer?

    (A) A business owner
    (B) An engineer
    (C) A reporter
    (D) A physician

88. What does the speaker ask the listeners to do?

    (A) Suggest ideas for a design
    (B) Wear protective gear
    (C) Refrain from taking pictures
    (D) Stay together as a group

___

89. What is the speaker mainly discussing?

    (A) An educational program
    (B) A registration fee
    (C) A library fundraiser
    (D) A community picnic

90. Why is the speaker concerned?

    (A) There is a shortage of funding.
    (B) A meeting space is not available.
    (C) Bad weather is expected soon.
    (D) Interest in a project has declined.

91. What does the speaker ask the listeners to do?

    (A) Register for an event
    (B) Send her property information
    (C) Meet in front of a building
    (D) Make a financial donation

___

92. Who most likely is the speaker?

    (A) A security guard
    (B) A college lecturer
    (C) A tour guide
    (D) A medical professional

93. What does the speaker mean when he says, "This is really valuable information"?

    (A) He encourages the listeners to complete a survey.
    (B) He is concerned that some documents will get lost.
    (C) He wants some data to be carefully protected.
    (D) He is pleased that so much information has been gathered.

94. What are the listeners reminded to do?

    (A) Keep their personal items with them
    (B) Call later for some test results
    (C) Be ready to present an ID card
    (D) Fill out a registration form in advance

___

Customer: Faye Segura	
Order number: 1223389	
Description	**Quantity**
Daffodil bulbs	35
Tulip bulbs	30
Rose bushes	15
Lavender bushes	6

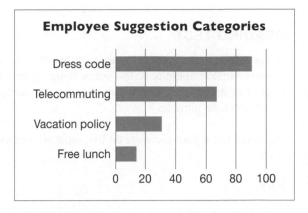

Employee Suggestion Categories

95. What is the purpose of the call?

(A) To change an appointment

(B) To verify an order

(C) To notify of a delivery error

(D) To request a payment

96. Look at the graphic. Which quantity does the speaker refer to?

(A) 35

(B) 30

(C) 15

(D) 6

97. What does the speaker say about Phillip?

(A) He can issue a refund.

(B) He can take a message.

(C) He can design a garden.

(D) He can pick up some plants.

98. Where do the listeners most likely work?

(A) At an insurance company

(B) At a law firm

(C) At a magazine publisher

(D) At an environmental agency

99. Look at the graphic. What topic will the company address in June?

(A) Dress code

(B) Telecommuting

(C) Vacation policy

(D) Free lunch

100. According to the speaker, what is available in the staff lounge today?

(A) A policy explanation

(B) Some survey forms

(C) Some refreshments

(D) A customer list

This is the end of the Listening test. Turn to Part 5 in your test book.

GO ON TO THE NEXT PAGE

READING TEST

In the Reading test, you will read a variety of texts and answer several different types of reading comprehension questions. The entire Reading test will last 75 minutes. There are three parts, and directions are given for each part. You are encouraged to answer as many questions as possible within the time allowed.

You must mark your answers on the separate answer sheet. Do not write your answers in your test book.

PART 5

Directions: A word or phrase is missing in each of the sentences below. Four answer choices are given below each sentence. Select the best answer to complete the sentence. Then mark the letter (A), (B), (C), or (D) on your answer sheet.

101. Most attendees at the conference confirmed that ------- learned a lot of useful information.

(A) theirs
(B) their
(C) them
(D) they

102. ------- in meeting the delivery demands is an important part of any courier business.

(A) Relied
(B) Relying
(C) Reliable
(D) Reliability

103. Keller Automotive's mini hybrid is the most affordable ------- among mini hybrids sold in the country.

(A) such
(B) one
(C) what
(D) each

104. Emerson Railways is interested in ------- its insurance provider in order to save money.

(A) covering
(B) emerging
(C) changing
(D) obtaining

105. Participants in the marathon will run ------- the Ness River and finish the race at Willow Park.

(A) along
(B) onto
(C) apart
(D) except

106. The new dryer from Chipley Appliances is designed ------- when the clothes are dry.

(A) to sense
(B) senses
(C) sensing
(D) sensed

107. The caterer was surprised that the seafood appetizers seemed ------- touched by the guests.

(A) conveniently
(B) apparently
(C) barely
(D) lightly

108. The peak season for winter wear is coming up, so it is ------- that we find a new manager for the Berka branch soon.

(A) imperative
(B) responsive
(C) exclusive
(D) persuasive

109. The construction of an additional lane on Highway 27 was delayed ------- a shortage of materials.

(A) because of
(B) since
(C) in case
(D) as a result

110. Community center officials were pleased that course ------- has increased by fifteen percent.

(A) description
(B) enrollment
(C) inventory
(D) attitude

111. Patrons may take out reference books from the library ------- they have received special permission from the head librarian.

(A) or else
(B) so
(C) whereas
(D) provided that

112. After the ticketing machines were installed, it was ------- to handle more passengers at the station.

(A) possible
(B) possibility
(C) possibly
(D) possibilities

113. Dewitt Communications ------- provides customer service training for its employees, so it has built a reputation for excellence.

(A) regularly
(B) firmly
(C) recently
(D) promptly

114. In compliance with regulations, we will give updates to those who are ------- involved in the matter.

(A) more direct
(B) directly
(C) direct
(D) directness

115. The research database maintained by Gyron Pharmaceuticals provides a ------- of information for physicians.

(A) quality
(B) similarity
(C) wealth
(D) mention

116. Once the transaction is complete, the person who requested the transfer will receive a message ------- the deposit.

(A) confirming
(B) confirms
(C) confirmed
(D) confirmation

117. Mr. Lincoln always flies with the same airline ------- he has joined a frequent flyer program.

(A) so that
(B) even if
(C) unless
(D) now that

118. After washing the car, Mr. Howard ------- a thin coat of wax to make the surface shine.

(A) to apply
(B) applying
(C) was applied
(D) applied

119. Ms. Mason forgot to take the fluctuations ------- currency rates into account when making the projections.

(A) often
(B) in
(C) finally
(D) on

120. Many potential customers were discouraged by ------- similar cell phone plans at Fletcher Mobile.

(A) confusing
(B) confusingly
(C) confusion
(D) confused

GO ON TO THE NEXT PAGE

121. Ms. Cheng added her ------- to the contract as a witness to the agreement.
    (A) signed
    (B) signs
    (C) signature
    (D) to sign

122. If you have lost or damaged your boarding pass, please speak to the gate agent, who can verify it and print -------.
    (A) another
    (B) each other
    (C) others
    (D) one another

123. Employees are asked to ------- the model number of the device that needs repairs.
    (A) intensify
    (B) specify
    (C) unify
    (D) testify

124. Lucy Berman has set a number of swimming records ------- her eight-year career as a professional swimmer.
    (A) above
    (B) regarding
    (C) throughout
    (D) of

125. Late for the meeting, Ms. Diaz took a seat in the back of the room to avoid -------.
    (A) noticed
    (B) being noticed
    (C) to notice
    (D) having noticed

126. The town's Independence Day Parade will commence with a brief speech by the newly ------- mayor.
    (A) elected
    (B) elects
    (C) electing
    (D) elect

127. Carla Stenton is an ------- entrepreneur who launched a start-up that expanded quickly across the nation.
    (A) embarrassed
    (B) acceptable
    (C) ambitious
    (D) alarmed

128. The sound quality of Vivico speakers is ------- superior compared to others on the market, but many people cannot afford them.
    (A) markedly
    (B) respectively
    (C) adamantly
    (D) permissibly

129. The first two rows in the auditorium are specially reserved for VIP guests, ------- are presenters.
    (A) the reason why
    (B) as a matter of fact
    (C) most of whom
    (D) on the contrary

130. Many participants in the tour were delighted to discover how ------- learning about the city's history could be.
    (A) considerable
    (B) accountable
    (C) enjoyable
    (D) transferable

PART 6

Directions: Read the texts that follow. A word, phrase, or sentence is missing in parts of each text. Four answer choices for each question are given below the text. Select the best answer to complete the text. Then mark the letter (A), (B), (C), or (D) on your answer sheet.

Questions 131-134 refer to the following advertisement.

During the first week of July, Twinkle Jewelry will hold a special event to celebrate its first anniversary. For one week only, get two items, and we ------- you for only one. For example, if
131.

you buy one necklace and one bracelet, you'll pay for the cheaper item only! You can choose

any two items you like from our wide ------- of jewelry. This offer applies to all of our products!
132.

-------, there is no limit to the number of times a person can benefit from it. However, jewelry will
133.

be given out on a first come, first served basis while supplies last. -------. The event starts on
134.

July 1.

131. (A) will charge
    (B) will be charged
    (C) were charging
    (D) have been charging

132. (A) select
    (B) selects
    (C) selection
    (D) selected

133. (A) In addition
    (B) As a result
    (C) Therefore
    (D) Accordingly

134. (A) That is why we have agreed to refund your purchase.
    (B) So come early to make sure you don't miss out.
    (C) We will set the items you request aside for you.
    (D) Please complete your payment as soon as possible.

Questions 135-138 refer to the following notice.

Public Seminar with Nora Devons
Thursday, May 14, 7 P.M.

Nora Devons, a prominent ------- of eliminating homelessness in Fredrick City, will be
135.

presenting a two-hour seminar at the Renner Convention Center. Ms. Devons is the president of

the Association of Social Workers, a group with over three hundred members. She ------- efforts
136.

to support the homeless community for the past eight years. During the seminar, she will tell the

audience about the seriousness of the homeless problem. ------- .
137.

The talk is open to audience members of all ages, and there is no entrance fee. ------- ,
138.

donations will be collected at the door to support the Marigold Homeless Shelter. For more

information, visit www.assocofsw.org.

---

135. (A) founder
(B) advocate
(C) candidate
(D) prosecutor

136. (A) had been leading
(B) has led
(C) is leading
(D) will lead

137. (A) She will also mention ways to help resolve it.
(B) The audience asked questions during the break.
(C) At that time, she served as a city council member.
(D) She plans to return to Grayson University to earn a master's degree.

138. (A) Accordingly
(B) Specifically
(C) Apparently
(D) However

Questions 139-142 refer to the following e-mail.

To: Natasha Seymour <nseymour@vicivenues.com>
From: Robert Thornton <r.thornton@hvelectronics.net>
Date: October 3
Subject: Event at Boulevard Hall

Dear Ms. Seymour,

I am part of a committee that is in charge of ------- a retirement dinner for one of my coworkers
139.
at HV Electronics. Several of your venues -------, but Boulevard Hall received the most support.
140.
This was due to ------- modern facilities and proximity to our office in Blakeley Towers.
141.

This will be our first time holding an event at Boulevard Hall. Could you confirm which dates are
available in November? We prefer November 20, so we hope that evening is still free. -------.
142.

Sincerely,

Robert Thornton

139. (A) inspiring
(B) arranging
(C) contributing
(D) visiting

140. (A) will be considered
(B) had considered
(C) were considered
(D) were considering

141. (A) their
(B) it
(C) its
(D) them

142. (A) We think you will be impressed with the spacious room.
(B) Even so, many people can walk from the office.
(C) This fee is within our estimated budget.
(D) If not, we have a few other possibilities in mind.

GO ON TO THE NEXT PAGE

To: Travel Times <info@traveltimes-magazine.com>
From: Christopher Venn <c.venn@frequenx.com>
Subject: Subscription #28571
Date: September 3

To Whom It May Concern:

I currently have a subscription to *Travel Times* magazine which is valid until the end of February. I'm wondering ------- it is possible to change the mailing address before the next issue comes
                           143.
out. -------. I'm currently receiving the magazine at work, but the new manager ------- that we
      144.   145.
no longer have personal mail delivered there. ------- residential address is 798 Trelawney Way,
                                               146.
Phoenix, AZ 85010. If there is a fee associated with this change, please e-mail me.

Thank you,

Christopher Venn

143. (A) what
    (B) if
    (C) while
    (D) for

144. (A) The information on Spain was particularly
        interesting.
    (B) The monthly bill had charged me for two
        subscriptions.
    (C) I couldn't find any information about doing this
        through your Web site.
    (D) I appreciate your printing the article I
        submitted.

145. (A) requested
    (B) facilitated
    (C) acknowledged
    (D) canceled

146. (A) Your
    (B) Its
    (C) Each
    (D) My

PART 7

Directions: In this part you will read a selection of texts, such as magazine and newspaper articles, e-mails, and instant messages. Each text or set of texts is followed by several questions. Select the best answer for each question and mark the letter (A), (B), (C), or (D) on your answer sheet.

Questions 147-148 refer to the following notice.

Warm Hands Warm Hearts (WHWH) is seeking new members for Melville's local group, which knits mittens and gloves to donate to the homeless. Our next meeting will be on Saturday, November 2, from 1 P.M. to 4 P.M. at the Lindale Coffee Shop. To get there, take subway line 5 to Kingstown Arena Station and use exit 5.

Participants should bring their own yarn and knitting needles. In addition, we would like a variety of colors and yarn types, so please let us know what you plan to bring for your project by commenting in the forum at warmhandswh.org/forum.

147. Where most likely would the notice be found?

(A) In a product catalog
(B) On a public bulletin board
(C) On a subway ticket receipt
(D) In a craft instruction book

148. According to the notice, why should people visit the Web site?

(A) To view photos of past projects
(B) To confirm registration for an event
(C) To request instructions by e-mail
(D) To report their choices of materials

Questions 149-150 refer to the following invoice.

Wallace Tools

Invoice Date: October 25
Invoice Number: 8395
Name: Dean Monette
Address: 805 Carriage Drive, Arlington Heights, IL 60005
Contact Number: 555-6950

One-week Rental: $49.99

[Contents]
Hadron-360 electric drill
Plastic carrying case
Charging device for unit battery
One-week insurance coverage (policy information printout)

Tax and Shipping: $8.95
Total: $58.94

Payment has been received in full for the above service. If you would like to keep the item longer, please call us at 555-2900. The device's user manual can be downloaded from our Web site at www.wallacetools.net.

149. What was NOT sent with the rental item?
(A) A user manual
(B) A battery charger
(C) Insurance details
(D) A portable container

150. Why should Mr. Monette call the number provided?
(A) To give feedback about a service
(B) To make a payment
(C) To request instructions
(D) To extend a rental period

Questions 151-152 refer to the following article.

BEIJING (July 5)—The price of raw silk is on the rise again after hitting a four-year low last quarter. This is in part due to trends in China and India, the world's largest producers of silk. Silk suppliers have been accumulating large quantities of the product at cheap prices and storing it rather than putting it on the market. This has led to an increase in price, which is expected to continue for the next few quarters. Clothing producers have enjoyed the low price of silk, but now that a higher cost of raw materials is projected, the fabric is much less attractive. As a result, many such producers are designing clothing made from man-made fabric, such as nylon and rayon, to avoid the unpredictability of the silk market.

151. According to the article, what has affected the price of silk?

(A) Some dealers are stocking up on the material.

(B) The currency value in China and India has dropped.

(C) Production has increased in efficiency.

(D) Customers are starting to prefer other fabrics.

152. How are clothing manufacturers dealing with a change?

(A) By negotiating directly with suppliers

(B) By developing products with alternative materials

(C) By purchasing supplies in bulk

(D) By changing the way goods are advertised

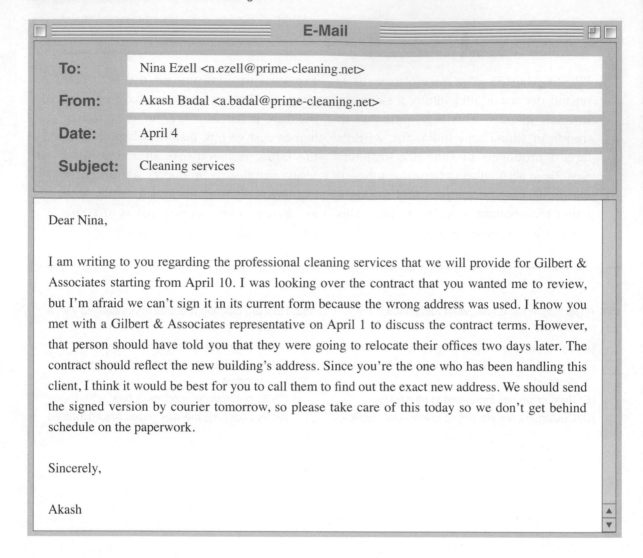

E-Mail

To:	Nina Ezell <n.ezell@prime-cleaning.net>
From:	Akash Badal <a.badal@prime-cleaning.net>
Date:	April 4
Subject:	Cleaning services

Dear Nina,

I am writing to you regarding the professional cleaning services that we will provide for Gilbert & Associates starting from April 10. I was looking over the contract that you wanted me to review, but I'm afraid we can't sign it in its current form because the wrong address was used. I know you met with a Gilbert & Associates representative on April 1 to discuss the contract terms. However, that person should have told you that they were going to relocate their offices two days later. The contract should reflect the new building's address. Since you're the one who has been handling this client, I think it would be best for you to call them to find out the exact new address. We should send the signed version by courier tomorrow, so please take care of this today so we don't get behind schedule on the paperwork.

Sincerely,

Akash

153. Why did Mr. Badal send the e-mail?

(A) To recommend a business
(B) To change a cleaning schedule
(C) To send an updated contract
(D) To point out an error

154. When did Gilbert & Associates move to a new building?

(A) March 28
(B) March 30
(C) April 1
(D) April 3

155. What should Ms. Ezell do by the end of the day?

(A) Negotiate some contract terms
(B) Contact the Gilbert & Associates office
(C) Send Mr. Badal a client recommendation
(D) Mail some documents to Prime Cleaning

Questions 156-157 refer to the following text-message chain.

Donald Graham [9:12 A.M.]
I've e-mailed you the estimate from the interior designer for remodeling our lobby.

Wei Lu [9:14 A.M.]
It's more expensive than I was expecting, especially since our lawyers don't even use that area much.

Donald Graham [9:15 A.M.]
Yes, it's slightly over budget, but I think it's worth it.

Wei Lu [9:16 A.M.]
Do you? It doesn't even include the cost of furniture.

Donald Graham [9:18 A.M.]
You have to understand that the lobby is the first thing people see when they arrive. It's essential that they have a good opinion of our business right from the start.

Wei Lu [9:19 A.M.]
You have a point. I guess it will give people more confidence in our services.

156. What are the writers mainly discussing?

(A) Hotel accommodations
(B) Budget limits
(C) Renovation costs
(D) Customer reviews

157. At 9:19 A.M., what does Ms. Lu most likely mean when she writes, "You have a point"?

(A) Attracting new customers is not easy.
(B) The business should be careful about spending.
(C) Making a good impression is important.
(D) The lobby needs to be expanded soon.

GO ON TO THE NEXT PAGE

NEW YORK (September 10)—Paula Frederick is known for her trendy and sophisticated fashions both on and off the runway. In addition to her retail business, she has created award-winning costumes for a number of films, most recently the sci-fi blockbuster *Golden Galaxy*. Now Ms. Frederick is lending her talents to a new project—designing warm-up uniforms and performance outfits for the national ice skating team. The team will wear them at the International Ice Skating Tournament, which will take place from January 3 to January 16.

Ms. Frederick was offered the project after meeting the team's coach, Vince Oliero, at an anniversary event for Charlotte Reeves, whose fashion house was Ms. Frederick's first employer after she graduated from design school. When Mr. Oliero mentioned that the team needed to update its look, the idea for the project was born.

Industry insiders are interested to see how Ms. Frederick's elaborate style will translate to the sports world. "I'm looking forward to the challenge," Ms. Frederick said at the debut event for *Golden Galaxy* earlier this week. "With the film, I was able to work with over-the-top designs and lavish embellishments. With my new project, I'll have limited fabric options and will need to prioritize comfort and practicality." *Golden Galaxy* producer Liam Hart, who accompanied Ms. Frederick to the event, also commented on the project, saying that he was certain Ms. Frederick's limitless creativity would help to make it a success.

Fans of Ms. Frederick's work can see *Golden Galaxy* costumes on the big screen and on her Web site. However, to see the uniforms they'll have to watch the tournament in person or live on television.

158. What is true about the *Golden Galaxy* costumes?

(A) They were Ms. Frederick's first project.
(B) They are practical and comfortable.
(C) They received an award.
(D) They are available for sale online.

159. Who most likely is Ms. Reeves?

(A) An ice skating coach
(B) A fashion designer
(C) A film producer
(D) A professional athlete

160. What is suggested about Mr. Hart?

(A) He has worked with Ms. Frederick on several projects.
(B) He recently attended a movie premiere.
(C) He met Ms. Frederick at an anniversary party.
(D) He knows Ms. Reeves personally.

Questions 161-163 refer to the following letter.

March 8

Store Manager Shawn Boyd
Outdoors Plus, Soulard Branch
1009 Ash Avenue
Saint Louis, MO 63146

Dear Mr. Boyd,

As you know, Camping Sphere Inc. is introducing a new lightweight backpack to its product line. For the entire months of April and May, we will hold a special promotion, offering the product at 30% off its suggested retail price. We'll start advertising the sale two weeks in advance. The official launch date will be April 1, and there will be a special launch event at the McKinley Heights branch. I know you also applied to hold the event at the Soulard branch, but we decided to go with a store that had already been in charge of large-scale events such as this. I will visit your store next week to drop off the displays for the new backpacks. These stands should be placed in a prominent area, and I can advise you on the arrangement at that time.

Sincerely,

Justin Dawson
Justin Dawson

---

161. How long will the discount on the new product be offered?

(A) One week
(B) Two weeks
(C) One month
(D) Two months

162. According to the letter, why was the McKinley Heights branch selected for an event?

(A) It needs the most improvement in its sales figures.
(B) Its employees have hosted similar events.
(C) It is the company's largest store.
(D) Its customers voted to hold the event there.

163. What will happen next week?

(A) A branch manager will print out some promotional material.
(B) Mr. Dawson will recommend some display strategies.
(C) A store will start selling a new line of backpacks.
(D) Mr. Boyd will oversee a product launch event.

GO ON TO THE NEXT PAGE

Clara Starnes 1:09 P.M.	Hi. I'm going to write about the Lafayette Art Museum for my next exhibit review. I know you've all been there before. Do you have any advice for me?
Radha Pai 1:18 P.M.	The size of the collection is enormous, so you need to plan ahead to see everything.
Clara Starnes 1:42 P.M.	I've heard that visitors aren't allowed to take pictures in some sections of the museum.
Joyce Garza 1:46 P.M.	You're right, Clara. Photos are not permitted in some sections, but signs are prominently displayed to inform visitors.
Clara Starnes 1:59 P.M.	I assume it's really busy on weekends, so I think I'll go on a weekday. Which day is best?
Joyce Garza 2:16 P.M.	It's always packed. But in my experience, Tuesday is the best day to go if you don't want to be around a lot of tourists and school groups.
Clara Starnes 2:25 P.M.	Then I think I'll go there on Tuesday.
Alyssa Verdi 2:37 P.M.	You can get information about their regulations from the Web site, information desk, and signs posted throughout the museum.
Radha Pai 2:51 P.M.	Right. Lafayette is better than the place I visited last week, Timber Museum. Timber Museum should follow its example.
Alyssa Verdi 2:55 P.M.	If you plan on going more than once, it's worth signing up for a membership. It costs $20 for a one-year membership, but you save $7 each time you visit.
Clara Starnes 3:39 P.M.	I appreciate your advice, everyone.

164. What does Ms. Starnes ask for?

(A) Recommendations for tourist sites
(B) Tips for visiting a place
(C) Advice for opening an exhibit
(D) Explanation about a schedule

165. Why does Ms. Starnes decide to make a visit on Tuesday?

(A) Because she wants to avoid the crowds.
(B) Because she can listen to a special lecture.
(C) Because the entrance fee is discounted.
(D) Because a guided tour is being offered.

166. At 2:51 P.M., what does Ms. Pai most likely mean when she writes, "Timber Museum should follow its example"?

(A) The attendance at Timber Museum has gone down significantly.
(B) The entrance fee at Timber Museum is too expensive for tourists.
(C) The policies at Timber Museum are not clearly explained.
(D) The collection at Timber Museum is not very big.

167. What does Ms. Verdi imply about a membership?

(A) It should be purchased online.
(B) It should be renewed annually.
(C) It offers a $20 discount each year.
(D) It allows members to buy a two-day pass.

Questions 168-171 refer to the following e-mail.

E-Mail

To: Aida Mazzanti <a.mazzanti@smindustries.net>
From: Li Zhang <zhangli@metrorealty99.com>
Date: June 10
Subject: From Metro Realty

Dear Ms. Mazzanti,

Thank you for meeting with me last week to tour some of the apartments available through our firm. Please note that the apartments in Elliot Tower and the one in Geo Suites have been rented. —[1]—. The two-bedroom apartment in the HSW Building is still available. I know this is larger than what you wanted. —[2]—. However, it's in the Arleta neighborhood, so you'd be able to walk to your office. —[3]—. The current tenant is moving out on June 20, so you can move in on June 21. If you are interested, I can send you a lease agreement, which should be signed and returned no later than June 14. At that time, we will collect a $200 holding fee. —[4]—. This apartment is in a popular building, so I hope to hear from you soon so that you don't miss your chance.

Sincerely,

Li Zhang

---

168. Why did Mr. Zhang send the e-mail?

(A) To accept a suggestion
(B) To schedule a tour
(C) To send a housing contract
(D) To update property information

169. What is suggested in the e-mail?

(A) Ms. Mazzanti prefers a two-bedroom home.
(B) Mr. Zhang will meet Ms. Mazzanti at her office.
(C) Ms. Mazzanti's workplace is located in Arleta.
(D) Metro Realty is gathering survey information.

170. According to Mr. Zhang, by when should Ms. Mazzanti submit some paperwork?

(A) June 10
(B) June 14
(C) June 20
(D) June 21

171. In which of the positions marked [1], [2], [3], and [4] does the following sentence best belong?

"Additionally, you will be expected to pay a deposit equal to one month's rent when you move in."

(A) [1]
(B) [2]
(C) [3]
(D) [4]

Cleanup Begins on Carriage Lake *By Jeremy Trigg*

September 9—Plans for an extensive cleanup project at Carriage Lake are finally underway after the city encountered several obstacles. — [1] —. Talks regarding the need to improve the lake's condition began earlier this year, and it didn't take long to gather the public support needed. The city opened the project up for bids from companies in late March. — [2] —. Fortunately, the second round of bids resulted in a suitable contract agreement with Morris Enterprises.

The work, which began last week, involves removing contaminated soil from the bottom of the lake. — [3] —. Crews from Morris Enterprises are using a Preston-680 hydraulic dredge to remove the sediment. This equipment has a pump that is 24 inches in diameter, and Morris Enterprises bought it to replace its Caramillo-55, which would not have been powerful enough for this project.

"While Carriage Lake used to be a major draw for boating and fishing enthusiasts, attendance figures have been on a downward trend for years," said city councilperson Jane Clifton. "This project is costing taxpayers tens of millions of dollars, but the finished result will attract tourists, and the revenue they bring along with them. When you take the environmental impact into account as well, it's a win-win situation for everyone."

Once the work is completed, mercury levels in the water are expected to be reduced by as much as 97%. — [4] —. Because of that, officials will once again permit swimming in the lake, which hasn't been the case for decades. The city will also build an outdoor stage at the site, which will host music concerts, awards ceremonies, and more. To follow the progress of the cleanup, visit www.carriagelakecleanup.org.

172. What is the article mainly about?
    (A) A project's progress
    (B) A machine's availability
    (C) A change in policy
    (D) A tourism trend

173. What does Ms. Clifton most likely think about the project?
    (A) It should have been started earlier in the year.
    (B) The people handling it do not have enough experience.
    (C) It will benefit the community despite its high costs.
    (D) The final cost should be paid by boaters and fishermen.

174. What is NOT true about Carriage Lake?
    (A) It is currently unsuitable for swimming.
    (B) Its number of visitors has been steadily declining.
    (C) It is the main source of drinking water in the town.
    (D) It will be the site of an outdoor performance area.

175. In which of the positions marked [1], [2], [3], and [4] does the following sentence best belong?

    "None of the prospective businesses could complete the scope of the work within the proposed budget."

    (A) [1]
    (B) [2]
    (C) [3]
    (D) [4]

GO ON TO THE NEXT PAGE

July 3

Anne Stein
414 Fulton Street
Winchester, KY 40391

Dear Ms. Stein,

You recently booked a vehicle rental through the Trivo Rentals mobile phone app. We appreciate your business and would like to get your feedback on the enclosed form about the rental in order to improve our services further. We conduct research such as this regularly because we find that it is the best way to understand our customers.

We hope you will also introduce us to a friend who might be interested in our service. If you do so, your friend will receive a voucher by e-mail for 10 percent off any rental, and you will be given a voucher for a free GPS rental for the next time you rent from us.

Thank you for your participation!

The Trivo Rentals Team

Trivo Rentals

Thank you for taking the time to complete this survey. Your opinion matters to us!

Name: _Anne Stein_   Most Recent Rental Date: _June 25_

Rental Location: _Winchester_   Duration of Rental: _1 week_

1. How often do you use Trivo Rentals and why?
My personal vehicle is a van, so a few times a year I rent a fuel-efficient car to go on business trips out of state.

2. Why did you choose Trivo Rentals?
It's great that Trivo Rentals keeps costs down by using cars that are a few years old, rather than brand-new ones. What really sets the company apart is that it sends a representative to my home to give me a ride to the Trivo Rentals office.
This is very convenient because I can't drive there myself without creating a parking issue.

3. How can we improve our services?
I think the added charges for insurance and extra services should be explained more clearly up front.

4. Would you like to recommend our services to a friend or family member? (Y) / N
Name: _Cliff Bower_   E-mail Address: _c.bower@ferrel.com_

176. What is the purpose of the letter?

(A) To request information about a customer's experience

(B) To gather feedback about a new product

(C) To thank a customer for their opinion

(D) To ask for some research results

177. What is implied about Trivo Rentals?

(A) It provides special packages to business professionals.

(B) It operates branches across the country.

(C) It offers a wide variety of insurance options.

(D) It has a smartphone application for reservations.

178. In the letter, the word "find" in paragraph 1, line 3, is closest in meaning to

(A) suggest

(B) discover

(C) believe

(D) acquire

179. What is true about Ms. Stein?

(A) She can collect reward points for her rental.

(B) She will be e-mailed a coupon for 10% off.

(C) She will be entered into a drawing for a GPS device.

(D) She can receive a free equipment rental.

180. What is one thing that Ms. Stein likes about Trivo Rentals?

(A) Its convenient location

(B) Its brand-new vehicles

(C) Its cheap insurance

(D) Its pick-up service

Questions 181-185 refer to the following memo and schedule.

To: Cervantes Incorporated Staff
From: Armando Dixon, General Manager
Subject: For your immediate attention
Attachment: Inventory Schedule

February 23

Following last year's merger, we are still downsizing our staff and looking for ways to cut overhead costs. As a result, we will be moving our offices next month from the Rinehart Building to the Werner Building, which has a lower rental fee. Those of you who drive will be pleased to know that the Werner Building has an underground parking lot for employees only, just like our current building does.

We have hired a professional moving company, Guerra Co., whose crew will visit our building on Friday, March 17. You do not need to report to work on that day. Prior to the move, employees will assist with taking inventory of the company's furniture, equipment, and supplies according to the attached schedule. The head of HR will supply boxes, tape, and labels for you to gather your personal belongings.

Inventory Schedule

DATE	LOCATION	DEPARTMENT	MANAGER
Monday, March 13	2nd Floor	Accounting	Naoto Kodama
Tuesday, March 14	3rd Floor	Sales	Troy Concord
		Marketing	Jesse Mateo *
Wednesday, March 15	4th Floor	Human Resources	Alana Templeton
		R&D	Kamal Bakshi
Thursday, March 16	1st Floor	Administration	Joan Pafford

* As Jesse Mateo will be absent that week, Joan Pafford from administration will fill in for him on his department's assigned day.

181. Why did Mr. Dixon send the memo?

(A) To announce a company merger

(B) To explain a relocation procedure

(C) To give an update on a construction project

(D) To ask employees to reduce spending

182. What is indicated about the Rinehart Building?

(A) It has a private parking area.

(B) It will become the Cervantes Incorporated headquarters.

(C) It will be torn down in March.

(D) It is larger than the Werner Building.

183. What is implied about Cervantes Incorporated's employees?

(A) They will be reassigned to different departments.

(B) They should work from home temporarily.

(C) They will be given a day off in March.

(D) They should report inventory problems to Mr. Dixon.

184. What is suggested about Ms. Templeton?

(A) She took a tour of the Werner Building.

(B) She works on the third floor.

(C) She made a suggestion to Mr. Dixon.

(D) She will distribute packing supplies.

185. What is scheduled to happen on March 14?

(A) A company will move to a new building.

(B) Ms. Pafford will assist a department that is not hers.

(C) Employees from Guerra Co. will visit the business.

(D) Mr. Concord will be absent from the office.

Wednesday Night Documentary Screenings at Elsberry Hall

Elsberry Hall is pleased to bring you award-winning documentaries followed by a question-and-answer session with the special guests listed.

June 7: *Hourglass* / Running Time: 2 hrs 21 mins
Special Guest: Orlando Briggs (director)
This film explores how tourism has affected the small island of Kihoa over the past fifty years.

June 14: *Powering the North* / Running Time: 2 hrs 18 mins
Special Guest: Bruce Morrison (Can-Elec Vice President)
This film explores how Canadian energy company Can-Elec has adapted its business model since its inception decades ago.

June 21: *In the Game* / Running Time: 2 hrs 5 mins
Special Guest: Shamba Metha (director)
Watch the development of soccer from its humble beginnings in 19th-century England to becoming the world's most popular sport today.

June 28: *Not for Sale* / Running Time: 1 hr 48 mins
Special Guest: Erin Hanson (director)
See how politician Benjamin Tribble's career has unfolded from his first election in 1982 to the present day.

Book ahead for big savings! Buy your tickets within the month of May to get $5 off the entrance fee.

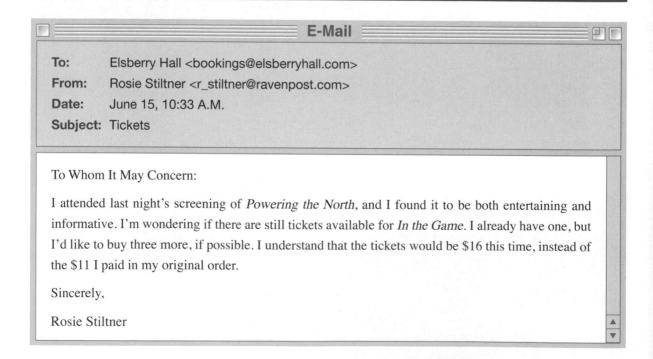

E-Mail

To: Elsberry Hall <bookings@elsberryhall.com>
From: Rosie Stiltner <r_stiltner@ravenpost.com>
Date: June 15, 10:33 A.M.
Subject: Tickets

To Whom It May Concern:

I attended last night's screening of *Powering the North*, and I found it to be both entertaining and informative. I'm wondering if there are still tickets available for *In the Game*. I already have one, but I'd like to buy three more, if possible. I understand that the tickets would be $16 this time, instead of the $11 I paid in my original order.

Sincerely,

Rosie Stiltner

To: Rosie Stiltner <r_stiltner@ravenpost.com>
From: Elsberry Hall <bookings@elsberryhall.com>
Date: June 15, 1:41 P.M.
Subject: RE: Tickets

Dear Ms. Stiltner,

Elsberry Hall enjoys a spacious seating area that can accommodate nearly five hundred people, so I'm pleased to inform you that we still have tickets available for the film you requested. However, you should note that the special guest for that date will be screenwriter Kevin Drummond, as the director cannot attend as planned. If you still want the tickets despite this change, you will have to call our box office at 555-3866 to give us your credit card details again, as we do not save information from previous transactions.

Sincerely,

Miles Rahn
Customer Service Agent, Elsberry Hall

186. What characteristic is shared by all of the films?

(A) They last longer than two hours.
(B) They explore a subject over time.
(C) They focus on business-related matters.
(D) They are made by well-known directors.

187. What is implied about Ms. Stiltner?

(A) She wants to exchange her tickets for a different film.
(B) She created a documentary film on her own.
(C) She booked her original ticket before June 1.
(D) She signed up for a theater membership program.

188. Which film's special guest has changed?

(A) Hourglass
(B) Powering the North
(C) In the Game
(D) Not for Sale

189. In the second e-mail, the word "enjoys" in paragraph 1, line 1, is closest in meaning to

(A) experiences
(B) possesses
(C) appreciates
(D) welcomes

190. According to Mr. Rahn, why should Ms. Stiltner call the box office?

(A) To verify a change
(B) To get an updated schedule
(C) To cancel a purchase
(D) To provide payment information

McCabe Home Appliances to Trim Its Product Line

August 27—McCabe Home Appliances plans to halt production of its PrimeAir-60 air purifier sometime in September, and stores carrying the product will sell it until it is sold out. Consumers who currently have the PrimeAir-60 are encouraged to stock up on filters, as the filters made for other McCabe air purifiers are a different shape and cannot be accommodated by the device.

A spokesperson for McCabe Home Appliances commented that the decision was made in order to focus on better-selling products. The PrimeAir-60 accounts for less than two percent of the company's revenue, so decision-makers at McCabe believed it was time to start promoting other designs. In addition, the majority of customers who did purchase the device complained about its loud operation. For a complete listing of McCabe Home Appliances' products, visit www. mccabehomeapp.com.

  www.mccabehomeapp.com

Home » Catalog » Sale Items » Clearance

The following items are on sale until all items are sold. *Updated October 1*

PrimeAir-60   ADD TO CART

Regular Price: $169.99   Clearance Price: $75.99

PrimeAir-60 is an air purifier that can be used in rooms up to 1,500 cubic feet. It has low energy usage and operates more efficiently than most air purifiers on the market today. Regular use of the PrimeAir-60 can reduce the presence of bacteria, viruses, and allergens in your home. The device is highly recommended for allergy sufferers and those with respiratory problems. The filter can be cleaned by hand and reused up to ten times.

PrimeAir-60 Replacement Filters 3-Pack   ADD TO CART

Regular Price: $59.99   Clearance Price: $39.99

PrimeAir-60 Replacement Filters 5-Pack   ADD TO CART

Regular Price: $89.99   Clearance Price: $55.99

All orders, including those containing clearance items, qualify for free delivery from October 1 to October 31.

```
● ● ●
◀ ▶  🏠  www.mccabehomeapp.com                    🔍
```

Home ≫ Reviews ≫ PrimeAir-60

Written by: Olivia Densmore   **Posted:** October 5

I will be sad to see this product go. I bought mine last year and have enjoyed using it constantly since then. I understand that the company has to take action on the most common complaint, but I've never experienced that problem. Even though the filters can be hand-washed and reused, I bought a 5-pack from the clearance sale today so I could ensure the use of the device for a long time.

191. What is the purpose of the article?

(A) To promote a new product in the line
(B) To notify consumers of a product recall
(C) To commemorate a company achievement
(D) To report the discontinuation of a product

192. In the article, the phrase "accounts for" in paragraph 2, line 2, is closest in meaning to

(A) uses
(B) represents
(C) happens
(D) explains

193. According to the Web page, what can customers receive in October?

(A) An extended warranty
(B) Free replacement filters
(C) An updated catalog
(D) Complimentary shipping

194. What does Ms. Densmore imply about the PrimeAir-60?

(A) She uses it during the daytime only.
(B) She will replace it with a newer model.
(C) She does not think it was too noisy.
(D) She made a complaint about it to the company.

195. What is most likely true about Ms. Densmore?

(A) She bought the PrimeAir-60 for $75.99.
(B) Her living room is less than 1,500 cubic feet.
(C) She spent $55.99 on replacement filters.
(D) Her purchase was delivered by express mail.

Volunteers Needed

Richmond Public Library provides essential educational services to the community, and we are looking for volunteers to assist us with our programs. You must be at least eighteen years old and be available for a minimum of four hours a week. To apply as a volunteer, fill out a form at the front desk by March 20. Please note that all volunteers must go to an orientation workshop at the library before they can begin volunteering. With help from members of the community, we can reach more people and help them to attain their literacy goals. We hope to get at least thirty new volunteers for our programs, so please encourage your family and friends to volunteer as well.

MEMO

To employees,

Thank you, everyone, for taking the time out of your busy schedules to train our new library volunteers. The training session will be held on April 7, starting at 1 P.M. There will be two hours of general library information followed by overviews of individual projects (30 minutes each) by the head of each program as below. At the end of the orientation, volunteers will be given a form on which they can indicate which programs they would like to assist with. I cannot guarantee that all volunteers will be matched with their first choice, but I will do my best.

Program Coordinators:

- Silvano Marchesi, Adult Literacy
- Walter Vance, Children's Storytime
- Elizabeth Lancaster, Homework Help
- Hariti Nayak, Early Readers

We didn't quite make our recruitment goal. However, I'm still pleased with the group's size. I will send a list of the volunteers later this week.

```
┌─────────────────────────────────────────────────────────────────────────────┐
│ ▓▓▓▓▓▓▓▓▓▓▓▓▓▓▓▓▓▓▓▓▓▓▓▓▓        E-Mail        ▓▓▓▓▓▓▓▓▓▓▓▓▓▓▓▓▓▓▓▓▓▓▓▓▓      │
├─────────────────────────────────────────────────────────────────────────────┤
```

To: Miriam Jarmillo <m.jarmillo@richmondpl.org>
From: Wen Lang <w.lang@richmondpl.org>
Date: April 29
Subject: Programs Update

Dear Ms. Jarmillo,

I'd like to give you an update on how the library programs are going. The new volunteers are settling into their roles nicely, and we've had a lot of positive feedback from the people participating in the programs. Because of the high demand for the Homework Help program, especially among middle school students, the director of that program plans to find a few more volunteers. I am tracking the weekly participation of each program and will have more detailed figures for you next month.

All the best,

Wen Lang
Richmond Public Library Program Coordinator

---

196. What is NOT expected from volunteers?

(A) Working over a certain number of weekly hours
(B) Attending an on-site training session
(C) Meeting a minimum age requirement
(D) Submitting a letter of recommendation

197. In the announcement, the word "reach" in paragraph 1, line 5, is closest in meaning to

(A) equal
(B) stretch
(C) achieve
(D) approach

198. What is suggested about the April 7 training session?

(A) It lasted for two hours in total.
(B) It assessed the volunteers' literacy.
(C) It had fewer than thirty participants.
(D) It got positive feedback from the volunteers.

199. Why will volunteers fill out a form at the training session?

(A) To express their preferences
(B) To rate the speakers' performances
(C) To confirm their schedules
(D) To suggest new programs

200. Who plans to recruit more volunteers?

(A) Mr. Marchesi
(B) Mr. Vance
(C) Ms. Lancaster
(D) Ms. Nayak

Stop! This is the end of the test. If you finish before time is called, you may go back to Parts 5, 6, and 7 and check your work.

Actual Test 3

LISTENING TEST

In the Listening test, you will be asked to demonstrate how well you understand spoken English. The entire Listening test will last approximately 45 minutes. There are four parts, and directions are given for each part. You must mark your answers on the separate answer sheet. Do not write your answers in your test book.

PART 1 🎧 09

Directions: For each question in this part, you will hear four statements about a picture in your test book. When you hear the statements, you must select the one statement that best describes what you see in the picture. Then find the number of the question on your answer sheet and mark your answer. The statements will not be printed in your test book and will be spoken only one time.

Statement (C), "They're sitting at the table," is the best description of the picture, so you should select answer (C) and mark it on your answer sheet.

1.

2.

GO ON TO THE NEXT PAGE

3.

4.

5.

6.

GO ON TO THE NEXT PAGE

Directions: You will hear a question or statement and three responses spoken in English. They will not be printed in your test book and will be spoken only one time. Select the best response to the question or statement and mark the letter (A), (B), or (C) on your answer sheet.

7. Mark your answer on your answer sheet.

8. Mark your answer on your answer sheet.

9. Mark your answer on your answer sheet.

10. Mark your answer on your answer sheet.

11. Mark your answer on your answer sheet.

12. Mark your answer on your answer sheet.

13. Mark your answer on your answer sheet.

14. Mark your answer on your answer sheet.

15. Mark your answer on your answer sheet.

16. Mark your answer on your answer sheet.

17. Mark your answer on your answer sheet.

18. Mark your answer on your answer sheet.

19. Mark your answer on your answer sheet.

20. Mark your answer on your answer sheet.

21. Mark your answer on your answer sheet.

22. Mark your answer on your answer sheet.

23. Mark your answer on your answer sheet.

24. Mark your answer on your answer sheet.

25. Mark your answer on your answer sheet.

26. Mark your answer on your answer sheet.

27. Mark your answer on your answer sheet.

28. Mark your answer on your answer sheet.

29. Mark your answer on your answer sheet.

30. Mark your answer on your answer sheet.

31. Mark your answer on your answer sheet.

PART 3 🎧

Directions: You will hear some conversations between two or more people. You will be asked to answer three questions about what the speakers say in each conversation. Select the best response to each question and mark the letter (A), (B), (C), or (D) on your answer sheet. The conversations will not be printed in your test book and will be spoken only one time.

32. Where most likely does the woman work?

(A) At a hospital

(B) At a university

(C) At a museum

(D) At a restaurant

33. What does the man ask about?

(A) How much a service costs

(B) What classes are being taught

(C) Which day is convenient

(D) How busy a location is

34. What information will the woman provide next week?

(A) A business's opening hours

(B) A detailed schedule

(C) The topic of a lecture

(D) The number of visitors

35. Who most likely is the man?

(A) A manager's assistant

(B) An applicant for a grant

(C) The director of a company

(D) The keynote speaker at a convention

36. What is the woman doing this week?

(A) Writing up a proposal

(B) Attending a conference

(C) Interviewing candidates

(D) Training at a new company

37. Why does the man want to meet the woman?

(A) To negotiate a deal

(B) To prepare a presentation

(C) To discuss a job opportunity

(D) To introduce a coworker

38. Where most likely are the speakers?

(A) At a clothing shop

(B) At a grocery store

(C) At a beauty salon

(D) At a paint retailer

39. What do first-time customers receive?

(A) A discount

(B) A free item

(C) A gift certificate

(D) A membership card

40. What will the man most likely do next?

(A) Make a purchase

(B) Wash some hair

(C) Choose a color

(D) Provide a refund

41. Why is the man calling?

(A) To complain about a rule

(B) To place an order

(C) To explain a service

(D) To ask about a price

42. What problem does the man mention about the lawn mower?

(A) It wasn't delivered on time.

(B) It doesn't work properly.

(C) It is the wrong model.

(D) It was incorrectly priced.

43. What does the woman say she will do?

(A) Contact a manager

(B) Issue a refund

(C) Organize a sales event

(D) Repair a device

GO ON TO THE NEXT PAGE

44. What does the woman say she plans to do?
 (A) Go on a cruise
 (B) Write a negative review
 (C) Work some extra hours
 (D) Resign from her position

45. What do the men imply about Gulliver Travel?
 (A) It has poor customer service.
 (B) It offers discounts to its employees.
 (C) It has the cheapest cruises on the market.
 (D) It is more expensive than Blue Green Travel.

46. According to the woman, what happened at the company while the men were away?
 (A) A coworker left her job.
 (B) A customer made a complaint.
 (C) A new person was hired.
 (D) A survey was conducted.

47. What are the speakers mainly discussing?
 (A) An article's contents
 (B) A course's difficulty
 (C) A product's packaging
 (D) A beverage's price

48. Why does the man say, "they went a little too far"?
 (A) He finds a design childish.
 (B) He thinks a product is expensive.
 (C) He wants to relocate a branch.
 (D) He disagrees with a policy.

49. What does the woman say she will do?
 (A) Return an item
 (B) Report a choice
 (C) Create an advertisement
 (D) Contact some customers

50. What are the speakers mainly discussing?
 (A) A new opening
 (B) A job change
 (C) A customer complaint
 (D) An office layout

51. What does the woman say she is looking forward to?
 (A) Talking to people directly
 (B) Working with the man
 (C) Reading some reviews
 (D) Joining a new company

52. What does the man suggest the woman do?
 (A) File a complaint
 (B) Consult a coworker
 (C) Find a different job
 (D) Provide some advice

53. What will happen on August 8?
 (A) A business will be relocated.
 (B) An author will be interviewed.
 (C) A contract will be signed.
 (D) A book signing will be held.

54. What does the woman suggest doing?
 (A) Putting away some items
 (B) Registering for an event
 (C) Waiting in line
 (D) Moving some furniture

55. What does the man say he will do?
 (A) Prepare an advertisement
 (B) Reserve some tickets
 (C) Write a summary
 (D) Visit a venue

56. What has the woman recently done?

(A) Attended a lecture series

(B) Registered for an event

(C) Reviewed a research study

(D) Given a presentation

57. What does the woman think the man should do?

(A) Meet a speaker

(B) Extend a deadline

(C) Submit a study

(D) Choose a topic

58. What does the woman imply about a review she wrote?

(A) It is outdated.

(B) It will be published soon.

(C) It took a long time to make.

(D) It was presented at a conference.

---

59. Who most likely is the man?

(A) A secretary

(B) A dentist

(C) A plumber

(D) A nutritionist

60. Why does the woman say, "Drinking cold water causes it"?

(A) To suggest a possible treatment

(B) To describe a healthy habit

(C) To give details about her diet

(D) To explain when a problem occurs

61. What does the man recommend the woman do?

(A) Follow a personal hygiene routine

(B) Make an appointment with a doctor

(C) Avoid drinking sweet beverages

(D) Take some time off from work

Interview Hours

Time Slot	Day	Time
1	Monday	3:00 P.M.
2	Wednesday	10:30 A.M.
3	Wednesday	5:00 P.M.
4	Friday	1:45 P.M.

62. What was announced in an e-mail?

(A) An employee has been promoted.

(B) A new branch is opening.

(C) A deadline has been extended.

(D) A company is relocating.

63. What is the man hesitating to do?

(A) Accept an offer

(B) Apply for a position

(C) Choose a candidate

(D) Talk to a supervisor

64. Look at the graphic. Which time slot is the man able to attend?

(A) Time Slot 1

(B) Time Slot 2

(C) Time Slot 3

(D) Time Slot 4

~ Special Menu ~

Each drink on the special menu comes with a free pastry!

black coffee ⟶ croissant — $2.50
single latte ⟶ éclair — $3.00
mocha ⟶ Danish — $3.50
cappuccino ⟶ cinnamon roll — $3.50

	Maximum passengers	Transmission
Vehicle 1	5	Manual
Vehicle 2	5	Automatic
Vehicle 3	8	Manual
Vehicle 4	8	Automatic

65. What does the woman ask about?

(A) What food is available
(B) How much an item costs
(C) Which coffee is best
(D) Where a menu is located

66. Look at the graphic. Which pastry will the woman get?

(A) A croissant
(B) An éclair
(C) A Danish
(D) A cinnamon roll

67. Why is the woman surprised?

(A) The prices have been lowered.
(B) The shop closes late.
(C) The menu options have changed.
(D) The coffee is strong.

68. Why does the man prefer renting a car to taking the train?

(A) It is cheaper.
(B) It is more convenient.
(C) It is faster.
(D) It is more reliable.

69. Look at the graphic. Which vehicle will the woman most likely reserve?

(A) Vehicle 1
(B) Vehicle 2
(C) Vehicle 3
(D) Vehicle 4

70. What does the man ask the woman?

(A) Where they will park
(B) How many people will drive
(C) How much the rental will cost
(D) When they should leave

PART 4 🎧 12

Directions: You will hear some talks given by a single speaker. You will be asked to answer three questions about what the speaker says in each talk. Select the best response to each question and mark the letter (A), (B), (C), or (D) on your answer sheet. The talks will not be printed in your test book and will be spoken only one time.

71. What industry does the speaker work in?
(A) Entertainment
(B) Fashion
(C) Automobile
(D) Marketing

72. According to the speaker, what should the company focus on?
(A) More comfortable products
(B) Better customer service
(C) More competitive prices
(D) Safer designs

73. What will the listeners most likely do next?
(A) Look at some designs
(B) Test-drive some vehicles
(C) Try on some clothes
(D) Review some materials

74. What type of business does the speaker work for?
(A) An insurance company
(B) A real estate agency
(C) A law firm
(D) An accounting business

75. What does the speaker mention about the position?
(A) Its salary can be negotiated.
(B) Its location has been changed.
(C) Its start date is fixed.
(D) Its duties require advanced skills.

76. What is the listener asked to do?
(A) Come in for an interview
(B) Return a phone call
(C) Submit a job application
(D) Modify a schedule

77. What department do the listeners most likely work in?
(A) Human resources
(B) Marketing
(C) Accounting
(D) Customer service

78. What can listeners find in the document the speaker sent last week?
(A) Contract terms
(B) Benefit options
(C) Employee information
(D) Required qualifications

79. What should listeners do by Wednesday?
(A) Read about some occupations
(B) Review job applications
(C) Advertise a job opening
(D) Update a Web site

80. What is the speaker preparing for?
(A) Hosting an event
(B) Entering a contest
(C) Moving to a new location
(D) Installing new equipment

81. Why does the speaker say, "The total is fourteen"?
(A) To request a payment
(B) To report the number of participants
(C) To explain a policy
(D) To provide the number of lectures

82. What does the speaker offer to do?
(A) Apply a discount
(B) Arrange a pickup
(C) Postpone a meeting
(D) Send directions

GO ON TO THE NEXT PAGE

83. According to the speaker, what recently happened?
(A) A branch was opened.
(B) Two companies merged.
(C) A product was launched.
(D) A restaurant changed its menu.

84. What did Mr. Boyle study in graduate school?
(A) Cooking
(B) Business administration
(C) Italian
(D) Art

85. What is Mr. Boyle currently doing?
(A) Touring a restaurant
(B) Designing a menu
(C) Ordering some food
(D) Attending a class

86. What type of business has the caller reached?
(A) A communications provider
(B) An electronics manufacturer
(C) A Web design company
(D) A device repair shop

87. What problem does the speaker mention?
(A) A service is slow.
(B) A machine is defective.
(C) A delivery is delayed.
(D) A Web site is down.

88. Why should callers press 0?
(A) To upgrade a plan
(B) To report an issue
(C) To cancel an order
(D) To request a refund

89. Who most likely are the listeners?
(A) Visiting clients
(B) Retired employees
(C) Branch managers
(D) New workers

90. What is the purpose of the talk?
(A) To outline some rules
(B) To announce break times
(C) To introduce a new manager
(D) To assess a performance

91. Why does the speaker say, "We work in close proximity to one another"?
(A) To justify a policy
(B) To provide directions
(C) To explain a layout
(D) To demand respect

92. Who most likely will the speaker interview next week?
(A) Computer repair technicians
(B) Sales executives
(C) Graphic designers
(D) Laboratory researchers

93. What does the speaker mean when she says, "it was twice what we expected"?
(A) A job opening got many applicants.
(B) A company's market share grew significantly.
(C) A candidate requested a larger salary.
(D) A hiring process took longer than planned.

94. According to the speaker, what will Timothy do?
(A) Reserve a conference room for an interview
(B) Review the résumés of applicants
(C) Create a vacation schedule for the team
(D) Find volunteers to give up their workspaces

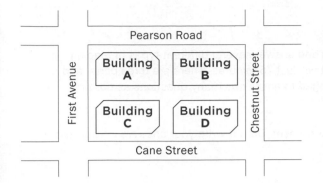

	Production Sections			
	Zone A	Zone B	Zone C	Zone D
	Plastics	Glass	Metal	Wood

95. Look at the graphic. Which building is under construction?

(A) Building A

(B) Building B

(C) Building C

(D) Building D

96. What has caused a delay in the construction project?

(A) Insufficient materials

(B) A car accident

(C) Weather conditions

(D) Financial problems

97. What will take place this afternoon?

(A) A grand opening

(B) A sales event

(C) An anniversary party

(D) An artisan fair

98. What is the speaker in charge of doing?

(A) Assuring the quality of goods

(B) Overseeing the hiring process

(C) Promoting the company's products

(D) Repairing production equipment

99. Who most likely are the listeners?

(A) Safety inspectors

(B) New employees

(C) Potential investors

(D) Department managers

100. Look at the graphic. In which area will the listeners spend the shortest amount of time?

(A) Zone A

(B) Zone B

(C) Zone C

(D) Zone D

This is the end of the Listening test. Turn to Part 5 in your test book.

READING TEST

In the Reading test, you will read a variety of texts and answer several different types of reading comprehension questions. The entire Reading test will last 75 minutes. There are three parts, and directions are given for each part. You are encouraged to answer as many questions as possible within the time allowed.

You must mark your answers on the separate answer sheet. Do not write your answers in your test book.

PART 5

Directions: A word or phrase is missing in each of the sentences below. Four answer choices are given below each sentence. Select the best answer to complete the sentence. Then mark the letter (A), (B), (C), or (D) on your answer sheet.

101. You may buy tickets for the May 11 concert in advance ------- at the door.

(A) for
(B) so
(C) or
(D) nor

102. For her lecture, Bridget Coleman provided ------- of foreign terms commonly used in court.

(A) translate
(B) translated
(C) translator
(D) translations

103. Most of Margos Electronics' devices are manufactured ------- factories overseas.

(A) by
(B) about
(C) past
(D) along

104. The team leader is too busy to pick up Colcott's CEO at the airport -------.

(A) her
(B) she
(C) hers
(D) herself

105. The ------- purpose of this meeting is to review our safety procedures.

(A) primary
(B) rigorous
(C) plentiful
(D) timely

106. Despite practicing, Peter Bertrand was not ------- prepared for the questions the interviewers asked him.

(A) suffice
(B) sufficiency
(C) sufficient
(D) sufficiently

107. Before his business trip to Mexico, Mr. Marcus studied Spanish so that he could ------- with the locals.

(A) state
(B) communicate
(C) reserve
(D) understand

108. ------- attendee will be given a folder with the program and notes about each presenter.

(A) Every
(B) Few
(C) Several
(D) All

109. Recent ------- in various scientific fields have caused a sudden increase in life expectancy.

(A) developments
(B) versions
(C) timelines
(D) ranges

110. Ms. Mander added six names to the ------- dinner guest list, bringing the number of expected diners up to twenty-three.

(A) origin
(B) originate
(C) original
(D) originally

111. The spring line of Vivi Fashion House's leather handbags was ------- at last week's runway show.

(A) consulted
(B) relieved
(C) attempted
(D) unveiled

112. Volunteers ------- in the lobby of the building at 11:00 A.M. next Saturday to prepare the fundraising event.

(A) gathered
(B) have gathered
(C) will be gathering
(D) will have been gathering

113. We can meet anytime that is convenient for you since my schedule is more flexible than -------.

(A) you
(B) yourself
(C) your
(D) yours

114. Gibson Department Store handed out small bags of free samples to customers to thank them for ------- its grand opening event.

(A) attend
(B) attending
(C) attendee
(D) attendance

115. Passengers traveling in first class are permitted to check in a maximum ------- three suitcases each.

(A) up
(B) beyond
(C) of
(D) to

116. Strict ------- with the company's policies is expected from employees at all times.

(A) application
(B) compliance
(C) management
(D) correction

117. Please enter the building through the north door, ------- is located on Sacramento Street.

(A) who
(B) what
(C) where
(D) which

118. According to the news anchor, the virus infected ------- ten thousand computers in just a few minutes.

(A) approximate
(B) approximately
(C) approximates
(D) approximation

119. Flucos Clothing plans on making a series of advertisements to appeal to a ------- clientele.

(A) diverse
(B) correct
(C) usual
(D) descriptive

120. This study indicates that customers would ------- shop online than try on items in a store.

(A) further
(B) probably
(C) rather
(D) mistakenly

GO ON TO THE NEXT PAGE

121. The new revelations about the emission of harmful gases by its factories has ------- as an issue for the company.

(A) become
(B) emerged
(C) resulted
(D) produced

122. Given the complex layout of the city, ------- the location of the Portville branch was difficult.

(A) choosing
(B) choice
(C) choose
(D) chosen

123. The restaurant manager reviewed food safety ------- with his staff to prepare for the monthly inspection.

(A) regulating
(B) regulated
(C) regulations
(D) regulates

124. To view a ------- explanation of presidential candidate Ann Lathrup's economic plans, visit her campaign Web site.

(A) repeated
(B) customized
(C) testified
(D) detailed

125. In order to receive a full refund for a returned item, the receipt ------- to the cashier.

(A) presented
(B) has presented
(C) would be presenting
(D) must be presented

126. By offering ------- prices, Ergo Supermarkets has become one of the most successful grocery stores in the area.

(A) competed
(B) competing
(C) competitive
(D) competitively

127. Abigail Hoskins was given a certificate of appreciation by the city ------- her efforts in improving educational standards.

(A) for
(B) into
(C) because
(D) when

128. Even though Maria's Grill is only ------- closer to the center of town, it gets a lot more customers than Primavera's.

(A) slightly
(B) overwhelmingly
(C) carefully
(D) popularly

129. The designer used a new type of software ------- the brochure advertising the convention.

(A) creates
(B) will create
(C) to create
(D) created

130. Management decided to hire Amy Volpert in spite of the ------- in her educational background because of her experience as an intern.

(A) attainments
(B) shortcomings
(C) submissions
(D) qualifications

PART 6

Directions: Read the texts that follow. A word, phrase, or sentence is missing in parts of each text. Four answer choices for each question are given below the text. Select the best answer to complete the text. Then mark the letter (A), (B), (C), or (D) on your answer sheet.

Questions 131-134 refer to the following e-mail.

To: Margaret Keeble <m_keeble@tysoncomm.com>
From: Juan Torres <j_torres@tysoncomm.com>
Date: November 18
Subject: Keep up the good work!

Dear Ms. Keeble,

I would like to thank you for handling the situation when Ms. Ferona came to our office upset because of a billing error. It is not always easy to know what to do in these situations, but the way you handled it was ------- . Pleasing our clients is an important part of the job. ------- , we
131.   **132.**
can't give them everything they demand. This would have a detrimental effect on our finances.

By explaining the reason for the error in a calm manner, you resolved the conflict quickly. -------
                                                                                                          133.
. The other managers and I agree that you deserve ------- from your hard work. Therefore, you
                                                                    134.
will be given an extra day of paid vacation.

Congratulations!

Juan Torres
Office Manager, Tyson Communications

131. (A) feasible
    (B) appropriate
    (C) steady
    (D) affordable

132. (A) In addition
    (B) Even if
    (C) Nonetheless
    (D) For instance

133. (A) Ms. Ferona will oversee this area from now on.
    (B) We have already reprinted your new bill showing the change.
    (C) It was also a good example to set for our junior staff members.
    (D) The company will upgrade its billing software soon.

134. (A) to benefit
    (B) will benefit
    (C) being benefits
    (D) it benefitted

GO ON TO THE NEXT PAGE

March 16, Narton—A new library _____ in the center of the small town of Narton will be opening
135.
its doors next month. The Narton Library will hold a collection of books, magazines, and videos

on all topics. In addition, it will offer free Internet access, host regular events, and provide

various workshops to _____ the community. "I think this library will be extremely helpful,"
136.
indicated _____ resident Samuel Prendy. "Narton is isolated in a remote location, and it is
137.
difficult for us to stay up-to-date on all the latest information." Mayor Brenkel is scheduled to give

a speech at the opening ceremony on April 2. _____. For more information about it, check
138.
Narton's official Web site.

135. (A) will be located
(B) locating
(C) is located
(D) located

136. (A) serve
(B) organize
(C) request
(D) visit

137. (A) expert
(B) dependent
(C) local
(D) active

138. (A) All are invited to attend this event.
(B) It will be announced on that day.
(C) You can pick up your books at that time.
(D) He was elected with a large majority.

As you know, the company donates to the F&Y homeless shelter every year. This year, instead of money, we have decided to donate various goods that the shelter is in need of. You'll see bins at the entrance of each department head's office. Employees are ------- to place items in good
139.

condition into these bins. When a bin is -------, it will be picked up by PR staff and taken to the
140.

shelter. A list of acceptable items will be posted in the staff lounge. -------. In particular, note that
141.

although clothing is welcome, certain ------- are not accepted due to common allergies and
142.

limited washing options. Thank you in advance for your donations.

Actual Test 3

139. (A) encouragement
(B) encourage
(C) encouraging
(D) encouraged

140. (A) open
(B) full
(C) finished
(D) consumed

141. (A) Please consult it carefully before placing anything in a bin.
(B) You may take anything that seems necessary to you.
(C) However, entrance is restricted to upper management only.
(D) If you agree with the terms, you may sign below.

142. (A) methods
(B) amounts
(C) materials
(D) payments

Questions 143-146 refer to the following letter.

September 14

Sterling Murray
25 Morocco Drive
Newtown, PA 18777

Dear Mr. Murray,

It is our pleasure to award you first place in the Graper Scientific Research Competition for your paper entitled "Quality Control in Pharmaceuticals: Testing Three Methods." The study you conducted and your findings were fascinating. -------. We trust that the rest of the readers in the

143.

scientific community will find your work -------. In addition, you ------- $2,500 for further

144.   145.

research. We hope that this will help in your future endeavors. Congratulations, and thank you

for your ------- to the field of medicine.

146.

Sincerely,

Richard Nelson
Director, Graper Science

143. (A) We highly recommend that you read this study.
(B) Many contestants have entered the competition.
(C) However, most of the information was already well-known.
(D) Your article will appear in next month's *Graper Science News*.

144. (A) inspires
(B) inspire
(C) inspirational
(D) inspiration

145. (A) will grant
(B) would have been granted
(C) would have granted
(D) will be granted

146. (A) distinction
(B) survey
(C) contribution
(D) knowledge

PART 7

Directions: In this part you will read a selection of texts, such as magazine and newspaper articles, e-mails, and instant messages. Each text or set of texts is followed by several questions. Select the best answer for each question and mark the letter (A), (B), (C), or (D) on your answer sheet.

Questions 147-148 refer to the following e-mail.

```
●  ●  ●                          E-Mail

To: Veronica Tessier <v.tessier@greatinterior.com>
From: Lucy Bracker <l.bracker@memail.net>
Subject: Sample Pictures
Date: January 18
_____

Dear Ms. Tessier,

Thank you for sending pictures of possible layouts for our living room. It is helpful to see
pictures of various colors and textures put together to get an idea of how things would look.
I am having trouble opening the last picture you sent, however. It seems to be in a different
format from the others, and my computer doesn't seem to be able to read it. Could you send
it again in the same format as the others?

Thank you very much.

Sincerely,

Lucy Bracker
```

147. Who most likely is Ms. Tessier?

(A) A professional photographer
(B) An interior designer
(C) An IT expert
(D) An art gallery owner

148. What problem is Ms. Bracker having?

(A) She doesn't have enough space.
(B) She doesn't like the color combinations.
(C) She is unable to view a file.
(D) She didn't receive an e-mail.

Mercer Real Estate New Employee Orientation Schedule
A

AUGUST						
Sunday	Monday	Tuesday	Wednesday	Thursday	Friday	Saturday
	1	2	3	4 **OR**	5	6
7	8	9	10	11	12	13
14	15	16	17	18	19	20
21	22	23	24 **DA**	25	26 **PRO**	27
28	29 **FFD**	30	31			

OR: First day of orientation. Walk-through of premises
DA: Individual department assignments announced
PRO: Pictures taken and creation of Web site profiles
FFD: First full day compensated as a full-time employee

149. On which day will employees tour the facilities?

(A) August 4
(B) August 24
(C) August 26
(D) August 29

150. What is indicated about the company's Web site pictures?

(A) They are required for finding one's department.
(B) They must be submitted on the first day of work.
(C) They are taken after departments have been assigned.
(D) They should be brought to work by employees on August 26.

Questions 151-152 refer to the following text-message chain.

Jimmie Kristof	[3:08 P.M.]
Rebecca, have you made arrangements for going to the conference next Monday?	
Rebecca Pauly	[3:09 P.M.]
I thought the company was taking care of that. Aren't they providing a bus for us?	
Jimmie Kristof	[3:10 P.M.]
No. They decided not to after all. So most people are taking the subway or driving.	
Rebecca Pauly	[3:13 P.M.]
Then I guess I'll drive. There aren't any subway stations near my place. But I've never been to that venue. I have no idea how to get there.	
Jimmie Kristof	[3:14 P.M.]
Well, that's why I contacted you. I was wondering if you'd like me to pick you up.	
Rebecca Pauly	[3:15 P.M.]
That would be much easier for me. Are you sure you don't mind?	
Jimmie Kristof	[3:17 P.M.]
Of course not. Your house is on my way. And I've been to that hall many times before.	

151. What is indicated about the writers' company?

(A) It is not handling transportation for employees.
(B) It has offices located near a subway station.
(C) It is organizing an event for its employees.
(D) It is moving to a new location.

152. At 3:15 P.M., what does Ms. Pauly mean when she writes, "That would be much easier for me"?

(A) She prefers to go by bus.
(B) She would like Mr. Kristof to drive her.
(C) She can pick up Mr. Kristof at the conference.
(D) She doesn't mind taking the subway.

CLARENCE CO.

Clarence Co. provides the best service in the area for businesses that are relocating. We provide a variety of options so that your transition to the new location is as smooth as possible.

If you sign up for our deluxe package, we will provide the following services:
- Unlimited plastic crates for packing belongings
- Packing of large equipment and furniture
- Special packing by our IT experts for your computers and other electronics
- Loading and unloading of all items
- Special clean-up service from our sister company, Sparkly Clean

Call us today at 553-0295 to schedule a time for us to come take a look at your facilities. We will provide a free estimate for our services.

---

153. What kind of company is Clarence Co.?

(A) A machinery manufacturer
(B) A delivery service
(C) A moving company
(D) A marketing consultant

154. What is indicated about Clarence Co.?

(A) It partners with a cleaning company.
(B) It can fix broken devices.
(C) It has branches in several locations.
(D) It is currently offering free upgrades.

155. What can customers learn if they have a consultation?

(A) How to set up some equipment
(B) How much they will have to pay
(C) Where to relocate their business
(D) When a delivery will be made

Questions 156-158 refer to the following online review.

Hotel Review: Bashiva Hotel, 1882 Hummingbird Way

Rating: ★★★★☆
Name: Stella Manning
Date(s) of stay: January 18–20   **Room type:** Regular Single Room

I stayed at Bashiva Hotel for two nights. I was on a business trip to meet some clients. Bashiva Hotel was ideal for my purposes. The rooms are comfortable, and the breakfast buffet is nice and well worth the price. — [1] —. Most importantly, despite being in a busy area of the city, I didn't hear much noise at night.

I chose this hotel because of its proximity to the downtown area. It was convenient for finding restaurants and getting to my meetings. — [2] —. I was supposed to catch a train early in the afternoon. I asked the front desk to call a taxi. I had to wait about fifteen minutes for it to arrive. — [3] —. Then, although the hotel staff said it would take about twenty minutes to get to the train station, it took closer to forty-five minutes. — [4] —. Fortunately, I managed to make it on time for my train because I had left early. However, all of this hassle could have been avoided had there been a bus from the hotel. The hotel already offers rides to and from the airport, but I think many of its guests come by train. Offering rides to the station as well would be very helpful.

156. What does Ms. Manning indicate about the hotel?
(A) It provides free breakfast.
(B) It is very noisy during the night.
(C) It is located near the city center.
(D) It is twenty minutes away from an airport.

157. In which of the positions marked [1], [2], [3], and [4] does the following sentence best belong?
"The only issue I had was when I was leaving."
(A) [1]
(B) [2]
(C) [3]
(D) [4]

158. What does Ms. Manning want the hotel to do?
(A) Add a shuttle service
(B) Adjust a timetable
(C) Clean its facilities
(D) Hire more staff

GO ON TO THE NEXT PAGE

Questions 159-160 refer to the following notice.

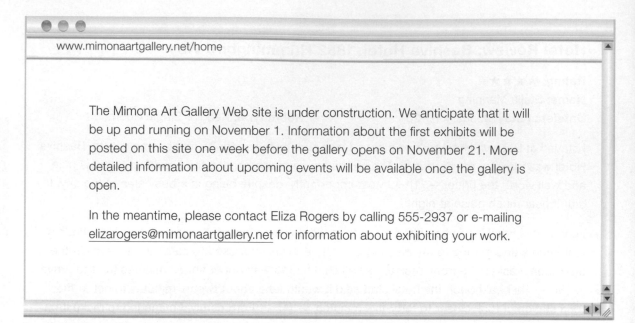

www.mimonaartgallery.net/home

The Mimona Art Gallery Web site is under construction. We anticipate that it will be up and running on November 1. Information about the first exhibits will be posted on this site one week before the gallery opens on November 21. More detailed information about upcoming events will be available once the gallery is open.

In the meantime, please contact Eliza Rogers by calling 555-2937 or e-mailing elizarogers@mimonaartgallery.net for information about exhibiting your work.

159. What is the purpose of the notice?

(A) To request reviews of an exhibit
(B) To announce the opening of a gallery
(C) To advertise artwork available for sale
(D) To provide a timeline for a new Web page

160. Why should Eliza Rogers be contacted?

(A) To make an appointment for a visit
(B) To purchase a work of art
(C) To ask about displaying artwork
(D) To register for an event

E-Mail

To:	Brandon Mosher <bmosher@trupal.biz>
From:	Karen Pesco <kpesco@trupal.biz>
Date:	March 31
Subject:	Tax Forms

Dear Mr. Mosher,

I am currently going over your tax documents. However, it has come to my attention that you worked at another company for two months last year. Although this is just a short period of time, your previous income must be taken into account and stated when submitting tax forms. While companies submit the necessary declarations when the employee leaves, it appears that your previous place of employment has not. I would be happy to take care of this for you, but for that, I need information about your compensation at your last job. If you could provide the two pay stubs you received for those two months, I will gladly adjust your documents for the tax year.

Let me know if you have any questions.

Sincerely,

Karen Pesco

---

161. In what department does Ms. Pesco most likely work?

(A) Accounting
(B) Marketing
(C) Customer service
(D) Research and Development

162. What problem does Ms. Pesco mention?

(A) Some income must be declared.
(B) A payment has been rejected.
(C) A tax rate has increased.
(D) Lots of employees have quit.

163. What does Ms. Pesco ask Mr. Mosher for?

(A) A job description
(B) Salary records
(C) Proof of employment
(D) Tax schedules

Clyde Mortensen [10:40 A.M.]	Hi, Jennifer and Henry. I want to get started on the design for the April issue's cover. Do you know who we are interviewing for the main article?
Jennifer Sydnor [10:41 A.M.]	It's going to be Jeff Blasio, a chef from an upcoming cooking show. I'll be writing that article, actually. I'm interviewing him next Tuesday.
Henry Tessor [10:42 A.M.]	And I'm the photographer for this one. So I'll be there on Tuesday as well to do the photo shoot of Mr. Blasio.
Clyde Mortensen [10:44 A.M.]	Oh, let me know when you're done. It would help to know what topics will be covered in the article and what the pictures will look like.
Jennifer Sydnor [10:45 A.M.]	How about we all meet on Wednesday? Henry, you can show us your pictures, and I can tell you both about the interview.
Clyde Mortensen [10:47 A.M.]	That works for me. I think the covers work best when the designers collaborate with the writers and photographers.
Henry Tessor [10:48 A.M.]	I couldn't agree more. Wednesday works for me too. Morning or afternoon? I can meet at any time.
Clyde Mortensen [10:49 A.M.]	The morning would be much better for me. Let's say at ten.
Jennifer Sydnor [10:50 A.M.]	Ten is good. I'll see you two then.

164. Where do the writers most likely work?

(A) At a photo studio
(B) At a restaurant
(C) At a design firm
(D) At a magazine publisher

165. What is indicated about Mr. Blasio?

(A) He owns a popular restaurant.
(B) He will be on television.
(C) He writes for a magazine.
(D) He applied for a new job.

166. What will Mr. Tessor do on Tuesday?

(A) Create an advertisement
(B) Take some pictures
(C) Write an article
(D) Choose a menu

167. At 10:48 A.M., what does Mr. Tessor most likely mean when he writes, "I couldn't agree more"?

(A) He doesn't like the design of one of the projects.
(B) He believes pictures are the most important element.
(C) He thinks people from different departments should work together.
(D) He isn't sure what topics will be covered in the interview.

Broken Pearls to Be Performed at the Marina Theater

January 21—*Broken Pearls*, a play in three acts, will be performed at the Marina Theater in Dresdon on February 13, 14, and 15. The script was written by Maria Deluz, who also directed the play. It will be the Marina Theater's first modern-era play. — [1] —.

Because of a limited marketing budget and a rather low-profile cast, the premiere, which was at the Golden Volcano Theater in Henryville, did not attract a large audience. However, the performance received such good reviews that the troupe was encouraged to start a tour of the region and perform at various local venues. — [2] —. What sent the play's popularity skyrocketing was one review in particular, by notorious critic Joshua Corbett. Mr. Corbett, who is known for his strict and often scathing reviews, called *Broken Pearls* "a jewel of modern theater" in a long-form article. Thus, the play suddenly went from obscure piece to famous work. — [3] —.

"We never expected *Broken Pearls* to become such a hit," lead actor Jeremy Moriah explained. "It is all very exciting. I look forward to performing at new venues. I hope to even travel overseas for a show someday." — [4] —. Indeed, several venues around Europe have contacted production manager Isabelle Morton about possible future events.

---

168. What is implied about the Marina Theater?

(A) It usually shows performances of older works.

(B) It has already hosted *Broken Pearls* several times.

(C) It has become Dresdon's most popular theater.

(D) It received a lot of negative reviews in the past.

169. What is indicated about the play's troupe?

(A) It spent a lot of money on advertising.

(B) It is composed of little-known actors.

(C) It is used to performing in renowned venues.

(D) It has performed in a variety of countries.

170. According to the article, who contributed the most to the play's popularity?

(A) Maria Deluz

(B) Joshua Corbett

(C) Jeremy Moriah

(D) Isabelle Morton

171. In which of the positions marked [1], [2], [3], and [4] does the following sentence best belong?

"This dream might just become a reality."

(A) [1]

(B) [2]

(C) [3]

(D) [4]

GO ON TO THE NEXT PAGE

Langda Goods Terms and Conditions

Thank you for choosing Langda Goods to carry your luggage on your next trip. All Langda luggage is covered by our one-year warranty. Please inspect your parcel carefully upon receiving it. If any part of the product is damaged, do not throw away any part of the product or its packaging. Immediately inform the delivery company. They will pick up the damaged goods and provide you with a claim form to fill out and a claim number. You may then follow the progress of your request on our Web site. It may take up to three weeks to review a claim.

A replacement will be sent to the customer if any of the following cases is reported within one year of purchase:
– Flaws in workmanship or material
– Tearing of the material
– Broken part
– Wearing of the wheels
– Color fading

Please note that in case of the following events, the customer is fully liable for the article and is entitled to no compensation:
– Unreasonable usage
– Staining
– Loss or theft

172. What is suggested about the recipients of the information?

(A) They have tried to return an item.

(B) They have recently purchased some luggage.

(C) They have just signed a contract with Langda Goods.

(D) They have posted a negative review of Langda Goods.

173. What does Langda Goods ask customers NOT to do if they receive a damaged item?

(A) Discard broken parts

(B) Notify the deliverer

(C) Complete a document

(D) Wait for a response

174. What can customers do on the Langda Goods Web site?

(A) Request faster delivery service

(B) Fill out a complaint form

(C) Check the status of a claim

(D) Extend the warranty of an item

175. In which case can a customer get a replacement?

(A) If the item is stolen.

(B) If the product has defects.

(C) If the material becomes stained.

(D) If the luggage is overused.

Arnett Co.

Arnett Co. has been providing high-quality services for the past five years. From May 1 to October 31, we're here to help you keep your yard and garden in excellent condition. We can provide mowing, tree-trimming, and weeding on a weekly or biweekly basis. If you are interested in having trees, flowers, or bushes planted, we can get you a discount with our partners at the Pineway Greenhouse, a reliable local business.

We have lots of returning customers every season, but slots are still available even if you've never used our services before. Please note that we do not serve corporate properties. If you'd like advice about the best way to care for your yard, we'll send one of our technicians to your home for a consultation at no charge. The monthly charge* for our basic service (mowing and cleanup only) is $425 for weekly visits or $250 for biweekly visits. There is also a premium service (the basic service plus weeding, bush trimming, and fertilizer treatments) for $675 for weekly visits or $450 for biweekly visits. Call us today at 555-5588.

*Applies to standard lots only. For oversized lots, please call to inquire about our rates.

Arnett Co. – New Customer Information

Customer: <u>Vickie Warnick</u>
Property: <u>226 Sunburst Drive, Portland, OR 97221</u>
Lot Type: <u>Standard</u>
* Equipment: <u>Lawnmower (model: Duncan-440)</u>
Type of Service requested: [ ] Basic   [X] Premium
                           [ ] Weekly   [X] Biweekly
Start Date of Service: <u>June 2</u>

- -

Consultation Date: <u>May 26</u>   Property Assessed by: <u>Robert Cass</u>

* If the customer prefers to use his/her own equipment, list the type and model name above.

176. What is the purpose of the flyer?

  (A) To announce a change in ownership
  (B) To promote a gardening care business
  (C) To advertise a sales event
  (D) To introduce a new service

177. What is indicated about Arnett Co.?

  (A) It collaborates with a greenhouse.
  (B) It accepts bookings by e-mail.
  (C) It sells several varieties of plants and flowers.
  (D) It offers services year-round.

178. What is NOT mentioned about Arnett Co.?

  (A) It only caters to residential properties.
  (B) It is not currently accepting new customers.
  (C) It has different prices for standard and
     oversized lots.
  (D) It offers a free consultation.

179. What is suggested about Ms. Warnick?

  (A) She will receive a discount for the first month.
  (B) She wants her own equipment to be used.
  (C) She was referred to Arnett Co. by a friend.
  (D) She has a property that is larger than
     average.

180. How much will Ms. Warnick be charged per
   month?

  (A) $250
  (B) $425
  (C) $450
  (D) $675

To: Gladwell Finance <info@gladwellfinance.com>

From: Keith Angulo <k.angulo@irvinemail.net>

Date: November 17

Subject: Transfer issue

To Whom It May Concern:

I tried to send money to my cousin in Vancouver using your online money transfer service. I applied a $5 credit toward the fees, which I got from signing up for your newsletter. He was able to pick up the cash at the Vancouver branch. However, after the transaction was completed, I noticed that I had been charged the full amount for the transfer fee. I looked over my account history to make sure I hadn't already used the credit, and I confirmed that I hadn't. However, the credit is no longer listed on my account. Please let me know why there was a problem with this transaction, request #45960, and what can be done to resolve it.

Thank you,

Keith Angulo

To: Keith Angulo <k.angulo@irvinemail.net>
From: Gladwell Finance <info@gladwellfinance.com>
Date: November 18
Subject: RE: Transfer issue

Dear Mr. Angulo,

On behalf of Gladwell Finance, I would like to apologize for the inconvenience you experienced. You did not mention the date that you sent the funds, but I was able to find it by using the number you provided. We were experiencing some problems when our internal server went down for a brief period on November 16, and this affected some customers. I have reissued you a credit of $5 to make up for the discount you should have gotten. My manager, Patrick Ogden, has also given me authorization to issue you a further $10 credit due to your inconvenience. This credit can be used toward our processing fees. You can verify that these amounts have been credited to you by clicking on the My Balance link after logging into your online account. You can use the credit anytime at your discretion. Should you have any further problems, you can call 555-3940, extension 31, rather than our customer service hotline. That way, you can get straight through to me.

Sincerely,

Brielle Stewart

181. What did Mr. Angulo do before contacting Gladwell Finance?

(A) He heard about the problem from his cousin.

(B) He received an invoice in the mail.

(C) He checked his past transactions.

(D) He reviewed his credit card bill.

182. What did Ms. Stewart use to look into Mr. Angulo's complaint?

(A) His transaction code

(B) His account number

(C) His request date

(D) His credit balance

183. In the second e-mail, the phrase "went down" in paragraph 1, line 3, is closest in meaning to

(A) deflated

(B) malfunctioned

(C) decreased

(D) lost

184. How can Mr. Angulo confirm that a credit was received?

(A) By reviewing an online page

(B) By checking a printed receipt

(C) By requesting a paper statement

(D) By e-mailing Ms. Stewart's manager

185. What is Mr. Angulo told to do if he has more issues?

(A) Call a customer service hotline

(B) Request a contract termination

(C) File a formal complaint online

(D) Contact Ms. Stewart directly

GO ON TO THE NEXT PAGE

Portrait Pro

Portrait Pro is a four-part series for people who have already mastered the basics of oil on canvas and want to move on to more advanced methods of painting. In these videos, renowned designer Gloria Hutton guides you through four steps to take your painting skills to the next level. In the first tutorial, you will learn how to choose the best brushes for various types of projects. The second video focuses on several advanced techniques. Third, you will create a portrait based on a provided model. Finally, you will learn how to paint your own ideas instead of using a model. The videos are available for download from all major Web sites.

Special Seminar at Hacksburg Museum of Arts and Crafts

On October 30, come to the Hacksburg Museum of Arts and Crafts for a special master class on painting. Artist Gloria Hutton will be giving a lecture based on the first video of her recently released four-part series, Portrait Pro.

Gloria Hutton is a prominent painter who created hundreds of breathtaking works that have been displayed in museums and festivals worldwide. Her natural talent has allowed Ms. Hutton to make a living off of her art early on, so money was not the motivation for making the videos. But she was receiving repeated requests for tips and private lessons and didn't have time to give regular classes. So she finally decided to release her tutorial series, which immediately became a bestseller.

Time: October 30, 3:00 P.M.
Place: Hacksburg Museum of Arts and Crafts, Shalandra Room
Fee: $35.00

Seating is limited for this event. Please register in advance by calling 555-8874.

Portrait Pro

Review by Margaret Jones

I highly recommend the *Portrait Pro* series to anyone passionate about art. I've been painting for several years now, and I thought all I could do to improve was to keep practicing. I never thought I'd learn so much simply by watching some videos. However, I've improved my skills tenfold by following Ms. Hutton's tutorials. She manages to explain complicated techniques in simple terms, and I was amazed by what I could accomplish by the time I finished watching these.

The only complaint I have is with the video about creating a project from scratch without referring to anything. I've watched that video dozens of times and still can't understand what Ms. Hutton is saying. However, because the three other videos were so helpful, I still think this series is worth the purchase.

186. According to the summary, who is the intended audience for the series?

(A) Professional artists with expert skills
(B) Beginners who never painted before
(C) People with experience in painting
(D) Collectors looking for artwork

187. What will attendants do at the seminar on October 30?

(A) Participate in filming a video
(B) Learn how to select utensils
(C) Create a portrait
(D) Practice some brushstrokes

188. According to the flyer, why did Ms. Hutton create the series?

(A) She needed more income.
(B) She wanted to advertise her classes.
(C) She was often asked for advice.
(D) She enjoyed her teaching experience.

189. In the review, the word "following" in paragraph 1, line 4, is closest in meaning to

(A) modifying
(B) coming after
(C) using
(D) testing

190. Which video of the *Portrait Pro* series does Ms. Jones say she watched many times?

(A) The first
(B) The second
(C) The third
(D) The fourth

GO ON TO THE NEXT PAGE

Divine Delights Caterer

For the best service in the area and the highest-quality food, choose Divine Delights Caterer! Summer is over, and our fall premium menus are here! See our Web site www.divinedelightscaterer.com for beverages and many other types of menus.

Premium Menu 1 ($50 per person)

Appetizer (choose one)
☐ Pumpkin soup
☐ Caesar salad

Main dish (choose one)
☐ Parmesan chicken
☐ Broccoli cream pasta

Dessert
Apple pie

Premium Menu 2 ($75 per person)
Includes one glass of wine

Appetizer (choose one)
☐ Onion soup
☐ Cobb salad

Main dish (choose one)
☐ Beef tenderloin
☐ Stuffed mushrooms

Dessert
Blueberry crumble

---

* Prices include service. Reservations for premium menus must be made at least one month in advance. A minimum of twenty people are required. Only one type of premium menu is possible per event. Please indicate each guest's dish preference at the time of reservation.

From: Rooter, Phil <prooter@glypha.com>
To: Stacker, Lindsay <lstacker@glypha.com>
Date: September 15
Subject: Corporate Dinner

Hi. I think your suggestion of holding a corporate dinner to celebrate the merger of Glypha Corp. and Baller Inc. is an excellent idea. You mentioned October 20 as a possible date. I've checked with everyone, and it seems to be a good day to hold the event. As requested, I've attached a flyer for a catering company I told you about. I know we want to have a nice meal, so I think we should get a premium menu. But I'm not sure what our budget is. Let me know which one you think would be best. I will then pass the menu around the office so that everyone can select their dish choices.

From: Tracy Meloy
To: Phil Rooter

Since Stephanie is out on vacation this week, I chose her dish preferences for her for the corporate dinner. I told you that she and I would both be having the same thing. However, I just found out that she is a vegetarian, so could you switch her selection to the broccoli cream pasta? Sorry about the change.

191. What is suggested about Divine Delights Caterer?

(A) It is closed in the winter and spring.
(B) It adapts its menus to the seasons.
(C) It offers only two types of menus.
(D) It has an online reservation system.

192. What is the purpose of the planned event?

(A) To congratulate a colleague
(B) To celebrate a successful quarter
(C) To impress a potential client
(D) To mark a new partnership

193. When should Glypha Corp. make the catering reservation by?

(A) September 15
(B) September 20
(C) October 15
(D) October 20

194. What is Mr. Rooter asked to do?

(A) Postpone a vacation
(B) Modify a meal choice
(C) Reschedule an event
(D) Add a guest to an attendance list

195. What main dish will Ms. Meloy most likely have at the corporate dinner?

(A) Parmesan chicken
(B) Broccoli cream pasta
(C) Beef tenderloin
(D) Stuffed mushrooms

GO ON TO THE NEXT PAGE

---

www.kikilafabrics.com/about

| HOME | **ABOUT** | PRODUCTS | CLEARANCE | CART |

Kikila Fabrics is famous for having the widest selection of fabrics. You can find any texture and color you need for all of your projects right here on our site.

Make sure you check out the CLEARANCE page, where all items are 50 percent off. There, you'll find the best value for your money. In addition, if you order more than 10 meters of any fabric, you are eligible for free delivery.

Fabric is cut to the size indicated in the order form. Please check your measurements carefully as we do not grant returns or exchanges if you entered the wrong numbers.

---

www.kikilafabrics.com/clearance

| HOME | ABOUT | PRODUCTS | **CLEARANCE** | CART |

SEPTEMBER CLEARANCE ITEMS

Flannel – print
Available prints: owls, cats, bears
Description: This single layer flannel is wonderful for quilts and children's apparel.
Washing: machine wash/tumble dry
Price: $9.50 per meter

Wool Blend
Available colors: green, red
Description: This is the perfect material for coats, jackets, blankets, and other winter favorites.
Washing: machine wash cold/tumble dry low; Note: do NOT iron
Price: $12.00 per meter

Faux leather
Available colors: brown, black
Description: This heavyweight imitation leather is great for luxurious pillows and other home decor elements.
Washing: wipe down with damp rag
Price: $6.00 per meter

To: Frances Olsen <folsen@pozmail.net>
From: Kikila Fabrics <cs@kikilafabrics.com>
Subject: Order Number 201483
Date: September 21

Dear Mr. Olsen,

We have received your request to exchange the faux leather you purchased. Please accept our sincerest apologies for sending you the wrong color. We have verified your original order and confirmed that you had in fact requested black. Your order of 6 meters of faux leather in black has been shipped. You can expect to receive it by Friday afternoon. In addition, we've included 5 meters of red wool blend as an apology. It can be easily combined with the faux leather to create a variety of winter apparel.

As for the material we originally sent, we kindly request that you send it back to us and we will refund you for its shipping.

Thank you for your patience and understanding.

Sincerely,

Kikila Fabrics

196. According to the first Web page, what is Kikila Fabrics known for?

(A) Its low prices
(B) Its fast delivery
(C) Its variety of items
(D) Its return policy

197. How should the flannel material be washed?

(A) By wiping it with a wet piece of cloth
(B) By taking it to a dry cleaner
(C) By putting it in a washing machine
(D) By using cold water only

198. What color material did Mr. Olsen originally receive?

(A) Green
(B) Red
(C) Black
(D) Brown

199. What is implied about Mr. Olsen?

(A) He received a discount on his purchase.
(B) He provided the wrong measurements.
(C) He tried to exchange some apparel.
(D) He did not pay a delivery fee for his order.

200. What does Kikila Fabrics offer as an apology to Mr. Olsen?

(A) Complimentary fabric
(B) A refund for his purchase
(C) An article of winter clothing
(D) Free shipping on a future order

Stop! This is the end of the test. If you finish before time is called, you may go back to Parts 5, 6, and 7 and check your work.

Actual Test 4

LISTENING TEST

In the Listening test, you will be asked to demonstrate how well you understand spoken English. The entire Listening test will last approximately 45 minutes. There are four parts, and directions are given for each part. You must mark your answers on the separate answer sheet. Do not write your answers in your test book.

PART 1 🎧13

Directions: For each question in this part, you will hear four statements about a picture in your test book. When you hear the statements, you must select the one statement that best describes what you see in the picture. Then find the number of the question on your answer sheet and mark your answer. The statements will not be printed in your test book and will be spoken only one time.

Statement (C), "They're sitting at the table," is the best description of the picture, so you should select answer (C) and mark it on your answer sheet.

1.

2.

GO ON TO THE NEXT PAGE

3.

4.

5.

6.

GO ON TO THE NEXT PAGE

PART 2 🎧 14

Directions: You will hear a question or statement and three responses spoken in English. They will not be printed in your test book and will be spoken only one time. Select the best response to the question or statement and mark the letter (A), (B), or (C) on your answer sheet.

7. Mark your answer on your answer sheet.

8. Mark your answer on your answer sheet.

9. Mark your answer on your answer sheet.

10. Mark your answer on your answer sheet.

11. Mark your answer on your answer sheet.

12. Mark your answer on your answer sheet.

13. Mark your answer on your answer sheet.

14. Mark your answer on your answer sheet.

15. Mark your answer on your answer sheet.

16. Mark your answer on your answer sheet.

17. Mark your answer on your answer sheet.

18. Mark your answer on your answer sheet.

19. Mark your answer on your answer sheet.

20. Mark your answer on your answer sheet.

21. Mark your answer on your answer sheet.

22. Mark your answer on your answer sheet.

23. Mark your answer on your answer sheet.

24. Mark your answer on your answer sheet.

25. Mark your answer on your answer sheet.

26. Mark your answer on your answer sheet.

27. Mark your answer on your answer sheet.

28. Mark your answer on your answer sheet.

29. Mark your answer on your answer sheet.

30. Mark your answer on your answer sheet.

31. Mark your answer on your answer sheet.

PART 3 🎧 15

Directions: You will hear some conversations between two or more people. You will be asked to answer three questions about what the speakers say in each conversation. Select the best response to each question and mark the letter (A), (B), (C), or (D) on your answer sheet. The conversations will not be printed in your test book and will be spoken only one time.

32. What does the woman want to buy?
    (A) A card
    (B) A desk
    (C) A computer
    (D) A shelf

33. What does the man say about the items?
    (A) Not all of them are discounted.
    (B) Most of them are out of stock.
    (C) Many of them are outdated.
    (D) Some of them are mislabeled.

34. What will the man most likely do next?
    (A) Verify a product's price
    (B) Speak to a manager
    (C) Check an account history
    (D) Print out a coupon

35. What is the purpose of the woman's call?
    (A) To make an appointment
    (B) To extend a deadline
    (C) To report some test results
    (D) To change work hours

36. What does the man mention about the company?
    (A) Its workers' shift schedules are flexible.
    (B) Its major tasks are done before noon.
    (C) Its medical office isn't open in the morning.
    (D) Its productivity is particularly high this week.

37. What does the man say he will do?
    (A) Inform a manager of a change
    (B) Reduce the workload for employees
    (C) Postpone a dental checkup
    (D) Promote the woman to a higher position

38. Why is the man calling?
    (A) To schedule the delivery of an item
    (B) To notify of a document's availability
    (C) To update his personal information
    (D) To request directions to a location

39. What does the man say is required?
    (A) Picture identification
    (B) Contact information
    (C) A local mailing address
    (D) A payment receipt

40. Why can't the woman meet the man today?
    (A) She forgot her passport.
    (B) She didn't make an appointment.
    (C) She is stuck in traffic.
    (D) She lives too far away.

41. Where most likely is the conversation taking place?
    (A) At a train station
    (B) At a bookstore
    (C) At a print shop
    (D) At a library

42. What does the woman ask Mr. Clayton?
    (A) Where a facility is located
    (B) Whether an exception can be made
    (C) How a process should be executed
    (D) How much an item costs

43. What will need to be paid on Friday?
    (A) An overdue fine
    (B) A transportation fee
    (C) A lost item charge
    (D) A luggage delivery bill

GO ON TO THE NEXT PAGE

44. What are the speakers mainly talking about?
    (A) An audience review
    (B) A musician's performance
    (C) An advertisement design
    (D) An informational handout

45. What problem does the woman mention?
    (A) A show's break time is too short.
    (B) A piece of music was poorly interpreted.
    (C) An entertainer is running late.
    (D) A schedule printout is incomplete.

46. What does the man mean when he says, "How is that possible"?
    (A) He doesn't understand how to do a task.
    (B) He wants the woman to explain a change.
    (C) He is surprised to notice an error.
    (D) He disagrees with the woman's statement.

47. What most likely is the woman's job?
    (A) Subway ticket vendor
    (B) Interior designer
    (C) Real estate agent
    (D) Taxi driver

48. What does the man ask about?
    (A) A meeting time
    (B) A place's location
    (C) Property values
    (D) Ticket prices

49. What will the woman most likely do next?
    (A) Find a property for the man
    (B) Help the man locate a place
    (C) Drive the man to a station
    (D) Send a document to the man

50. Where most likely is the conversation taking place?
    (A) At a fire station
    (B) At a real estate agency
    (C) At a jewelry store
    (D) At an interior designer's

51. What characteristic do Maria and Clyde want?
    (A) An old-fashioned appearance
    (B) A contemporary look
    (C) A traditional system
    (D) A high energy production

52. What is mentioned about the Windsor Gold?
    (A) It has sold out.
    (B) It's a customer favorite.
    (C) It has a gold finish.
    (D) It's in a modern style.

53. Who most likely is the man?
    (A) A hotel manager
    (B) A restaurant worker
    (C) A private caterer
    (D) An event organizer

54. What does the woman plan on doing after work tomorrow?
    (A) Going straight home
    (B) Dining with colleagues
    (C) Shopping for groceries
    (D) Meeting her friends

55. What does the woman ask the man to do?
    (A) Cancel her request
    (B) Add items to her order
    (C) Meet her at her office
    (D) Make a reservation

56. What is the purpose of the woman's call?

(A) To ask for directions

(B) To schedule a meeting

(C) To inquire about a package

(D) To report a missing item

57. What does the man mean when he says, "I should have been clearer"?

(A) He needs to explain a new strategy.

(B) He thinks the woman went the wrong way.

(C) He is going to provide a status update.

(D) He is confused by the woman's statement.

58. What does the woman say about the intersection?

(A) She has already passed it.

(B) She used to work in an office near it.

(C) She doesn't know where it is.

(D) She has found a post office by it.

---

59. Who most likely is the man?

(A) A pastry chef

(B) A business consultant

(C) A newspaper reporter

(D) A fitness expert

60. What are the speakers mainly discussing?

(A) A business strategy

(B) A product launch

(C) A shortage of materials

(D) A training event

61. What does the woman say will happen next month?

(A) Free refreshments will be served.

(B) A new location will be opened.

(C) A class will be offered.

(D) More employees will be hired.

WEEKDAY TRAIN SCHEDULE

Train Number	Destination	Departure Time	Arrival Time
105	Atlanta	6:20 A.M.	7:40 A.M.
207	Atlanta	10:30 A.M.	11:50 A.M.
482	Atlanta	2:20 P.M.	3:40 P.M.
553	Atlanta	5:50 P.M.	7:10 P.M.

62. What type of company do the speakers most likely work at?

(A) A travel agency

(B) A clothing store

(C) A transportation company

(D) A food producer

63. What will the man do tomorrow?

(A) Depart for Atlanta

(B) Attend an event

(C) Search for a hotel

(D) Leave the office early

64. Look at the graphic. Which train will the man most likely take?

(A) Train 105

(B) Train 207

(C) Train 482

(D) Train 553

GO ON TO THE NEXT PAGE

**Amateur Art Contest
Call for entries**

Submission period: February 3–5
Awards Ceremony: February 7 at 6 P.M.
Show opens to the public: February 8
Show closes: February 20

Willow Art Museum

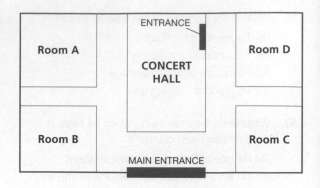

65. What will the man do tomorrow?

(A) Write an article
(B) Meet with a reporter
(C) Tour a museum
(D) Purchase some artwork

66. Look at the graphic. When does the man need extra help?

(A) February 3
(B) February 5
(C) February 7
(D) February 20

67. What does the woman say she will do?

(A) Move to a new home
(B) Submit an original painting
(C) Come to the museum early
(D) Create a registration form

68. Who most likely is the man?

(A) A conductor
(B) A musician
(C) A ticket agent
(D) An audience member

69. What does the man mention about the lecture?

(A) It costs extra to attend.
(B) It doesn't have any more seats available.
(C) It started a few minutes ago.
(D) It will be about tonight's music.

70. Look at the graphic. Where will the woman most likely go next?

(A) Room A
(B) Room B
(C) Room C
(D) Room D

PART 4 🎧16

Directions: You will hear some talks given by a single speaker. You will be asked to answer three questions about what the speaker says in each talk. Select the best response to each question and mark the letter (A), (B), (C), or (D) on your answer sheet. The talks will not be printed in your test book and will be spoken only one time.

71. Where is this talk most likely being heard?
(A) At a museum
(B) At a department store
(C) At a concert hall
(D) At a souvenir shop

72. What will the speaker do at eleven thirty?
(A) Host an auction
(B) Play a song
(C) Explain a device
(D) Start a guided tour

73. What does the speaker recommend the listeners do at twelve o'clock?
(A) Meet with a specialist
(B) Attend a lecture
(C) Observe a specific item
(D) Exit the building

74. Why does the speaker apologize?
(A) There is a lack of seats.
(B) A machine malfunctioned.
(C) A meeting is starting late.
(D) A location has changed.

75. What is the purpose of the meeting?
(A) To introduce an employee
(B) To select group members
(C) To explain a new policy
(D) To review a project's goals

76. According to the speaker, why should the questions be written down?
(A) They should be reviewed by a supervisor.
(B) They will be read aloud for a recording.
(C) They need to be sorted by category.
(D) They are limited to one per person.

77. What kind of product does the report describe?
(A) Athletic shoes
(B) An electronic device
(C) Natural cosmetics
(D) A home appliance

78. According to the speaker, what is special about the product?
(A) Its safety features
(B) Its recyclable materials
(C) Its compact size
(D) Its lightweight design

79. What does the speaker recommend doing?
(A) Comparing prices
(B) Testing products
(C) Visiting a Web site
(D) Calling with questions

80. Who most likely are the listeners?
(A) Tour guides
(B) Job applicants
(C) Beach visitors
(D) Hotel guests

81. What are the listeners asked to do?
(A) Explain a problem
(B) Fill out a survey
(C) Find a partner
(D) Do a role-play activity

82. What will the listeners most likely do next?
(A) Pick up a handout
(B) Follow the speaker
(C) Take a break
(D) Sign up for a session

Actual Test 4

GO ON TO THE NEXT PAGE

141

83. Where is this announcement most likely being heard?
    (A) At a grocery store
    (B) At an airport
    (C) At a daycare center
    (D) At a zoo

84. Why does the speaker say, "This will only slow the process"?
    (A) To prevent rude behavior
    (B) To clarify an estimate
    (C) To encourage purchases
    (D) To announce a delay

85. What does the speaker offer some young visitors?
    (A) Priority seating
    (B) Free entry
    (C) A toy animal
    (D) Photographs of animals

86. What is the purpose of the message?
    (A) To modify an order
    (B) To make an apology
    (C) To explain a process
    (D) To request a payment

87. What is mentioned about *The Grand Hope*?
    (A) It was written by a best-selling author.
    (B) It is less expensive than *Agents and Foes*.
    (C) It is currently out of stock.
    (D) It was given as a birthday present.

88. What does the speaker ask the listener to do?
    (A) Provide a refund
    (B) Use a fast delivery service
    (C) Update a Web site
    (D) Return a phone call

89. What task are the listeners expected to do?
    (A) Taste some beverage samples
    (B) Record some music performances
    (C) Review some advertisements
    (D) Assess some job candidates

90. What does the speaker imply when he says, "Don't pay attention to them"?
    (A) The company wants independent opinions.
    (B) Some handouts contain an error.
    (C) The listeners were given the wrong instructions.
    (D) Some employees will be monitoring the activity.

91. What will the listeners most likely do next?
    (A) Print some documents
    (B) Write down questions
    (C) Put on name tags
    (D) Form small groups

92. What is the purpose of the talk?
    (A) To introduce an author
    (B) To advertise a book
    (C) To criticize an idea
    (D) To request nominations

93. What does the speaker imply when she says, "Trust me"?
    (A) She has read the book.
    (B) She will write a novel.
    (C) She plans on answering questions.
    (D) She has won several awards.

94. What will most likely happen next?
    (A) A book will be signed.
    (B) A passage will be read.
    (C) Some questions will be asked.
    (D) An award will be presented.

EMERALD PARK TOUR SCHEDULE

DEPARTURE TIME	GUIDE
11:00 A.M.	Cindy
12:30 P.M.	Sandra
2:00 P.M.	Josh
3:30 P.M.	Richard

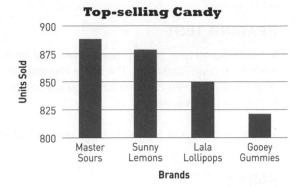

Top-selling Candy

95. Why has one of the tours been canceled?

(A) Weather conditions are unfavorable.

(B) An employee was injured.

(C) An area needs renovations.

(D) Not enough people registered.

96. Look at the graphic. At what time was the canceled tour supposed to leave?

(A) At 11:00 A.M.

(B) At 12:30 P.M.

(C) At 2:00 P.M.

(D) At 3:30 P.M.

97. What are the visitors prohibited from doing?

(A) Leaving children unattended

(B) Entering without a guide

(C) Running in the park

(D) Joining several tours

98. According to the speaker, how can the company increase profits?

(A) By selling a new product

(B) By changing suppliers

(C) By purchasing more goods

(D) By targeting different customers

99. Look at the graphic. What will the company buy less of?

(A) Master Sours

(B) Sunny Lemons

(C) Lala Lollipops

(D) Gooey Gummies

100. What will the speaker most likely do next?

(A) Place an order

(B) Finalize a plan

(C) Give out documents

(D) Negotiate a price

This is the end of the Listening test. Turn to Part 5 in your test book.

GO ON TO THE NEXT PAGE

READING TEST

In the Reading test, you will read a variety of texts and answer several different types of reading comprehension questions. The entire Reading test will last 75 minutes. There are three parts, and directions are given for each part. You are encouraged to answer as many questions as possible within the time allowed.

You must mark your answers on the separate answer sheet. Do not write your answers in your test book.

PART 5

Directions: A word or phrase is missing in each of the sentences below. Four answer choices are given below each sentence. Select the best answer to complete the sentence. Then mark the letter (A), (B), (C), or (D) on your answer sheet.

101. Ms. Anita always ------- participates in fundraisers by baking cookies and selling them.

(A) active
(B) acts
(C) actively
(D) activity

102. The parade for the town festival is ------- to start at 1 P.M. tomorrow.

(A) scheduled
(B) remained
(C) considered
(D) celebrated

103. Once the door opened, the usher showed the audience members to their ------- seats.

(A) respective
(B) respect
(C) respectful
(D) respecting

104. All of the furniture sold in our store comes with easy-to-follow ------- for fast assembly.

(A) estimates
(B) instructions
(C) comforts
(D) refunds

105. Mr. Crob had to wait fifteen minutes for an ------- when he called customer service.

(A) answer
(B) answering
(C) answered
(D) answers

106. Being fluent in at least two languages is a necessary qualification ------- working as a concierge at the Summertime Resort.

(A) about
(B) through
(C) by
(D) for

107. Technicians must turn off the power to the entire building when ------- the electrical system.

(A) repair
(B) repaired
(C) repairing
(D) repairs

108. The video ------- various ways in which the software can help a business to organize its data.

(A) inquires
(B) focuses
(C) terminates
(D) demonstrates

109. Recommend a friend of ------- to join our gym, and we will provide a discounted membership fee.
(A) you
(B) your
(C) yourself
(D) yours

110. The manager ------- asked that Ms. Nicola be the one to lead the negotiations with Cinta Corp.
(A) utterly
(B) specifically
(C) broadly
(D) gradually

111. Many candidates ------- applications for the sales associate position, so it will take time to go over all of them.
(A) to submit
(B) were submitted
(C) submission
(D) have submitted

112. It is impossible to get a shuttle bus from the airport to the hotel ------- any reservations.
(A) unless
(B) without
(C) except
(D) besides

113. Mr. Moss expressed interest in ------- a workshop to help improve his public speaking skills.
(A) joined
(B) join
(C) joining
(D) to join

114. The airline's new policy increases the baggage ------- from one suitcase per passenger to two for international flights.
(A) claim
(B) involvement
(C) allowance
(D) acquisition

115. Patrons of the Mencer Public Library can renew ------- checked-out books online and thus avoid overdue fines.
(A) their
(B) theirs
(C) they
(D) them

116. Not only senior staff members but also new employees will benefit ------- the revisions to the pay scale.
(A) of
(B) among
(C) from
(D) to

117. The branch supervisor decided to close the store early to let the staff go home ------- the snowstorm started.
(A) so as to
(B) before
(C) ahead of
(D) rather than

118. The date and venue for the convention have been chosen, but the program ------- needs to be finalized.
(A) still
(B) lately
(C) once
(D) exactly

119. Colleagues will offer to give money for gas to ------- who volunteer to drive them to the annual picnic.
(A) them
(B) those
(C) other
(D) anyone

120. The price of gold was rising steadily for a few months, but it started ------- at the end of June.
(A) to impede
(B) to decline
(C) to spend
(D) to eliminate

GO ON TO THE NEXT PAGE

121. In response to severe ------- concerning its high pollution levels, the factory took measures to protect the surrounding environment.

(A) critical
(B) criticizes
(C) critically
(D) criticism

122. Now that the bookstore's Web site has been updated, regular customers can get reading recommendations ------- their purchase history.

(A) on behalf of
(B) such as
(C) based on
(D) in spite of

123. Pearly White Toothpaste, though ------- recommended by dentists nationwide, is not as popular among buyers as its main competitor.

(A) strong
(B) strength
(C) strongest
(D) strongly

124. Engineers must have a master's degree or ------- work experience to be considered for senior management openings.

(A) deliberate
(B) lucrative
(C) equivalent
(D) systematic

125. To alleviate traffic congestion in the downtown area, the city planner ------- some roadways to one-way streets.

(A) has been converted
(B) are converted
(C) is converting
(D) convert

126. While the final winners will be kept secret, the top ------- for the talent awards will be revealed two weeks before the ceremony.

(A) subscriptions
(B) confidences
(C) congratulations
(D) nominations

127. Denny Marlow became more and more ------- about his chances of getting the accounting job as the interview progressed.

(A) hope
(B) hopefully
(C) hopeful
(D) hoping

128. Guests are expected to reply to the invitation by the end of the month ------- they plan on attending the event or not.

(A) either
(B) whether
(C) since
(D) though

129. Chef Francis Gales opened a restaurant ------- menu changes daily depending on the best fish and produce available each morning.

(A) that
(B) when
(C) whose
(D) while

130. The directors of Hencer Inc. are very ------- about who they allow into the biannual meeting for setting the company's objectives.

(A) selective
(B) prominent
(C) accessible
(D) ambitious

PART 6

Directions: Read the texts that follow. A word, phrase, or sentence is missing in parts of each text. Four answer choices for each question are given below the text. Select the best answer to complete the text. Then mark the letter (A), (B), (C), or (D) on your answer sheet.

Questions 131-134 refer to the following e-mail.

To: All members <memberlist@bettermegym.com>
From: Dennis Primus <dprimus@bettermegym.com>
Subject: New Weekend Hours
Date: August 4

Dear members,

Thank you to all who ------- our survey to share ideas concerning Better Me Gym. We strive to
                        131.
keep our gym the most modern and convenient for our clients, so feedback such as yours is

highly ------- to us. While we cannot reply to each of you individually, we are happy to make
       132.
changes to address the most common -------. The first of these was about our closing times.
                                   133.
Many of you complained about our short weekend hours. -------. We hope that you will enjoy
                                                       134.
these added hours.

See you at the gym!

Dennis Primus
Manager, Better Me Gym

---

131. (A) completing
　　　(B) completes
　　　(C) are completing
　　　(D) completed

132. (A) values
　　　(B) value
　　　(C) valuable
　　　(D) valuing

133. (A) demands
　　　(B) schedules
　　　(C) routines
　　　(D) patrons

134. (A) Unfortunately, we cannot extend our hours of
　　　　operation.
　　　(B) In response, we have decided to stay open
　　　　until 9 P.M. on Saturdays.
　　　(C) Members are free to work out as many hours
　　　　as they wish.
　　　(D) These are described in detail in your gym
　　　　membership contract.

GO ON TO THE NEXT PAGE

Secure your house with Houseguard! Our ------- security system has all the latest features you
135.
need to feel safe and comfortable in your own home. We will set up security cameras, motion

sensors, and an alarm system that will cover all areas of your property. -------, we will equip
136.
your home with our smart control robot, which constantly monitors your appliances to eliminate

any danger. -------. For example, should you leave the gas on when you leave, it will ------- turn
131. **138.**
it off for you, thus preventing a potential fire. Make your home safer today! Visit www.
houseguard.com today to schedule an installation.

135. (A) second-hand
(B) ill-equipped
(C) out-of-date
(D) state-of-the-art

136. (A) Therefore
(B) Nonetheless
(C) In addition
(D) On the other hand

137. (A) Indeed, burglaries have been on the rise
lately.
(B) The Houseguard robot could save your house.
(C) There are many control systems to choose
from.
(D) You can now cook amazing meals from your
own kitchen.

138. (A) automatic
(B) automates
(C) automation
(D) automatically

Questions 139-142 refer to the following letter.

November 25

Eric Closter
2957 Marisol Avenue
Willows, PA 18765

Dear Mr. Closter,

We are writing to inform you that the latest payment for your subscription to *Monthly Talks* was declined. Thus, we were unable to process the transaction. -------. **139.** If you cannot determine the cause of the error after ------- **140.** all of your information, contact your bank.

Since your payment did not go through, we have ------- **141.** shipment of the latest issue to your address. In order to receive the December issue, you must ------- **142.** provide valid payment information as we will be sending out the last issues soon.

If you have any questions about your *Monthly Talks* subscription, please call us at 555-3548.

Sincerely,

The *Monthly Talks* Staff

139. (A) However, we do not have the correct credit card information.
(B) A cancelation fee of $12.99 will be deducted from your account.
(C) Attached is a form for renewing your subscription to our magazine.
(D) This problem may be due to an address change or card expiration.

140. (A) verifying
(B) verification
(C) verify
(D) verified

141. (A) timed
(B) refunded
(C) canceled
(D) measured

142. (A) incorrectly
(B) surely
(C) promptly
(D) temporarily

GO ON TO THE NEXT PAGE

Local Companies Commit to Change

BETHOS (January 22)— -------. According to this potential contract, Frester Corp., Alphet Inc.,
143.
and Proga Corp. would commit to limiting their factories' energy consumption and emission
levels. Such changes could cost each company a large amount of money by slowing their
production rates. -------, the directors agreed that focusing on environmentally friendly methods
144.
would be beneficial in the long run. "If all three companies ------- to the agreement, then no one
145.
will lose too much, and the environment will gain," argued a director of Frester Corp. ------- of
146.
the sixteen directors volunteered any details about the logistics of the plan, but they did confirm
that an agreement was reached and will be made public soon.

143. (A) A recent study shows that pollution levels in
Bethos are at an all-time high.
(B) Several local companies are currently seeking
to hire entry-level workers.
(C) The directors of three large companies met
yesterday to discuss an agreement.
(D) Solar energy is just one example of renewable
energy that is easy to harvest.

144. (A) Furthermore
(B) Nevertheless
(C) Similarly
(D) Otherwise

145. (A) propose
(B) follow
(C) compare
(D) adhere

146. (A) Those
(B) Any
(C) None
(D) Neither

PART 7

Directions: In this part you will read a selection of texts, such as magazine and newspaper articles, e-mails, and instant messages. Each text or set of texts is followed by several questions. Select the best answer for each question and mark the letter (A), (B), (C), or (D) on your answer sheet.

Questions 147-148 refer to the following receipt.

Tina's Treasures

Date: 11/15
Member number: 194538838

- -

Silk Tie	$22.99
Leather belt	$39.99
Linen shirt	$45.00
Subtotal	$107.98
Tax (6%)	$6.48
Total	**$114.46**
Cash	$120.00
Change	-$5.54

- -

Member points earned	110
Total member points	1,005

Congratulations! You have reached more than one thousand member points and have earned this coupon:

Good for $5.00 at Tina's Treasures
Coupon Code: A2225SG56

Find us online at www.tinastreasures.com, where you can browse our merchandise, write product reviews, and place orders. You can also sign up for our newsletter to receive special promotions by e-mail.

147. What kind of store most likely is Tina's Treasures?

(A) A fabrics distributor
(B) A clothing outlet
(C) A hardware store
(D) A jewelry shop

148. According to the receipt, how did the buyer receive a coupon?

(A) By winning a contest
(B) By reviewing a product
(C) By being a loyal customer
(D) By subscribing to a newsletter

GO ON TO THE NEXT PAGE

151

Laura Fisher [6:58 P.M.]
Thomas, are you still at the office by any chance?

Thomas Volpert [6:59 P.M.]
Yes, I'm still here, but I was just about to leave for Jarrod's retirement party.

Laura Fisher [7:00 P.M.]
I was supposed to bring Jarrod's gift to the restaurant, but I just noticed that I left it at the office. I'm almost at the restaurant already.

Thomas Volpert [7:01 P.M.]
No problem. Just tell me where it is, and I'll bring it.

Laura Fisher [7:02 P.M.]
Oh, that's such a relief. You'll see a box under my desk. It's blue and black. It has a label from Galinda's Collection Shop on it.

Thomas Volpert [7:03 P.M.]
Okay, hold on. Let me check.

Thomas Volpert [7:07 P.M.]
Got it. The invitation says seven thirty, right? I'd better get going.

Laura Fisher [7:08 P.M.]
Yes. Thank you so much! You're a lifesaver.

149. At 7:07 P.M., what does Mr. Volpert mean when he writes, "Got it"?

(A) He found the present.
(B) He understands the directions.
(C) He received a party invitation.
(D) He has a gift receipt.

150. Where is Mr. Volpert most likely going next?

(A) To the office
(B) To Ms. Fisher's home
(C) To a restaurant
(D) To a store

Questions **151-152** refer to the following e-mail.

E-mail

To: Sooyeon Baek <baeksooyeon@harligen.net>
From: Gerald Finn <finngerald@harligen.net>
Date: January 18
Subject: Urgent

Dear Ms. Baek,

I need your help. The foreman at the 171 Dutton Street property has informed me that his team has nearly run out of the gravel for the water barrier. They need more as soon as possible not to fall behind schedule. I'll be away from the office the rest of the day performing safety checks at our other sites, so I can't take care of this myself. Would you please call the supplier and ask for more gravel to be delivered? The type we're using is listed in the database under that property's name. It should be easy to find.

Thank you!

Gerald Finn

---

151. For what kind of business does Mr. Finn most likely work?
(A) A construction company
(B) A manufacturing facility
(C) A hardware store
(D) A real estate firm

152. What is Ms. Baek asked to do?
(A) Meet a potential customer
(B) Place an order
(C) Update a database
(D) Pick up a delivery

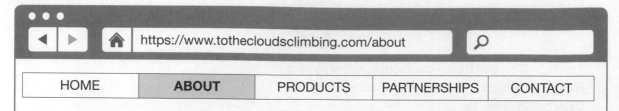

To the Clouds was established over fifteen years ago and has continuously strived to create the most innovative climbing gear and apparel around. Contact us today to become an official To the Clouds distributor. We are one of the top-selling brands on the market, and you will want to have our products in your store to attract the climbing community. By selling To the Clouds equipment, you will gain a reputation as a trustworthy store that sells excellent gear and apparel. Moreover, all of our products come with lifetime warranties to reassure customers that they are buying superior equipment. And we supply high-quality posters, banners, and leaflets. Our merchandise is thus simple to market and always sells out quickly.

153. Who should contact To the Clouds?

(A) Sporting goods retailers
(B) Professional athletes
(C) Climbing club leaders
(D) Equipment manufacturers

154. What is NOT mentioned about To the Clouds products?

(A) Their warranty doesn't expire.
(B) They are sold at affordable prices.
(C) They are popular among climbers.
(D) They are easy to advertise.

Employee Notice: Annual Juny Fundraising Gala

The annual fundraising gala for Juny Children's Organization will be held at the Sarcona Convention Center on Sunday, April 30, from 6 P.M. to 8:30 P.M. Attendance for Dream Voyages employees is optional but strongly encouraged. As usual, our company will be sponsoring the event. However, instead of donating money as we have every other year, we are donating prizes for the raffle. For those of you who have not been to this event before, please note the dress code.

Dress code

Men do not need to wear tuxedos but must wear dark-colored suits, with a white shirt and solid-color tie. Please avoid loud prints and patterns.

Acceptable attire for women includes long gowns and pantsuits. Please do not wear short-cut dresses. If you decide to wear high heels, make sure you can comfortably stand in the shoes for a long period of time.

Prize donations

Dream Voyages will be donating one all-inclusive tour package to Europe, three vacation packages to resorts in Mexico, and ten weekend spa packages. Please note that anyone affiliated with Dream Voyages is not eligible to win any of these prizes.

Actual Test 4

155. What has Dream Voyages changed?

(A) Its dress code for employees
(B) Its contribution to the organization
(C) Its policy on attendance to the event
(D) Its type of rewards for customers

156. What are women NOT allowed to wear?

(A) Dark-colored dresses
(B) High-heel shoes
(C) Long pants
(D) Short skirts

157. What is suggested about the prizes donated by Dream Voyages?

(A) They may not be won by Dream Voyages employees.
(B) They do not include expenses related to plane tickets.
(C) They will be awarded to the best-performing workers.
(D) They are the most expensive gifts at the fundraiser.

To: Garfield, Anna <annagarfield76@peoplesnet.com>
From: Customer Service <cs@featherflights.com>
Date: July 12
Subject: Flight reservation – Action needed

Dear Anna Garfield,

We are writing to inform you that payment for your flight to Los Angeles has not been processed. Please make a payment through our Web site in the amount of $636.88. — [1] —. Your reservation will not be complete until this amount has been received. If payment is not submitted within twenty-four hours after the request was made, the seats will be forfeited. — [2] —.

For your reference, you have requested two seats for a round-trip flight to Los Angeles departing from Austin on Saturday, August 7, at 3:20 P.M. and returning on Sunday, August 29, at 10:10 A.M. — [3] —.

Please note that the price you were originally quoted for the tickets may no longer be available after today. This is why we urge you to complete the reservation as soon as possible. If you require assistance, you may call our customer service line at 555-293-5892 between 9 A.M. and 5 P.M. on weekdays. — [4] —.

Thank you for choosing with Feather Flights. We look forward to serving you.

Regards,

The Feather Flights Customer Service Team

158. What is the purpose of the e-mail?
(A) To confirm a reservation
(B) To explain a flight change
(C) To acknowledge a cancelation
(D) To notify a customer of a due payment

159. In which of the positions marked [1], [2], [3], and [4] does the following sentence best belong?
"Thus, you will have to start the reservation process again."
(A) [1]
(B) [2]
(C) [3]
(D) [4]

160. What is indicated about the ticket price?
(A) It might change in the future.
(B) It is temporarily discounted.
(C) It includes only one way.
(D) It is payable only by phone.

January 30—After an unprecedented successful fourth quarter, it was rumored that Habbart Corp. would be giving large year-end bonuses to all of its employees. — [1] —. Habbart Corp. spokesperson Mr. Bryan Caster announced that the company would instead be making a large donation to Enviro First, an environmental foundation.

The revelation came as a surprise, as Habbart Corp. has a reputation for ignoring environmental issues. — [2] —. Controversy was especially intense after one of Habbart's plants had a small explosion that caused a chemical leak, contaminating a nearby river. Although the leak was quickly contained, local residents took to the streets to protest, denouncing the company's lack of care for ecological concerns. — [3] —.

Yet Habbart Corp.'s latest decision seems to contradict those claims. Mr. Caster emphasized that the company took matters related to sustainable production very seriously. "We want to support and work in collaboration with organizations that fight to protect the environment," Mr. Caster declared. — [4] —. The total amount of the donation has not been revealed, but it is expected to be the largest one Enviro First has yet received. Mr. Caster insisted that all of Habbart Corp.'s extra profits would go to the organization.

Actual Test 4

161. What is the purpose of the article?

(A) To criticize a corporation's approach to environmental issues

(B) To advocate stronger measures against natural disasters

(C) To announce a company's contribution to a nonprofit

(D) To report an accident that happened at a local factory

162. What is indicated about Habbart Corp.?

(A) It is known for its environment-friendly methods.

(B) It will be giving extra compensation to its employees.

(C) It had an exceptionally profitable fourth quarter.

(D) It is planning on building a new plant near a river.

163. According to the article, what caused people to protest against Habbart Corp.?

(A) Its neglect of the environment

(B) Its employee benefits packages

(C) Its frequent explosion accidents

(D) Its small charitable donations

164. In which of the positions marked [1], [2], [3], and [4] does the following sentence best belong?

"However, this was denied at a press conference held yesterday."

(A) [1]

(B) [2]

(C) [3]

(D) [4]

GO ON TO THE NEXT PAGE

★ ★ ★ ★ ★   ★ ★ ★ ★ ★

Boca Chocolates is seventy-five years old, and to celebrate, the factory will be opening its doors to the public for one week, from May 6 to May 12. This is your chance to visit the premises and find out how Boca Chocolates makes its delicious sweets!

First, you will take a guided tour that will show you every step of the process from the bean to the box. You will see our workers operating the machinery, and our chocolate artists decorating the final products.

After you learn all about how chocolate is made, you can taste special samples of upcoming products, enjoy our magical chocolate fountain, and purchase gift baskets at a discount. In addition, every visitor will go home with a box of chocolates as a gift.

For security purposes, the number of visitors is limited, so make your reservation early! Tours are $45 for adults, $30 for students, and $20 for children under twelve. Call 555-9963 to schedule a time.

★ ★ ★ ★ ★   ★ ★ ★ ★ ★

165. What is being advertised?

(A) A new kind of chocolate

(B) A special anniversary tour

(C) A sales event at a grocery store

(D) An innovative candy-making machine

166. What will be given out for free?

(A) Gift baskets

(B) Fountains

(C) Decorations

(D) Boxes of sweets

167. What are readers encouraged to do?

(A) Reserve a time slot

(B) Place an order

(C) Taste a product

(D) Try a piece of equipment

Questions 168-171 refer to the following online chat discussion.

Selam Habte [4:26 P.M.]	I know you two had to miss my announcements at the end of the weekly staff meeting, so I wanted to fill you in.
Anna Morgan [4:28 P.M.]	Thanks. What did we miss?
Selam Habte [4:29 P.M.]	Our company is going to release a new long-lasting lipstick.
Kikuyo Tsuruta [4:30 P.M.]	That's great news. I'm glad the R&D department took my advice about adding another product to the line.
Anna Morgan [4:31 P.M.]	When will we start advertising the new lipstick?
Selam Habte [4:32 P.M.]	Mr. Catteneo is putting together a marketing plan now.
Kikuyo Tsuruta [4:34 P.M.]	Wouldn't this be a better job for a senior marketing executive?
Anna Morgan [4:35 P.M.]	Yeah. Mr. Catteneo is new to our company and doesn't know much about our products.
Selam Habte [4:39 P.M.]	I realize that, but he has a marketing background in cosmetics.
Anna Morgan [4:41 P.M.]	I see. Well, it wouldn't hurt for him to see some of our previous work. I could send him a portfolio of previous projects.
Kikuyo Tsuruta [4:42 P.M.]	And I'd be happy to review his work.
Selam Habte [4:43 P.M.]	I don't think that'll be necessary, Kikuyo, but I like your idea, Anna.
Anna Morgan [4:44 P.M.]	Okay. I'll do that now.

SEND

168. What is mainly being discussed?

(A) A policy update
(B) A new client
(C) A schedule change
(D) A product launch

169. What is implied about Ms. Tsuruta?

(A) She thinks the company needs to control spending.
(B) She made a suggestion about the company's goods.
(C) She asked Mr. Habte for some advice.
(D) She developed a new line of cosmetics.

170. At 4:41 P.M., what does Ms. Morgan most likely mean when she writes, "I see"?

(A) Mr. Catteneo is too busy to work on a project.
(B) Mr. Catteneo cannot help Ms. Morgan with a problem.
(C) Mr. Catteneo has already reviewed a portfolio.
(D) Mr. Catteneo may be qualified for a task.

171. What will Ms. Morgan most likely do next?

(A) Review documents prepared by Mr. Catteneo
(B) Send information about previous projects
(C) Set up a meeting with Mr. Catteneo
(D) Recommend a new marketing director

GO ON TO THE NEXT PAGE

E-Mail

To: Katrina Simon <ksimon@presslerlibrary.org>
From: Nora Yales <nyales@presslerlibrary.org>
Date: November 30
Subject: Opening tomorrow

Dear Ms. Simon,

I was told that you were willing to open the library in my place tomorrow morning and work my shift. I wanted to send you a quick reminder to help you out with the opening procedure. It's been a while since you last did this, and there are several steps, so I thought it would be helpful.

First, I wanted to make sure you know the code to disarm the alarm: 0358. Remember to pick up the mail, including the newspapers. You can leave the mail on my desk. Stamp the newspapers with the library stamp, and display them on the news shelf in the journals section. Make sure you take off yesterday's papers and classify them with the other past newspapers.

The key to the cash register is in the top drawer of my desk. Double check that there is $48 in it to start the day.

After you turn on the lights on every floor, you should be ready to unlock the front doors. The keys for that are in the key cabinet in my office.

The weather forecast says there will be a huge snowstorm, and since I live far away, I'd rather not drive in that weather, so I'm taking the whole day off and not leaving the house. But if you run into any trouble or have any questions, feel free to call me. I will also be available to chat online if you need my advice.

I am very thankful that you live close enough to be able to walk to the library. Thank you for being willing to do this.

Good luck!

Nora Yales
Library Assistant

---

172. What is the purpose of the e-mail?

    (A) To warn of weather conditions

    (B) To recommend a schedule change

    (C) To offer a position

    (D) To outline a procedure

173. What is suggested about Ms. Simon?

    (A) She has opened the library before.

    (B) She will drive to work tomorrow.

    (C) She reads the newspaper every day.

    (D) She usually closes the library.

174. What is NOT something Ms. Simon is expected to do?

    (A) Disable a security system

    (B) Open the front doors

    (C) Read the mail

    (D) Count money

175. What will Ms. Yales do tomorrow?

    (A) Retire from her job

    (B) Drive Ms. Simon to work

    (C) Stay home for the day

    (D) Handle customer questions

GO ON TO THE NEXT PAGE

To: Cage, Peter <pcage@jaysmail.net>
From: Topher, Edward <etopher@sapphireflowers.com>
Date: May 8
Subject: Free Voucher

Dear Mr. Cage,

We are very sorry for the late delivery of your floral arrangement on May 5. We understand that because of this delay, the celebration of your daughter's acceptance into Boston University was not as special as it could have been.

Unfortunately, we ran out of roses on that day and had failed to set some aside for your afternoon delivery. We placed another order, but since our supplier is located in Stratton, it took time to get the flowers. We are in the process of switching to a more modern inventory management program, and we can assure you that this kind of mistake will not happen again. We hope that you will continue to choose Sapphire Flowers for your future special occasions.

To express our regret, we are offering you a voucher for a complimentary bouquet of your choice to be delivered at any address in the area. You will find it attached to this e-mail. Please print it and fill it out when you wish to order a delivery.

Sincerely,

Edward Topher
Sapphire Flowers

~ Sapphire Flowers ~
Voucher Code: XS564813

Good for one floral arrangement and its delivery within Jayville.

Choose from the following selection:

☐ Classic Roses ☐ Blue Bunch ☐ Dream Bouquet ☐ Spring Special

Delivery date: Monday, May 18   Delivery time: 10 A.M.
Address: Janice Richards
            Frontier Corp. finance department
            514 Enterprise Drive

Message(Optional):
Dear Janice,

I am sad to see you go. It was great working with you all these years. I hope you enjoy your new job in Bendertown!

Regards,
Peter Cage

176. What is the purpose of the e-mail?

    (A) To notify of a delay

    (B) To offer an apology

    (C) To report a system error

    (D) To congratulate a coworker

177. What does Mr. Topher indicate happened on May 5?

    (A) His store's inventory was mismanaged.

    (B) His daughter was accepted into college.

    (C) His supplier was replaced.

    (D) His flowers were all delivered late.

178. In the e-mail, the word "assure" in paragraph 2, line 4, is closest in meaning to

    (A) convince

    (B) remind

    (C) guarantee

    (D) compensate

179. Who most likely is Janice Richards?

    (A) Mr. Cage's colleague

    (B) Mr. Topher's supervisor

    (C) Mr. Cage's customer

    (D) Mr. Topher's supplier

180. Where most likely is Mr. Topher's store located?

    (A) Boston

    (B) Stratton

    (C) Jayville

    (D) Bendertown

GO ON TO THE NEXT PAGE

July 31

Jerome Madison
2675 Chenoweth Drive
Nashville, TN 37214

Dear Mr. Madison,

I heard that you are searching for a new assistant manager for the marketing team. As you know, I have been the manager of Gamma Motors' design team for eleven years. Ms. Skye Armand started working on my team six years ago and has proven to be a strong asset. She has informed me of her intention to apply for the position of assistant manager with the marketing team, and I offered to write a reference letter.

I believe that Ms. Armand's transfer could be beneficial to the company. Her understanding of design strategies and how to appeal to customers is evident in her work, and this talent would be of high value in the marketing team. Moreover, her experience within Gamma Motors and her intimate knowledge of its various models would contribute greatly to creating effective marketing campaigns. I know that you will soon be focusing on preparing for the launch of the new Gamma SUV 6. Ms. Armand has been involved in several aspects of the vehicle's design, and I think she will have some great ideas about how to present it in its best light.

If you have any questions about Ms. Armand's work, feel free to contact me.

Sincerely,

Melanie Yoder

Melanie Yoder, Design Manager

To: Marketing employees <marketingteam@gammamotors.com>
From: Jerome Madison <jmadison@gammamotors.com>
Date: September 2
Subject: Marketing Campaign

The campaign for our newest model has proven highly successful. Our teaser video has been shared all over social media and has reached millions of views. A reporter for a popular car magazine has even asked to interview one of our managers.

Congratulations to everyone, but especially to Ms. Armand. This was her first campaign, and we were able to come up with the best features to highlight in our advertisements thanks to her experience in developing its design. We already have a high number of test drive requests, and we expect the launch to be even more successful than our minivan's.

Regards,

Jerome Madison, Marketing Manager

181. Why did Ms. Yoder write to Mr. Madison?

    (A) To recommend a worker

    (B) To submit her résumé

    (C) To offer him a position

    (D) To advertise a product

182. In the letter, the word "intimate" in paragraph 2, line 4, is closest in meaning to

    (A) private

    (B) detailed

    (C) objective

    (D) faithful

183. What is mentioned about the teaser video?

    (A) Many people have watched it.

    (B) It features a talk with a Gamma employee.

    (C) It became a top-rated movie.

    (D) It was released by Gamma's competitor.

184. What is Mr. Madison congratulating his team about?

    (A) A minivan's advertisement

    (B) An SUV's marketing

    (C) A member's promotion

    (D) A magazine's popularity

185. What is suggested about Ms. Armand?

    (A) She turned down a job offer.

    (B) She has been promoted to manager.

    (C) She recently switched teams.

    (D) She wrote an article for a magazine.

GO ON TO THE NEXT PAGE

Help Center

What can we help you with?

I have ☐ a Question ☐ a Request/Problem ☐ a Comment
My Message to Fuchsia Foods:

> I've been receiving Fuchsia Foods' organic food delivery boxes for three months now. I really enjoy receiving my package each afternoon, so I wish to upgrade my plan to the next level. When you make the switch, please keep in mind that I am a vegetarian and continue to send me the packages that don't include meat or eggs. If this change is possible, please bill me accordingly.
>
> Thank you very much.
>
> Sebastian Palmer

Do you expect a reply? **If yes, please provide your e-mail address:**
☐ Yes ☐ No

sebpalmer@yourmail.net

SUBMIT

Thank you for contacting us.
If you requested a reply, we will be in contact with you shortly regarding your inquiry.
If you have a question that requires immediate assistance, please call us at 352-555-2948.

March 15 Deliveries

	Basic	Deluxe	Basic vegetarian	Deluxe vegetarian	Delivery Time
86 Tassen Road			✓		11:35 A.M.
15 Jordan Drive				✓	11:50 A.M.
56 Preston Avenue		✓			2:12 P.M.
12 Mesca Street				✓	2:26 P.M.

To: Sebastian Palmer <sebpalmer@yourmail.net>
From: Customer Service <cservice@fuchsiafoods.com>
Date: March 15
Subject: About your upgrade request

Dear Mr. Palmer,

This is to confirm that we have switched your package delivery plan. Your first package of the new plan was delivered this afternoon. The credit card that we have on record for your account was billed accordingly.

Please note that we do not customarily allow plan switches before the end of a month since we preschedule our orders ahead of time. However, another member asked to change to your original plan, so we were able to simply switch your two deliveries. This was a lucky coincidence, but please note that if you wish to make future changes, you will have to wait until the end of a month to do so.

Thank you for your understanding, and enjoy your new food deliveries!

Sincerely,

Rebecca Lars
Customer Service Representative

186. Why did Mr. Palmer post on the Web page?

(A) To cancel an erroneous payment
(B) To ask for a non-vegetarian option
(C) To stop receiving packages
(D) To modify his current plan

187. What kind of package was Mr. Palmer originally receiving?

(A) Basic
(B) Deluxe
(C) Basic vegetarian
(D) Deluxe vegetarian

188. Where does Mr. Palmer most likely live?

(A) 86 Tassen Road
(B) 15 Jordan Drive
(C) 56 Preston Avenue
(D) 12 Mesca Street

189. In the e-mail, in paragraph 2, line 1, the word "customarily" is closest in meaning to

(A) normally
(B) fairly
(C) naturally
(D) rarely

190. According to the e-mail, why was Mr. Palmer's request granted?

(A) He waited until the end of the month.
(B) He asked to switch in advance.
(C) Another customer requested a plan switch.
(D) The desired plan is more expensive.

GO ON TO THE NEXT PAGE

OFFICIAL INVITATION

Dear Mr. Pratt,

As a longtime investor of Barton Electronics, you are invited to Barton's Future and Progress Event on April 24. I will be making a major announcement that you do not want to miss.

Date: April 24
Time: From 2 P.M. to 4 P.M.
Location: Falcon Room (third floor), Hiver Hotel
Entrance: Free (must present this card)

Looking forward to seeing you,

Vin Vecino

Barton Electronics' Upcoming Announcement

Barton Electronics will be holding a special event on April 24. The company is to make what its CEO called a "major announcement" in the invitations that were sent out. It has since then been confirmed that Barton Electronics will be presenting a new device. Yet the type of device is still unconfirmed, and rumors have been flooding the Internet.

It all started when photos of a new laptop design were leaked on social media last week. However, the source of these leaks is unknown, and their authenticity has not been verified.

Mr. Vecino was also caught on camera meeting with Ms. Beatrix Starling, the famous fitness expert who created a popular series of training videos. Fitness trackers have recently seen a surge in popularity, so this meeting sparked rumors about a possible Barton fitness tracker. When asked about his reason for meeting with Ms. Starling, Mr. Vecino refused to comment.

Finally, it is likely that Barton Electronics will announce their new smartphone model. The company has released a new phone every year for the past four years, and their last model, the Barton 44, is close to a year old.

From: Vin Vecino
To: Steven Parker

Ms. Starling sent me a copy of the speech she intends to give. In it, she explains the advantages of the device's main features. Originally, we were going to have her present at the end, but I think it would be better if she went before we show the pictures of the device. So I've decided to save the pictures for last to build up anticipation. I'll e-mail her speech to you now. Take a look at it and tell me if you agree.

191. What is Mr. Pratt required to do for the event?

   (A) Show the invitation
   (B) Bring a device
   (C) Reserve the room
   (D) Prepare a presentation

192. Who is Vin Vecino?

   (A) A special guest
   (B) A company CEO
   (C) A fitness expert
   (D) A private investor

193. In the article, the word "caught" in paragraph 3, line 1, is closest in meaning to

   (A) recorded
   (B) scheduled
   (C) arrested
   (D) expected

194. What new device is Barton Electronics most likely launching?

   (A) A smartphone
   (B) A camera
   (C) A laptop
   (D) A fitness tracker

195. When will people see pictures of the new device?

   (A) Before the event
   (B) At the start of the event
   (C) At the end of the event
   (D) After the event

GO ON TO THE NEXT PAGE

Questions 196-200 refer to the following advertisement, online form, and review.

Yula School Programs

Yula School provides the most comprehensive programs for event decorators. Learn how to design a space to create the best customized environment. Our programs take just one year to complete! At Yula, you will take several core courses before moving on to your two specialty courses, which depend on the curriculum you choose. The specialty courses included in each curriculum are listed below.

Curriculum A: Weddings and Showers
– Draping and Fabrics
– Using Plants and Trees

Curriculum B: Private Holiday Celebrations
– Choosing a Color Scheme
– Mood Creation with Lighting

Curriculum C: Corporate Events
– Choosing a Color Scheme
– Creating a Stage

Curriculum D: Themed Children's Parties
– Balloon Sculptures
– Creating a Stage

* The deadlines for applying are August 15 for the fall semester and November 15 for the spring semester. Submit a résumé, motivation letter, and letter of recommendation to admissions@yula.com to apply.

Questions & Comments

STUDENT
Jeremy Forester

I am in my last class to complete my Yula event decorator program. However, I was wondering if it would be possible to take one more class after this semester. My friend Kelly Leonard is in the Private Holiday Celebrations program, and she is really enjoying her current course, which is not offered in any other curriculum. Is it possible to add just this class without following the entire curriculum? If so, how much would it cost?

SUBMIT

Review: ★★★★★
Name: J. Forester

Shortly after I completed the curriculum, I was contacted by a company to decorate their venue for a new product launch party. Everyone was praising the decorations, and the company was so pleased with my work that they asked me to deal with their tenth anniversary celebration. I never expected to be so quickly hired for such a big event. Thanks to all the hands-on experience I received at Yula School, everyone thought I'd been in the business for years! Yula really prepares you well by giving you excellent tips and training you in everything you'll need for your decorating business. I highly recommend Yula to anyone who wants to become a professional decorator.

196. What is NOT mentioned about Yula School's programs?

(A) How to submit an application
(B) What the specialty courses are
(C) How long a program lasts
(D) When each semester begins

197. Which class is Ms. Leonard currently taking?

(A) Draping and Fabrics
(B) Choosing a Color Scheme
(C) Mood Creation with Lighting
(D) Creating a Stage

198. In the review, the phrase "deal with" in paragraph 1, line 3, is closest in meaning to

(A) handle
(B) touch
(C) inform
(D) compensate

199. What is suggested about Mr. Forester?

(A) He has not worked as a decorator for very long.
(B) He now teaches courses at Yula School.
(C) He recently designed a new product.
(D) He will start a new program at Yula School.

200. Which curriculum did Mr. Forester most likely study?

(A) Curriculum A
(B) Curriculum B
(C) Curriculum C
(D) Curriculum D

Stop! This is the end of the test. If you finish before time is called, you may go back to Parts 5, 6, and 7 and check your work.

Actual Test 5

LISTENING TEST

In the Listening test, you will be asked to demonstrate how well you understand spoken English. The entire Listening test will last approximately 45 minutes. There are four parts, and directions are given for each part. You must mark your answers on the separate answer sheet. Do not write your answers in your test book.

PART 1 🎧 17

Directions: For each question in this part, you will hear four statements about a picture in your test book. When you hear the statements, you must select the one statement that best describes what you see in the picture. Then find the number of the question on your answer sheet and mark your answer. The statements will not be printed in your test book and will be spoken only one time.

Statement (C), "They're sitting at the table," is the best description of the picture, so you should select answer (C) and mark it on your answer sheet.

1.

2.

GO ON TO THE NEXT PAGE ➤

3.

4

5.

6

GO ON TO THE NEXT PAGE

PART 2 🎧 18

Directions: You will hear a question or statement and three responses spoken in English. They will not be printed in your test book and will be spoken only one time. Select the best response to the question or statement and mark the letter (A), (B), or (C) on your answer sheet.

7. Mark your answer on your answer sheet.

8. Mark your answer on your answer sheet.

9. Mark your answer on your answer sheet.

10. Mark your answer on your answer sheet.

11. Mark your answer on your answer sheet.

12. Mark your answer on your answer sheet.

13. Mark your answer on your answer sheet.

14. Mark your answer on your answer sheet.

15. Mark your answer on your answer sheet.

16. Mark your answer on your answer sheet.

17. Mark your answer on your answer sheet.

18. Mark your answer on your answer sheet.

19. Mark your answer on your answer sheet.

20. Mark your answer on your answer sheet.

21. Mark your answer on your answer sheet.

22. Mark your answer on your answer sheet.

23. Mark your answer on your answer sheet.

24. Mark your answer on your answer sheet.

25. Mark your answer on your answer sheet.

26. Mark your answer on your answer sheet.

27. Mark your answer on your answer sheet.

28. Mark your answer on your answer sheet.

29. Mark your answer on your answer sheet.

30. Mark your answer on your answer sheet.

31. Mark your answer on your answer sheet.

Directions: You will hear some conversations between two or more people. You will be asked to answer three questions about what the speakers say in each conversation. Select the best response to each question and mark the letter (A), (B), (C), or (D) on your answer sheet. The conversations will not be printed in your test book and will be spoken only one time.

32. What are the speakers discussing?

(A) A product description

(B) A seating chart

(C) An entrance code

(D) A supplies order

33. What does the man give the woman?

(A) A product catalog

(B) An ID badge

(C) A new form

(D) A training manual

34. What does the man recommend doing?

(A) Canceling an order

(B) Directing questions to a coworker

(C) Viewing an example online

(D) Getting approval in advance

35. Who most likely are the speakers?

(A) Salespeople

(B) Researchers

(C) Lecturers

(D) Photographers

36. What does the man ask the woman to do?

(A) Contact a supplier right away

(B) Put some information on display

(C) Finish a project ahead of schedule

(D) Make some suggestions for improvements

37. What does the woman say she wants to do?

(A) Check the inventory

(B) Adjust a fee

(C) Arrange a meeting

(D) Confirm the attendance

38. What problem does the man mention?

(A) A board member hasn't arrived yet.

(B) A sales promotion didn't go well.

(C) A document is missing some information.

(D) A branch is performing more poorly than expected.

39. What does the woman ask about?

(A) The topic of a report

(B) The cost of a service

(C) The number of board members

(D) The start time of a meeting

40. What does the woman suggest doing?

(A) Hiring a different printing service

(B) Contacting the Fletcher branch

(C) Changing the meeting date

(D) Completing a task on site

41. What is the woman interested in buying?

(A) A refrigerator

(B) A television

(C) A smartphone

(D) A software program

42. Why does Barrett recommend the Stinson brand?

(A) It has the widest selection.

(B) It is currently on sale.

(C) It is the most popular brand.

(D) It has long-lasting products.

43. What will the woman probably do next?

(A) Watch a demonstration

(B) Ask for a discount

(C) Extend a warranty

(D) Fill out a registration form

GO ON TO THE NEXT PAGE

Actual Test 5

44. What are the speakers mainly discussing?
    (A) A hiring decision
    (B) An employee evaluation
    (C) A registration process
    (D) A business trip

45. Why was the man unable to read some materials?
    (A) He had a problem with his computer.
    (B) He recently returned from a vacation.
    (C) He had to visit an important client.
    (D) He was working on a coworker's task.

46. What does the woman imply when she says, "You shouldn't have to do that alone"?
    (A) She will help train the new employees.
    (B) She can assign an extra task to Liam.
    (C) She can help the man finish a report.
    (D) She will speak to the man's supervisor.

47. What kind of business do the speakers probably work for?
    (A) A delivery service
    (B) A printing company
    (C) A clothing outlet
    (D) An insurance agency

48. According to the man, what is the problem?
    (A) There is a shortage of supplies.
    (B) An order form contained an error.
    (C) There are not enough workers.
    (D) A client has made a complaint.

49. What do the speakers decide to do?
    (A) Work additional hours
    (B) Purchase some equipment
    (C) Cancel a project
    (D) Request a deadline extension

50. What does the man say he likes about the store?
    (A) Its wide selection
    (B) Its friendly employees
    (C) Its convenient hours
    (D) Its member rewards

51. Why is the man unable to use his coupon?
    (A) It has already expired.
    (B) It has a minimum purchase amount.
    (C) It is for a different store.
    (D) It cannot be used with other offers.

52. What does the woman mean when she says, "I'll go there shortly"?
    (A) She can drop off some paperwork for the man.
    (B) She will help the man carry his items.
    (C) She plans to take a break soon.
    (D) She will try to find some merchandise for the man.

53. What field does the man most likely work in?
    (A) Tourism
    (B) Ecology
    (C) Construction
    (D) Agriculture

54. What kind of project will the man explain?
    (A) A local cleanup
    (B) A building renovation
    (C) A marketing campaign
    (D) A company picnic

55. What is the woman concerned about?
    (A) Staying within a budget
    (B) Getting official approval
    (C) Finding enough volunteers
    (D) Starting a study on time

56. Where most likely is the conversation taking place?
    (A) At a bus terminal
    (B) At an airport
    (C) At a hotel
    (D) At a theater

57. According to the man, what is the additional fee for?
    (A) A transportation service
    (B) A room upgrade
    (C) A cancellation fee
    (D) A deposit

58. What will Alexandra most likely give Ms. Brooks next?
    (A) A ticket
    (B) A receipt
    (C) A schedule
    (D) A business card

59. What are the speakers mainly discussing?
    (A) Vacation plans
    (B) An opening celebration
    (C) An end-of-year event
    (D) A catering service

60. What will the woman ask her coworkers?
    (A) What type of venue they want
    (B) When their vacations are
    (C) Who they plan to invite
    (D) Which date they prefer

61. What does the man say he will do?
    (A) Select menu items
    (B) Reserve a restaurant
    (C) Prepare a meal
    (D) Contact guests

Dark Tan Shades	
Brand	Product Code
Bridgeport	147
Lancaster	295
Reiser	466
Saldana	803

62. Why did the man change his mind?
    (A) He asked a colleague's opinion.
    (B) He tested some free samples.
    (C) He found a cheaper item.
    (D) He reviewed a product catalog.

63. Look at the graphic. Which product will the man purchase?
    (A) Product 147
    (B) Product 295
    (C) Product 466
    (D) Product 803

64. What is the man asked to do?
    (A) Call back again later
    (B) Provide room measurements
    (C) Update an order form online
    (D) Return some unused goods

GO ON TO THE NEXT PAGE

INTERPRETATION RATES	
Number of Hours	Price per Hour
1 hour	$80
2-4 hours	$75
5-6 hours	$70
More than 6 hours	$65

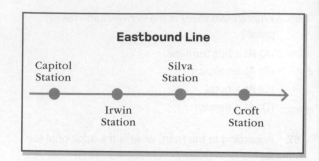

Eastbound Line

Capitol Station   Irwin Station   Silva Station   Croft Station

65. Who most likely is the man?

(A) An event organizer

(B) A language specialist

(C) An information technology expert

(D) A chemistry professor

66. What information does the woman ask for?

(A) The date of the event

(B) The address of a venue

(C) The languages needed

(D) The registration fee

67. Look at the graphic. How much will the man most likely pay per hour?

(A) $80

(B) $75

(C) $70

(D) $65

68. What does the man want to do?

(A) Find a sports facility

(B) Pick up a map

(C) Change a train ticket

(D) Get to a theater

69. Look at the graphic. To which stop is the man told to go?

(A) Capitol Station

(B) Irwin Station

(C) Silva Station

(D) Croft Station

70. What is the man concerned about?

(A) Having to buy another ticket

(B) Moving his luggage by himself

(C) Missing the next train

(D) Walking through a crowded station

Directions: You will hear some talks given by a single speaker. You will be asked to answer three questions about what the speaker says in each talk. Select the best response to each question and mark the letter (A), (B), (C), or (D) on your answer sheet. The talks will not be printed in your test book and will be spoken only one time.

71. Where most likely are the listeners?
    (A) At a fashion show
    (B) At an art institute
    (C) At a hardware store
    (D) At a community center

72. According to the speaker, what can be found in the west wing?
    (A) A promotional video
    (B) A demonstration
    (C) Some free samples
    (D) Some paintings

73. What does the speaker encourage listeners to do?
    (A) Enroll in a rewards program
    (B) Share their feedback
    (C) Make some suggestions
    (D) Sign up for a workshop

74. Where most likely does the speaker work?
    (A) At a construction company
    (B) At a property management firm
    (C) At an insurance agency
    (D) At a plumbing company

75. What is the call mainly about?
    (A) Arranging a repair
    (B) Scheduling a tour
    (C) Announcing renovations
    (D) Signing a lease

76. Why should the listener call the speaker back?
    (A) To pay for a service
    (B) To register a complaint
    (C) To approve a charge
    (D) To change an appointment

77. Who is Jackie Galvani?
    (A) A radio host
    (B) A researcher
    (C) A painter
    (D) An art critic

78. What did Ms. Galvani recently do?
    (A) Started a school
    (B) Gave a lecture
    (C) Opened a gallery
    (D) Reviewed a sculpture

79. What does the speaker ask listeners to do?
    (A) Register for a class
    (B) Buy a painting
    (C) Speak with the guest
    (D) Submit questions

80. Who is this advertisement intended for?
    (A) Job seekers
    (B) Business owners
    (C) New employees
    (D) Interns

81. What field does the speaker's company specialize in?
    (A) Pharmaceuticals
    (B) Journalism
    (C) Fashion
    (D) Computer science

82. What are listeners asked to send?
    (A) A description of their facilities
    (B) A selection of preferred candidates
    (C) An explanation of their needs
    (D) A list of interview questions

GO ON TO THE NEXT PAGE

Actual Test 5

83. Why is the business closed?

(A) An emergency happened.

(B) Renovations are being made.

(C) A dentist recently retired.

(D) Workers are on vacation.

84. What does the speaker imply when he says, "Otherwise, tell us if you have a preferred dentist"?

(A) New customers may choose a dentist.

(B) A new dentist will be hired.

(C) Patients can write reviews of their dentists.

(D) Regulars may select a new dentist.

85. When will the clinic reopen?

(A) On July 30

(B) On July 31

(C) On August 8

(D) On August 9

86. Why did the speaker schedule the meeting?

(A) To give a demonstration of a product

(B) To make corrections to a sales report

(C) To provide information about an industry event

(D) To request volunteers for a trade fair booth

87. What recently changed about the Kenosha-50?

(A) Its battery weight was reduced.

(B) Its warranty period was extended.

(C) Its processing speed was improved.

(D) Its screen size was increased.

88. What does the speaker mean when she says, "it's currently just under five hundred grams"?

(A) The price is too high for the weight.

(B) A device does not meet the industry standard.

(C) Supplies are running out faster than expected.

(D) The product is inconvenient to carry around.

89. Who does the speaker introduce?

(A) An author

(B) A history professor

(C) A director

(D) A movie producer

90. What does the speaker apologize for?

(A) A leaflet has an error.

(B) A presentation is delayed.

(C) A movie screening is canceled.

(D) A guest cannot come.

91. What does the speaker imply when he says, "I hope you brought your own"?

(A) Items will not be available on site.

(B) Listeners need an entrance ticket for the talk.

(C) Mr. Stroud will answer some prepared questions.

(D) Listeners may suggest their own ideas.

92. Why does the speaker congratulate the listeners?

(A) They improved their work efficiency.

(B) They exceeded a sales goal.

(C) They hired a hard-working employee.

(D) They attracted a new client.

93. According to the speaker, what was the most impressive part of a presentation?

(A) Its simple explanations

(B) Its variety of photographs

(C) Its accompanying handout

(D) Its helpful charts

94. What will the speaker probably do next?

(A) Introduce a coworker

(B) Present some awards

(C) Write a list of companies

(D) Assign the listeners to teams

Elliot Bay Ferries
Seattle → Bainbridge Island

Departure: 9:20 A.M.   Arrival: 10:10 A.M.

Ticket Type: Walk-on Passenger
Ticket Fee: $8.20

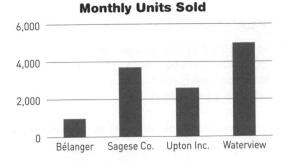

Monthly Units Sold

95. What does the speaker remind listeners to do?
(A) Direct questions to terminal employees
(B) Keep their belongings with them
(C) Check the departure dock
(D) Have their tickets ready

96. Look at the graphic. When should the ticket holder board the ferry?
(A) At 8:50 A.M.
(B) At 9:00 A.M.
(C) At 9:20 A.M.
(D) At 10:10 A.M.

97. What will be given to listeners soon?
(A) A ticket receipt
(B) A safety briefing
(C) A terminal map
(D) A seat assignment

98. What did the speaker do on Tuesday?
(A) Met with a consultant
(B) Tested product samples
(C) Checked the inventory
(D) Processed an order

99. What is causing a change in product supplies?
(A) A building expansion
(B) A business closure
(C) An inventory error
(D) A training event

100. Look at the graphic. Which brand will have more items added?
(A) Bélanger
(B) Sagese Co.
(C) Upton Inc.
(D) Waterview

This is the end of the Listening test. Turn to Part 5 in your test book.

READING TEST

In the Reading test, you will read a variety of texts and answer several different types of reading comprehension questions. The entire Reading test will last 75 minutes. There are three parts, and directions are given for each part. You are encouraged to answer as many questions as possible within the time allowed.

You must mark your answers on the separate answer sheet. Do not write your answers in your test book.

PART 5

Directions: A word or phrase is missing in each of the sentences below. Four answer choices are given below each sentence. Select the best answer to complete the sentence. Then mark the letter (A), (B), (C), or (D) on your answer sheet.

101. Mr. Wexler bought lunch for ------- team as a way of showing appreciation.

(A) he
(B) him
(C) his
(D) himself

102. ------- the past three months, the number of members at Slate Gym has doubled.

(A) Under
(B) While
(C) At
(D) Over

103. The letter to the editor was written by Janice Reeves, a ------- to *National Gardening Magazine*.

(A) subscribed
(B) subscribes
(C) subscriber
(D) subscription

104. Bothell Manufacturing will ------- be streamlining its production line with modern equipment.

(A) quite
(B) soon
(C) else
(D) ever

105. Now that the bakery has brought in a long-term investor, it is in good shape -------.

(A) finances
(B) finance
(C) financial
(D) financially

106. Benz Athletics was able to increase sales thanks to the ------- of a new line of clothing designed for children.

(A) delivery
(B) suggestion
(C) content
(D) addition

107. Consumers can save a lot of money on furniture if the components ------- at home.

(A) assembling
(B) to be assembled
(C) have assembled
(D) are assembled

108. Nature enthusiasts enjoy taking hikes ------- the woods located at the northern section of Derby National Park.

(A) through
(B) onto
(C) regarding
(D) except

109. The guests seated at the VIP table at the company's banquet include ------- for the annual employee awards.
(A) nominated
(B) nominations
(C) nominees
(D) nominate

110. Security guards at Mayfair International Airport need to be ------- of the rules and regulations for travelers.
(A) alert
(B) precise
(C) aware
(D) strict

111. Since the director was not available that day, the members of the sales team gave the product presentation to the buyers by -------.
(A) themselves
(B) them
(C) they
(D) theirs

112. Shobe Utilities ------- the information on its Web site to Spanish and Chinese so that it can be understood by more customers.
(A) is translated
(B) have translated
(C) has translated
(D) be translated

113. The current IT department is indeed the most ------- group in the company's history.
(A) diversely
(B) diversification
(C) diverse
(D) diversify

114. The manuscript for Ms. Colby's award-winning bestseller was ------- rejected by the publisher.
(A) rather
(B) nearby
(C) yet
(D) almost

115. Ms. Simpson, who is the Carolina branch's top salesperson, requested that ------- be promoted to team leader.
(A) herself
(B) she
(C) her
(D) hers

116. EZ Couriers will purchase three more vans for its fleet in an effort to ------- the rise in demand for its services.
(A) predict
(B) accommodate
(C) attribute
(D) generate

117. Tourists and locals alike visit the farmers' market because the produce there is very ------- priced.
(A) reason
(B) reasoned
(C) reasonably
(D) reasonable

118. ------- arriving at their final destination, the airline passengers waited for their belongings at the luggage carousel.
(A) Along
(B) Upon
(C) Unlike
(D) During

119. The newly trained cook forgot two of the ------- ingredients in the soup, so it did not turn out right.
(A) essential
(B) inherent
(C) equal
(D) reliable

120. The company's image is built on trust, ------- employees are expected to be open and honest with customers at all times.
(A) never
(B) so
(C) what
(D) then

GO ON TO THE NEXT PAGE

121. Mr. Vaughn wants to prepare a working model of the prototype ------- collaborating on the details with others.

(A) even so
(B) before
(C) so that
(D) instead

122. Lavola Restaurant is almost always filled to capacity and has earned a ------- for excellent food and service.

(A) clarification
(B) statement
(C) commitment
(D) reputation

123. The department store provided sample bottles of perfume ------- allow customers to try them.

(A) by far
(B) as a result of
(C) in order to
(D) above all

124. As its expansion project is completed, Lintz Hotel will ------- more staff members to handle the higher volume of guests.

(A) forfeit
(B) recruit
(C) dedicate
(D) delegate

125. The quality of the first draft of the report was not -------, so the manager asked for it to be rewritten.

(A) accepting
(B) acceptably
(C) acceptable
(D) acceptability

126. Event planners selected the Ingram Center for the software convention due to its ------- to major highways.

(A) publicity
(B) proximity
(C) regularity
(D) locality

127. Dr. Kapadia, who has conducted ------- research in the field of genetic engineering, is a highly respected biologist.

(A) furnished
(B) extensive
(C) perishable
(D) punctual

128. ------- gently the criticism of a staff member is made, it could still cause offense to a sensitive person.

(A) Somewhat
(B) However
(C) Entirely
(D) Seldom

129. Gabriel Falcone created a fully automated system that allowed the pharmaceutical company to more ------ evaluate a medical test's accuracy.

(A) narrowly
(B) increasingly
(C) partially
(D) efficiently

130. A number of board members questioned ------- Mr. Woodworth had the right qualifications for the position.

(A) both
(B) unless
(C) because
(D) whether

Directions: Read the texts that follow. A word, phrase, or sentence is missing in parts of each text. Four answer choices for each question are given below the text. Select the best answer to complete the text. Then mark the letter (A), (B), (C), or (D) on your answer sheet.

Questions 131-134 refer to the following advertisement.

Jacobs Interiors

Why move when you can just upgrade for a fraction of the cost? Our experienced designers

have ------- homes, offices, and even television studios! They will help you every step of the
      131.

way, starting with the selection of materials. -------. Nevertheless, we are willing to get items
                                                132.

imported or shipped to get you exactly what you want. We will also keep your safety in mind, as

we have engineers inspect structures ------- to the building's support system before making any
                                      133.

changes. Visit our Web site at www.jacobsint.com to see photos of past projects and read

testimonials about how we fulfilled customers' -------.
                                               134.

131. (A) related
     (B) transformed
     (C) invested
     (D) toured

132. (A) The business offers a money-back guarantee
         on the work.
     (B) Don't hesitate to share your project ideas with
         the designer.
     (C) Some colors remain popular from year to year.
     (D) We try to use locally sourced supplies as often
         as we can.

133. (A) vitally
     (B) vital
     (C) vitalize
     (D) vitality

134. (A) orders
     (B) relations
     (C) behaviors
     (D) forms

Questions 135-138 refer to the following memo.

To: All Haynes Airlines Ticket and Gate Agents
From: Crystal Lecuyer
Date: October 25

In preparation for the busy holiday travel season, we will be ------- two extra lines in our check-
135.
in area. We believe this will help us to reduce the long wait times for check-in.

Under this new plan, part-time workers will have additional shifts ------- January 5. You may also
136.

------- to work at the gate, as boarding is an important factor in on-time departures. Your
137.

supervisors plan to set a schedule soon. -------.
138.

Thank you for your hard work and cooperation.

135. (A) opening
(B) relocating
(C) decorating
(D) suspending

136. (A) within
(B) until
(C) during
(D) following

137. (A) assigning
(B) be assigned
(C) assigned
(D) having assigned

138. (A) Gate numbers should be posted as soon as possible.
(B) A copy of it is attached to this memo.
(C) Travelers are expected to request this service.
(D) Please notify them of any potential scheduling conflicts.

188

Questions 139-142 refer to the following article.

Golf Club to Raise Funds for Local Museum

HOLTONVILLE, August 7—The Holtonville Golf Club will hold its first-ever tournament at Greenway Golf Course to raise money for the Contemporary Art Museum. ------- . Winners will
139.
take home a trophy as well as gift cards. The club hopes that participants will not only have a good time but will also become ------- informed about the importance of art in the community.
140.
------- , the event provides a great opportunity for young golfers to play in a friendly competition.
141.
All ------- from the event will go toward making urgent roof repairs at the museum.
142.

---

139. (A) The city's mayor praised organizers for their focus on the environment.
(B) Golf lessons are offered at the site throughout the summer months.
(C) The prizes for the competition will be announced at a later date.
(D) The competition will grant participants prizes donated by local businesses.

140. (A) full
(B) fullness
(C) fuller
(D) fully

141. (A) Otherwise
(B) Thus
(C) Furthermore
(D) In fact

142. (A) interest
(B) proceeds
(C) materials
(D) separation

GO ON TO THE NEXT PAGE

To: Pamela Rardin <p.rardin@montoyainc.net>
From: Aarom Communications <info@aaromcomm.com>
Date: September 4
Subject: Aarom-6 Phone

Dear Ms. Rardin,

Our records show that you recently made a ------- of an Aarom-6 smartphone from Aarom
143.
Communications. We are delighted to offer you our noise-canceling wireless headphones for

just $89.99. -------. These headphones provide premium sound quality, a comfortable fit, and a
144.
long battery life.

If you are interested, please ------- to this e-mail no later than September 10 with your preferred
145.
mailing address. We will then make a charge to your Aarom customer account. ------- will
146.
appear on your monthly statement as "Aarom Headphones." We hope you will take advantage
of this great deal, and we look forward to serving you.

Sincerely,

Sharon Kearney

Customer Service Agent, Aarom Communications

---

143. (A) review
(B) repair
(C) purchase
(D) profit

144. (A) This special price reflects a thirty percent
discount.
(B) They come as a standard accessory at no
extra charge.
(C) You can read more about this in your product
warranty.
(D) We appreciate your notifying us of the issue
promptly.

145. (A) respond
(B) subscribe
(C) disregard
(D) feel free

146. (A) Those
(B) Few
(C) Another
(D) It

PART 7

Directions: In this part you will read a selection of texts, such as magazine and newspaper articles, e-mails, and instant messages. Each text or set of texts is followed by several questions. Select the best answer for each question and mark the letter (A), (B), (C), or (D) on your answer sheet.

Questions 147-148 refer to the following notice.

Crestar Maintenance Project

From June 3 to July 18, we will be working on several maintenance projects on our network. This work may affect your departure time and/or journey duration. Signs are posted throughout the station to inform you of the changes to the timetable for each day. Please be sure to view this posted information to ensure that you know what to expect. Thank you for your patience.

147. For whom is the notice most likely intended?
(A) Safety inspectors
(B) Travel agents
(C) Construction workers
(D) Train passengers

148. What does the notice instruct people to do?
(A) Check an adjusted schedule
(B) Provide feedback about a service
(C) Report problems to the company
(D) Make a payment in advance

GO ON TO THE NEXT PAGE

Barrington Roofing
305 Acres Lane, Brentwood, TN 37027
(615) 555-8483

Customer: Leonard Harper
Property Site: 4651 Guevara Street, Brentwood, TN 37027
Description of Work: Replace roof on residential property

Original Quote	$7,500	Issue Date	May 3
Updated Quote	$6,300	Issue Date	May 7

Notes: The original quote included the entire roof replacement process. Now the client will remove the old shingles before the project begins and handle their disposal separately.

Start Date	May 15	End Date	May 16
Deposit and first payment received			$300 on May 7

* Half of the balance ($3,000) is due as a second payment on the first day of work. The final payment is due one week after the completion of the work. Please note that payments must be made in accordance with this schedule regardless of weather delays.

149. Why has a charge on the invoice been changed?

(A) The price of materials has increased.

(B) The customer presented a coupon.

(C) The permit had to be paid for separately.

(D) The customer will take care of some of the work.

150. When should Mr. Harper make his second payment?

(A) On May 15

(B) On May 16

(C) On May 22

(D) On May 23

Cynthia Spencer [11:13 A.M.]

Hi, Ralph. You're away from the office today, right?

Ralph Wallace [11:16 A.M.]

Yes. I'll be attending meetings with representatives from one of our largest accounts. Why?

Cynthia Spencer [11:17 A.M.]

I'm wondering if I could borrow your laptop just for today. Mine isn't working, and the IT team doesn't have a replacement.

Ralph Wallace [11:18 A.M.]

Of course. Just return it when you're done.

Cynthia Spencer [11:19 A.M.]

I will. Thanks a lot! It's in the common department locker, right?

Ralph Wallace [11:20 A.M.]

Yes, it should be. And there isn't a password, so you should be fine.

Actual Test 5

151. What is Mr. Wallace doing today?

(A) Meeting some clients off-site

(B) Training some IT workers

(C) Setting up a meeting room

(D) Giving some customers a tour

152. At 11:18 A.M., what does Mr. Wallace mean when he writes, "Of course"?

(A) He will call the IT team to make a request.

(B) He does not mind lending some equipment to Ms. Spencer.

(C) He can help repair Ms. Spencer's malfunctioning laptop.

(D) He will order a replacement item for Ms. Spencer.

GO ON TO THE NEXT PAGE

To: All Osage Consulting Employees
From: Carla Watson, Branch Supervisor
Date: October 17
Subject: Employee break room

Now that the employee break room is open again following the renovations, we want to make sure that this area is kept clean and tidy for all who use it. Therefore, from now on, we are changing the policy on the usage of the refrigerator. Whenever you put something in the refrigerator, it must have your name and the date marked on it clearly. Every Friday afternoon, the refrigerator will be cleaned out, and items that have expired and those that do not have names on them will be thrown out. This will ensure that the refrigerator does not get too full and does not have any spoiled food in it. Thank you in advance for your cooperation.

153. Why did Ms. Watson write the memo?

(A) To notify staff of a renovation
(B) To explain a break schedule
(C) To report a room closure
(D) To announce a new rule

154. What are readers of the memo asked to do?

(A) Refrain from eating food in the office
(B) Empty the refrigerator every Friday
(C) Label their food and drink items
(D) Volunteer for a weekly cleanup job

Questions 155-157 refer to the following Web page.

http://www.bloomfieldpublib.org/news

| HOME | ABOUT | SERVICES | **NEWS** | SEARCH |

The Bloomfield Public Library is proud to be one of the venues for the city's first-ever Spring Literary Festival, which runs from April 16 to 20. The event will feature talks all over the city from professional writers who have had their works published recently, including Jiang Li, Linda Atchison, Yamuna Bose, and Patrick Corona. Ms. Atchison's talk, which will be held at our library, is expected to be a particularly big draw, as her latest mystery novel, *Onward North*, has spent thirty weeks on the bestseller list. The book also took home the prestigious Larochelle Prize last month.

Tickets for the event can be purchased at the Bloomfield Community Center.

155. What is NOT true about the Spring Literary Festival?

(A) It has never been held before.
(B) It will last for less than a week.
(C) It includes an author awards ceremony.
(D) It will take place in several locations.

156. Who has recently won an award?

(A) Jiang Li
(B) Linda Atchison
(C) Yamuna Bose
(D) Patrick Corona

157. What is mentioned about Bloomfield Public Library?

(A) It will be closed in preparation for the festival.
(B) It organizes the literary festival every year.
(C) It will host a lecture by a professional writer.
(D) It is seeking volunteers to assist with the festival.

GO ON TO THE NEXT PAGE

E-Mail

To: Gwen Landry <gwenlandry@milagrosinc.com>
From: Amanda Morgan <amanda@nsrmembers.org>
Date: July 29
Subject: Important Notice

Dear Ms. Landry,

According to our records, you have been a member of the National Society of Realtors for the past three years. —[1]—. Thank you for your patronage, and we hope you are enjoying the benefits of being a part of this group.

We are currently holding our annual membership drive and would like to ask for your assistance. —[2]—. If you have friends or colleagues who would be suitable for our group, please have them complete the attached application form. This form has a special number so we can determine that the referral came from you. —[3]—.

For each member you refer, you will receive $10 off your monthly dues. In addition, you will have a seat reserved for you in the VIP section at our annual conference. —[4]—. We will also enter your name into a prize drawing for a five-day vacation in the Bahamas.

If you have inquiries about recruitment, please feel free to e-mail me anytime.

Sincerely,

Amanda Morgan
Membership Services

---

158. Who most likely is Ms. Landry?

(A) A group founder
(B) A real estate agent
(C) A homeowner
(D) A bank teller

159. What is NOT an advantage of referring members?

(A) A chance to win a trip
(B) Priority seating at an event
(C) A reduction in membership fees
(D) Discounted tickets to a conference

160. In which of the positions marked [1], [2], [3], and [4] does the following sentence best belong?

"It can be found at the bottom of the page."

(A) [1]
(B) [2]
(C) [3]
(D) [4]

Aiden Holt

739 Kessler Way

Syracuse, NY 13202

Dear Mr. Holt,

We hope you have enjoyed the free one-month trial of our Premium Sports Package. Your access to the four international football channels, two basketball channels, and two mixed sports channels will end on April 30 if you take no further action. To make sure you don't miss any of the sports coverage you love, sign up for a one-year subscription to the Premium Sports Package, which will add just $7.95 to your monthly bill. You can do so by changing the settings on your online account with Chapman Cable through our Web site. There you can also check your user agreement for details about how to add or discontinue premium packages.

Enclosed you will also find a postage-paid postcard, on which you can share your suggestions, ideas, and complaints. We'd love to hear how you are finding your Chapman Cable experience so far.

Warmest regards,

The Chapman Cable Accounts Team

Actual Test 5

161. What is the purpose of the letter?

(A) To encourage a customer to continue a service

(B) To announce which channels will be added next month

(C) To introduce a new package of sports channels

(D) To remind a customer to make a payment on his account

162. What will happen on April 30?

(A) A free trial will expire.

(B) A sports event will take place.

(C) A discount will be applied.

(D) An online account will be disabled.

163. What is enclosed with the letter?

(A) A discount coupon

(B) A broadcast schedule

(C) An updated user agreement

(D) A comment card

GO ON TO THE NEXT PAGE

Latika Nair 1:23 P.M.	Renovations on our office will not start next week as planned.
Chet Matthews 1:25 P.M.	I heard that the company we were supposed to use went out of business unexpectedly.
Latika Nair 1:26 P.M.	Right. So I'm looking for another construction firm, preferably one endorsed by someone I know. Any ideas?
Diane Perdue 1:27 P.M.	I was very pleased with the work done by Norris Construction at my house last year.
Chet Matthews 1:28 P.M.	But that business was sold to another person last month, so the quality might not be the same.
Diane Perdue 1:29 P.M.	I didn't know that. We'd better not take any chances.
Chet Matthews 1:30 P.M.	The dental clinic across the street recently had its interior redesigned, and it looks great.
Latika Nair 1:31 P.M.	We should try to find out the address and contact number of their contractor.
Motoshi Tenno 1:32 P.M.	I actually have an appointment there on Friday, so I'll do that during my visit.

164. Why did Ms. Nair start the online chat?

(A) To get a business recommendation
(B) To introduce a new contractor
(C) To review some contract terms
(D) To approve a renovation schedule

165. What is indicated about Norris Construction?

(A) It was endorsed by a dental clinic.
(B) It canceled a contract unexpectedly.
(C) It is under new ownership.
(D) It has lower prices than its competitors.

166. At 1:29 P.M., what does Ms. Perdue most likely mean when she writes, "We'd better not take any chances"?

(A) She wants to retract her suggestion.
(B) She thinks they should do a safety check.
(C) She plans to do further research.
(D) She needs more time for a decision.

167. What will Mr. Tenno do on Friday?

(A) Contact Norris Construction
(B) Gather information about a business
(C) Reschedule an appointment
(D) Visit a new contractor

To: Gregory Pearlman <g.pearlman@oakway.com>

From: Tibbs Inc. <inquiries@tibbsinc.com>

Date: August 26

Subject: RE: Inquiry

Dear Mr. Pearlman,

I received your message about your recent participation in our sightseeing boat ride around Nieves Bay. I've checked our lost-and-found box, and there are indeed a few men's watches in there, one of which might be yours. Unfortunately, I cannot provide you with a photograph of these items as requested, as our company regulations do not allow it. To claim a lost item, you should come to our office at the harbor and give a description of the item. If possible, showing the ticket from your boat ride will make the process faster. That's because we will be able to determine exactly which boat you were on, and our found items are cataloged by date and boat.

There is no need to book an appointment in advance. Simply stop by during our office hours, which are 9 A.M. to 6 P.M. daily. Please note that we are a seasonal business, and the season is wrapping up at the end of the month. Therefore, you only have a few days to visit us before the office closes for the low season, so please do so if you can, as returning your item will become a lot more complicated after that.

Sincerely,

Lucy Wooldridge

Administrative Assistant, Tibbs Inc.

168. What kind of service does Tibbs Inc. most likely provide?

(A) Event photography

(B) Swimming lessons

(C) Group tours

(D) Hotel bookings

169. Why was Ms. Wooldridge unable to send Mr. Pearlman a picture?

(A) A Web site is not working.

(B) It is against company policy.

(C) Some equipment is missing.

(D) The image needs to be edited.

170. According to the e-mail, how can Mr. Pearlman expedite a process?

(A) By avoiding the peak times

(B) By paying an additional fee

(C) By booking an appointment

(D) By presenting a ticket

171. What does Ms. Wooldridge recommend doing?

(A) Purchasing a season pass

(B) Contacting her manager

(C) E-mailing a description

(D) Taking action quickly

Investment at GT Communications

March 3—GT Communications has confirmed its plans to invest heavily in technology for its facilities. Customers have shifted away from landlines, which previously made up GT Communications' entire business, and started using mobile phone networks and the Internet. Therefore, the company is adapting its business model by changing its infrastructure. — [1] —.

The smallest of the company's facilities—located in Nashville—already received the new machines so that the plan could be tried out on a small scale before rolling out the changes companywide. — [2] —. GT Communications is taking measures to ensure that its staff members are not negatively affected by the upgrades. "During the transition at Nashville, we looked for areas where we could retrain our people instead of laying them off," said company spokesperson Katherine Coyle. "— [3] —. We expect similar figures at the rest of our facilities."

GT Communications is now ready for Phase 2 of its transition, which is installing the state-of-the-art equipment at all sites. — [4] —. The work will begin with the Detroit site later this year, followed by the Kansas City branch early next year, and the Houston branch late next year. Once all of the upgrades have been completed, the final site will be open for public tours so that people can see the operations for themselves.

172. According to the article, what caused GT Communications to transform its business plan?

(A) A new government regulation
(B) A complaint from the workforce
(C) A change in consumer behavior
(D) An increase in shareholders

173. What is mentioned about the company's facility in Nashville?

(A) It was used as a testing site.
(B) It received a technology award.
(C) It is the first factory opened by GT Communications.
(D) It was the meeting place of investors.

174. Where does GT Communications plan to offer public tours of a site?

(A) Nashville
(B) Detroit
(C) Kansas City
(D) Houston

175. In which of the positions marked [1], [2], [3], and [4] does the following sentence best belong?

"We were thus able to keep ninety percent of staff members at that location."

(A) [1]
(B) [2]
(C) [3]
(D) [4]

GO ON TO THE NEXT PAGE

Four intense workshops are being made available to employees of HTT Corp. Employees must choose one of the four courses below. Each course comprises three three-hour sessions unless otherwise specified. The sessions will be held on Fridays (March 14, 21, and 28) from 2 P.M. to 5 P.M.

Exchange Rates Risk Management
❏ Instructor: Frederic Masker
This course will look closely at how exchange rates affect markets, explain how predictions are made, and go over the best strategies for investing in an international context. This course has one additional two-hour session on April 4.

International Capital Flows
❏ Instructor: Lydia Benson
This course will explain how capital flows globally, introduce a few key relationships among countries, and go over the major effects of these flows on the global economy.

Multinational Corporations
❏ Instructor: Sylvia Glazkova
This course will introduce three major multinational corporations and give an in-depth analysis of their functioning and budget management.

Case Studies
❏ Instructor: Trenton Blair
This hands-on course will have students work in groups to analyze a case and determine the best strategy for the sample corporation to take. Each group will present their findings in the last session.

To: Linda Kay <lindakay@httcorp.com>
From: Peter Moreno <petermoreno@httcorp.com>
Subject: Friday Afternoon
Date: Thursday, March 27

Dear Ms. Kay,

Ms. Benson has changed the last session for the workshop from tomorrow to next Tuesday. I am thus free to work tomorrow afternoon. However, I was wondering if it would be acceptable for me to watch the presentations from Mr. Blair's class. Several coworkers taking that course have told me about their work, and I am highly interested in seeing the results. Of course, if I am needed in the office at that time, I will be available to work.

Thank you for your consideration.

Sincerely,

Peter Moreno
Budget Analyst, HTT Corp.

176. Where will the information most likely appear?

    (A) In a brochure

    (B) On a bulletin board

    (C) In a magazine

    (D) On a flyer

177. When will Ms. Glazkova's last class be held?

    (A) March 14

    (B) March 21

    (C) March 28

    (D) April 4

178. Which instructor will have students collaborate on a project?

    (A) Frederic Masker

    (B) Lydia Benson

    (C) Sylvia Glazkova

    (D) Trenton Blair

179. Which course has Mr. Moreno been attending?

    (A) Exchange Rates Risk Management

    (B) International Capital Flows

    (C) Multinational Corporations

    (D) Case Studies

180. What is NOT true about Mr. Moreno?

    (A) He has already attended several classes.

    (B) He wants to see his coworkers' projects.

    (C) He is scheduled to give a presentation.

    (D) He is able to come to the office on Friday.

GO ON TO THE NEXT PAGE

To: MMH Law Firm Employees
From: Tamara Caudill, Attorney
Subject: Re: Building for Sale

April 16

As discussed in the weekly meeting, the owner of Midland Tower will put the building up for sale next month, and we will relocate our offices. Aldridge Co., the realtor handling the sale of the building, would like professionals to take photos for the property listing on its Web site. This photo shoot will take place on April 24 and will be carried out in all parts of the building. I have attached a schedule with the offices that are going to be photographed. In preparation for the photographers' visit, all items must be cleared from your desk except your computer and phone. We will provide plastic bins for you, and you should put your items in them for the short duration of the shoot. A maintenance worker will visit you ten minutes before your appointed time to collect these bins with a cart. Furniture might be rearranged in your office, but it will be returned to its original placement before you get back. The entire process will take about twenty minutes maximum, during which time you can take a break in the staff lounge. This does not count toward your usual daily break time.

Thank you for your cooperation, and we apologize for any inconvenience this may cause.

[Attachment: Final Schedule]

Aldridge Co. Schedule: April 24

TIME	OFFICE	OCCUPANT(S)
9:00 A.M.	201	Harriet Duncan
9:20 A.M.	202	Ranjan Singh
9:40 A.M.	203	Dale Mumford, Michael Bellamy
10:00 A.M.	204	Shirley Swain
10:20 A.M.	205	Brandon Parra, Huan Ren

Brandon Parra will handle room 202 because the occupant won't be in the office that day.

181. What is the purpose of the memo?

(A) To introduce a new building owner to employees

(B) To explain how an office relocation will occur

(C) To distribute a schedule for a renovation project

(D) To announce a plan for photographing a building

182. What does Ms. Caudill advise the memo recipients to do?

(A) Direct their questions to Aldridge Co.

(B) Use containers to temporarily move items

(C) Contact her regarding their availability on April 24

(D) Leave their personal belongings at home

183. What can the memo recipients do on April 24?

(A) Take an additional break

(B) Work part of the day from home

(C) Leave work early

(D) Have an extended lunchtime

184. At what time will a maintenance worker arrive at Ms. Swain's office on April 24?

(A) 9:40 A.M.

(B) 9:50 A.M.

(C) 10:00 A.M.

(D) 10:10 A.M.

185. What is implied about Mr. Singh?

(A) He will move to office 203.

(B) He shares an office with Mr. Parra.

(C) He will be absent on April 24.

(D) He requested a change in the schedule.

GO ON TO THE NEXT PAGE

Questions 186-190 refer to the following product description, online review, and online response.

The Bag of the Future: Zimmer-40

The Zimmer-40 will revolutionize the way you think about backpacks. It features a fold-out solar panel that can be used to charge your personal electronics. The advanced battery ensures that you always have the power you need on the go. The outer section is fully resistant to water, so your devices are always protected. In addition, all plastic parts on the backpack come from recycled plastic.

The Zimmer is sold at department stores and sporting goods outlets. Sign up for our monthly newsletter at the time of purchase to get a free second battery.

  www.ucanreview.net/customer_reviews/accessories

Brand: Zimmer
Reviewer: Tyson Quintero

Item: Zimmer-40
Post Type: New

After researching several technology-enabled backpacks on the market, I selected the Zimmer-40 because of Zimmer's solid reputation. The color of the bag was darker than it appeared in the catalog, but that wasn't a problem for me. I'm impressed with how long the battery holds its charge, and I'm glad to have the second free one. The only thing that disappointed me was that my 15-inch laptop does not fit inside the bag. Despite this, I highly recommend this product, and I intend to buy it as a gift for several friends.

www.ucanreview.net/customer_reviews/accessories

Brand: Zimmer
Commenter: Phillip Sandoval

Item: Zimmer-40
Post Type: Reply

As a Zimmer customer service agent, I'm sorry you were not completely satisfied with your purchase. Based on your needs, you might want to consider the Zimmer-40B. It has a special charging compartment on the inside that can accommodate up to a 17-inch laptop. It has the same gel-filled shoulder straps as the Zimmer-40, so you can still wear it comfortably even if it is loaded with heavy items. Since you already have the Zimmer-40, there isn't any point in buying a new battery because the same one can be used in all of our bags. I hope this resolves your issue.

186. What is NOT indicated about the Zimmer-40?

(A) It has a waterproof exterior.

(B) It makes use of renewable energy.

(C) It is partially made from recycled materials.

(D) It is light enough to use during sports.

187. What can be inferred about Mr. Quintero?

(A) He will receive monthly updates from Zimmer.

(B) He purchased the bag at a department store.

(C) He doesn't like the color of the bag.

(D) He mainly uses the bag for outdoor activities.

188. What is suggested in the online review?

(A) Zimmer is a relatively new company.

(B) Mr. Quintero plans to purchase more bags.

(C) Zimmer sells a line of laptop computers.

(D) Mr. Quintero noticed some damage on his bag.

189. Why does Mr. Sandoval recommend the Zimmer-40B to Mr. Quintero?

(A) It is the only bag with gel-filled straps.

(B) It can charge items more quickly.

(C) It has a larger carrying capacity.

(D) It is more durable than the Zimmer-40.

190. In the online response, the word "point" in paragraph 1, line 6, is closest in meaning to

(A) opinion

(B) reason

(C) aspect

(D) spot

GO ON TO THE NEXT PAGE

=== **E-Mail** ===

To: Kimberly Garrett <kgarrett@saezinc.net>
From: Marietta Convention Center <info@mariettacc.com>
Date: February 19
Subject: Information

Dear Ms. Garrett,

Thank you for taking a tour of the Marietta Convention Center on February 18. I hope you enjoyed viewing our technology-enabled facilities, including the expansion of the west wing. Based on your description of the banquet your company plans to hold, I believe we would be the perfect site. Each room comes equipped with a stage, which could be used to present awards to your art instructors and give speeches, and there are a variety of amenities to suit your needs. Furthermore, I can confirm that we currently have no reservations booked for your desired date of March 31. Attached, please find the detailed information you requested about each room. If you would like to make a booking, or if you have any further questions, do not hesitate to contact me at 555-6677, extension 21. I hope to hear from you soon.

Sincerely,

Ralph Shelby
Guest Services Representative, Marietta Convention Center

Marietta Convention Center Room Descriptions

Daisy Room—Maximum Capacity: 50 / Rental Fee: $2,600
4 x 8 m stage, podium, projector, pull-down video screen

Sunflower Room—Maximum Capacity: 50 / Rental Fee: $2,900
4 x 8 m stage, podium, projector, pull-down video screen, exterior doorway to garden

Peony Room—Maximum Capacity: 100 / Rental Fee: $3,500
6 x 10 m stage, podium, projector, flat-screen built-in television, full-service bar

Orchid Room—Maximum Capacity: 100 / Rental Fee: $4,800
6 x 12 m stage, podium, projector, flat-screen built-in television, full-service bar, view of Lochmere Bay

Various seating arrangements are available. Guests may use south or west parking lot for a nominal fee.

E-MAIL MESSAGE

To: Amina Jeffries, Dean McGraw, Kimberly Garrett, Bai Tan
From: Amil Rao
Date: February 20
Subject: Banquet plans

Hi Everyone,

It seems like we are making progress on our committee's plans for the upcoming banquet for our staff and their families. Thank you, Kimberly, for taking over the Marietta Convention Center visit for me, since I had to fly to Toronto that day for an unexpected business matter. I'm still waiting for the reports from the rest of you regarding the caterers you were assigned to research. Please e-mail that information to me by Thursday afternoon.

As for the venue options, I'd love our ninety guests to be able to overlook Lochmere Bay as they dine, but I don't think this will be feasible, given our limited budget. Instead, I think it would be best to rent the cheaper room that fits our size needs. We can discuss this further at Friday's meeting. See you then!

Amil

191. Where does Ms. Garrett most likely work?

(A) At a technology company
(B) At a fitness center
(C) At an art institute
(D) At a performance venue

192. Which room amenity is indicated in the information?

(A) Special lighting for the stage area
(B) A view of the city skyline
(C) Complimentary parking for guests
(D) Access to an outdoor space

193. What is implied about Mr. Rao?

(A) He joined the committee at the last minute.
(B) He visited several meeting venues.
(C) He wrote a review of a caterer.
(D) He took a business trip on February 18.

194. What can be inferred about Mr. McGraw?

(A) He is in charge of the committee's budget.
(B) He is gathering information about caterers.
(C) He is unable to attend Friday's meeting.
(D) He visited the Marietta Convention Center.

195. Which room would Mr. Rao most likely want to rent?

(A) Daisy Room
(B) Sunflower Room
(C) Peony Room
(D) Orchid Room

GO ON TO THE NEXT PAGE

Questions 196-200 refer to the following article, Web page, and review.

Theater Fundraiser a Success

Last night's charity banquet to raise funds for the Gilcrest Theater was deemed a remarkable success by event planners, who reported proceeds of nearly $12,000, approximately $2,000 over the goal. The money will be used for the installation of a cutting-edge sound system in the theater, which will serve as a much-needed replacement for the outdated system currently being used.

The work will be completed just in time for the Regional Film Festival, of which the Gilcrest Theater is a hosting site. While the facility usually presents live theater performances, it is equipped with a large projection screen for movies. Other theaters across the region will also participate, but Gilcrest Theater has the highest seating capacity among them, more than double that of the second-largest one, Corinth Theater.

Tickets for the film festival go on sale next week. Movie fans can take in intense dramas by critically acclaimed directors. Or for those looking for something light, there are plenty of films with comedic writing.

---

www.regionalfilmfestival.com/schedule

| HOME | ABOUT | **SCHEDULE** | SEATING | DIRECTION |

Regional Film Festival

| Thursday, September 6 | Friday, September 7 | **Saturday, September 8** | Sunday, September 9 |

Venue / Phone Number	Film	Start Time	
24th Street Theater / 555–4102	*Underground*	7:00 P.M.	[More Info]
Corinth Theater / 555–0578	*A Summer's Day*	7:30 P.M.	[More Info]
Gilcrest Theater / 555–5855	*The Tale of Marco*	7:05 P.M.	[More Info]
Palacios Theater / 555–9360	*Wilson's Army*	8:10 P.M.	[More Info]

Customers should select the seat number and row when purchasing tickets, so please review the map of the venue's seating sections, downloadable at www.regionalfilm festival.com/seating, before calling to order tickets. This will speed up the ordering process.

Underground: Best Thriller of the Year
****

By Casey Ashton

If you're looking for a thriller that will keep you guessing until the very end, look no further than *Underground*, the latest masterpiece by director Mia Camacho. I recently saw it at the Regional Film Festival, and I was extremely impressed with the character development, intriguing plot, and fantastic acting. This film is a must-see!

196. In the article, the word "deemed" in paragraph 1, line 2, is closest in meaning to

(A) considered
(B) expected
(C) admired
(D) caused

197. How will the raised funds be used at Gilcrest Theater?

(A) To launch an advertising campaign
(B) To purchase a projection screen
(C) To upgrade an outdated Web site
(D) To install new audio equipment

198. When will the largest theater start its screening event on September 8?

(A) At 7:00 P.M.
(B) At 7:05 P.M.
(C) At 7:30 P.M.
(D) At 8:10 P.M.

199. What are ticket purchasers advised to do?

(A) Download a digital receipt
(B) Check a seating chart in advance
(C) Read some online movie reviews
(D) Receive tickets by express mail

200. Where did Mr. Ashton watch a film?

(A) 24th Street Theater
(B) Corinth Theater
(C) Gilcrest Theater
(D) Palacios Theater

Stop! This is the end of the test. If you finish before time is called, you may go back to Parts 5, 6, and 7 and check your work.

分數換算表

本分數換算表是為了換算教材中收錄之五回分量的測驗分數而製成。完成各回測驗後，試著預估看看自己的預期分數區間吧！

LISTENING RAW SCORE （答對題數）	LISTENING SCALED SCORE （換算分數）	READING RAW SCORE （答對題數）	READING SCALED SCORE （換算分數）
96-100	475-495	96-100	460-495
91-95	435-495	91-95	425-490
86-90	405-475	86-90	395-465
81-85	370-450	81-85	370-440
76-80	345-420	76-80	335-415
71-75	320-390	71-75	310-390
66-70	290-360	66-70	280-365
61-65	265-335	61-65	250-335
56-60	235-310	56-60	220-305
51-55	210-280	51-55	195-270
46-50	180-255	46-50	165-240
41-45	155-230	41-45	140-215
36-40	125-205	36-40	115-180
31-35	105-175	31-35	95-145
26-30	85-145	26-30	75-120
21-25	60-115	21-25	60-95
16-20	30-90	16-20	45-75
11-15	5-70	11-15	30-55
6-10	5-60	6-10	10-40
1-5	5-50	1-5	5-30
0	5	0	5

註：上述表格僅供參考，實際計分以官方分數為準。

Answer Sheet

READING SECTION

Questions 101–200, each with options Ⓐ Ⓑ Ⓒ Ⓓ

101	102	103	104	105	106	107	108	109	110
111	112	113	114	115	116	117	118	119	120
121	122	123	124	125	126	127	128	129	130
131	132	133	134	135	136	137	138	139	140
141	142	143	144	145	146	147	148	149	150
151	152	153	154	155	156	157	158	159	160
161	162	163	164	165	166	167	168	169	170
171	172	173	174	175	176	177	178	179	180
181	182	183	184	185	186	187	188	189	190
191	192	193	194	195	196	197	198	199	200

LISTENING SECTION

Questions 1–100, each with options Ⓐ Ⓑ Ⓒ Ⓓ

1	2	3	4	5	6	7	8	9	10
11	12	13	14	15	16	17	18	19	20
21	22	23	24	25	26	27	28	29	30
31	32	33	34	35	36	37	38	39	40
41	42	43	44	45	46	47	48	49	50
51	52	53	54	55	56	57	58	59	60
61	62	63	64	65	66	67	68	69	70
71	72	73	74	75	76	77	78	79	80
81	82	83	84	85	86	87	88	89	90
91	92	93	94	95	96	97	98	99	100

TOEIC TEST 1

Answer Sheet

READING SECTION

LISTENING SECTION

TOEIC TEST 2

101 102 103 104 105 106 107 108 109 110
Ⓐ Ⓑ Ⓒ Ⓓ

111 112 113 114 115 116 117 118 119 120
Ⓐ Ⓑ Ⓒ Ⓓ

121 122 123 124 125 126 127 128 129 130
Ⓐ Ⓑ Ⓒ Ⓓ

131 132 133 134 135 136 137 138 139 140
Ⓐ Ⓑ Ⓒ Ⓓ

141 142 143 144 145 146 147 148 149 150
Ⓐ Ⓑ Ⓒ Ⓓ

151 152 153 154 155 156 157 158 159 160
Ⓐ Ⓑ Ⓒ Ⓓ

161 162 163 164 165 166 167 168 169 170
Ⓐ Ⓑ Ⓒ Ⓓ

171 172 173 174 175 176 177 178 179 180
Ⓐ Ⓑ Ⓒ Ⓓ

181 182 183 184 185 186 187 188 189 190
Ⓐ Ⓑ Ⓒ Ⓓ

191 192 193 194 195 196 197 198 199 200
Ⓐ Ⓑ Ⓒ Ⓓ

1 2 3 4 5 6 7 8 9 10
Ⓐ Ⓑ Ⓒ Ⓓ

11 12 13 14 15 16 17 18 19 20
Ⓐ Ⓑ Ⓒ Ⓓ

21 22 23 24 25 26 27 28 29 30
Ⓐ Ⓑ Ⓒ Ⓓ

31 32 33 34 35 36 37 38 39 40
Ⓐ Ⓑ Ⓒ Ⓓ

41 42 43 44 45 46 47 48 49 50
Ⓐ Ⓑ Ⓒ Ⓓ

51 52 53 54 55 56 57 58 59 60
Ⓐ Ⓑ Ⓒ Ⓓ

61 62 63 64 65 66 67 68 69 70
Ⓐ Ⓑ Ⓒ Ⓓ

71 72 73 74 75 76 77 78 79 80
Ⓐ Ⓑ Ⓒ Ⓓ

81 82 83 84 85 86 87 88 89 90
Ⓐ Ⓑ Ⓒ Ⓓ

91 92 93 94 95 96 97 98 99 100
Ⓐ Ⓑ Ⓒ Ⓓ

Answer Sheet

TOEIC TEST 3

READING SECTION

#	A	B	C	D
101	Ⓐ	Ⓑ	Ⓒ	Ⓓ
102	Ⓐ	Ⓑ	Ⓒ	Ⓓ
103	Ⓐ	Ⓑ	Ⓒ	Ⓓ
104	Ⓐ	Ⓑ	Ⓒ	Ⓓ
105	Ⓐ	Ⓑ	Ⓒ	Ⓓ
106	Ⓐ	Ⓑ	Ⓒ	Ⓓ
107	Ⓐ	Ⓑ	Ⓒ	Ⓓ
108	Ⓐ	Ⓑ	Ⓒ	Ⓓ
109	Ⓐ	Ⓑ	Ⓒ	Ⓓ
110	Ⓐ	Ⓑ	Ⓒ	Ⓓ
111	Ⓐ	Ⓑ	Ⓒ	Ⓓ
112	Ⓐ	Ⓑ	Ⓒ	Ⓓ
113	Ⓐ	Ⓑ	Ⓒ	Ⓓ
114	Ⓐ	Ⓑ	Ⓒ	Ⓓ
115	Ⓐ	Ⓑ	Ⓒ	Ⓓ
116	Ⓐ	Ⓑ	Ⓒ	Ⓓ
117	Ⓐ	Ⓑ	Ⓒ	Ⓓ
118	Ⓐ	Ⓑ	Ⓒ	Ⓓ
119	Ⓐ	Ⓑ	Ⓒ	Ⓓ
120	Ⓐ	Ⓑ	Ⓒ	Ⓓ
121	Ⓐ	Ⓑ	Ⓒ	Ⓓ
122	Ⓐ	Ⓑ	Ⓒ	Ⓓ
123	Ⓐ	Ⓑ	Ⓒ	Ⓓ
124	Ⓐ	Ⓑ	Ⓒ	Ⓓ
125	Ⓐ	Ⓑ	Ⓒ	Ⓓ
126	Ⓐ	Ⓑ	Ⓒ	Ⓓ
127	Ⓐ	Ⓑ	Ⓒ	Ⓓ
128	Ⓐ	Ⓑ	Ⓒ	Ⓓ
129	Ⓐ	Ⓑ	Ⓒ	Ⓓ
130	Ⓐ	Ⓑ	Ⓒ	Ⓓ
131	Ⓐ	Ⓑ	Ⓒ	Ⓓ
132	Ⓐ	Ⓑ	Ⓒ	Ⓓ
133	Ⓐ	Ⓑ	Ⓒ	Ⓓ
134	Ⓐ	Ⓑ	Ⓒ	Ⓓ
135	Ⓐ	Ⓑ	Ⓒ	Ⓓ
136	Ⓐ	Ⓑ	Ⓒ	Ⓓ
137	Ⓐ	Ⓑ	Ⓒ	Ⓓ
138	Ⓐ	Ⓑ	Ⓒ	Ⓓ
139	Ⓐ	Ⓑ	Ⓒ	Ⓓ
140	Ⓐ	Ⓑ	Ⓒ	Ⓓ
141	Ⓐ	Ⓑ	Ⓒ	Ⓓ
142	Ⓐ	Ⓑ	Ⓒ	Ⓓ
143	Ⓐ	Ⓑ	Ⓒ	Ⓓ
144	Ⓐ	Ⓑ	Ⓒ	Ⓓ
145	Ⓐ	Ⓑ	Ⓒ	Ⓓ
146	Ⓐ	Ⓑ	Ⓒ	Ⓓ
147	Ⓐ	Ⓑ	Ⓒ	Ⓓ
148	Ⓐ	Ⓑ	Ⓒ	Ⓓ
149	Ⓐ	Ⓑ	Ⓒ	Ⓓ
150	Ⓐ	Ⓑ	Ⓒ	Ⓓ
151	Ⓐ	Ⓑ	Ⓒ	Ⓓ
152	Ⓐ	Ⓑ	Ⓒ	Ⓓ
153	Ⓐ	Ⓑ	Ⓒ	Ⓓ
154	Ⓐ	Ⓑ	Ⓒ	Ⓓ
155	Ⓐ	Ⓑ	Ⓒ	Ⓓ
156	Ⓐ	Ⓑ	Ⓒ	Ⓓ
157	Ⓐ	Ⓑ	Ⓒ	Ⓓ
158	Ⓐ	Ⓑ	Ⓒ	Ⓓ
159	Ⓐ	Ⓑ	Ⓒ	Ⓓ
160	Ⓐ	Ⓑ	Ⓒ	Ⓓ
161	Ⓐ	Ⓑ	Ⓒ	Ⓓ
162	Ⓐ	Ⓑ	Ⓒ	Ⓓ
163	Ⓐ	Ⓑ	Ⓒ	Ⓓ
164	Ⓐ	Ⓑ	Ⓒ	Ⓓ
165	Ⓐ	Ⓑ	Ⓒ	Ⓓ
166	Ⓐ	Ⓑ	Ⓒ	Ⓓ
167	Ⓐ	Ⓑ	Ⓒ	Ⓓ
168	Ⓐ	Ⓑ	Ⓒ	Ⓓ
169	Ⓐ	Ⓑ	Ⓒ	Ⓓ
170	Ⓐ	Ⓑ	Ⓒ	Ⓓ
171	Ⓐ	Ⓑ	Ⓒ	Ⓓ
172	Ⓐ	Ⓑ	Ⓒ	Ⓓ
173	Ⓐ	Ⓑ	Ⓒ	Ⓓ
174	Ⓐ	Ⓑ	Ⓒ	Ⓓ
175	Ⓐ	Ⓑ	Ⓒ	Ⓓ
176	Ⓐ	Ⓑ	Ⓒ	Ⓓ
177	Ⓐ	Ⓑ	Ⓒ	Ⓓ
178	Ⓐ	Ⓑ	Ⓒ	Ⓓ
179	Ⓐ	Ⓑ	Ⓒ	Ⓓ
180	Ⓐ	Ⓑ	Ⓒ	Ⓓ
181	Ⓐ	Ⓑ	Ⓒ	Ⓓ
182	Ⓐ	Ⓑ	Ⓒ	Ⓓ
183	Ⓐ	Ⓑ	Ⓒ	Ⓓ
184	Ⓐ	Ⓑ	Ⓒ	Ⓓ
185	Ⓐ	Ⓑ	Ⓒ	Ⓓ
186	Ⓐ	Ⓑ	Ⓒ	Ⓓ
187	Ⓐ	Ⓑ	Ⓒ	Ⓓ
188	Ⓐ	Ⓑ	Ⓒ	Ⓓ
189	Ⓐ	Ⓑ	Ⓒ	Ⓓ
190	Ⓐ	Ⓑ	Ⓒ	Ⓓ
191	Ⓐ	Ⓑ	Ⓒ	Ⓓ
192	Ⓐ	Ⓑ	Ⓒ	Ⓓ
193	Ⓐ	Ⓑ	Ⓒ	Ⓓ
194	Ⓐ	Ⓑ	Ⓒ	Ⓓ
195	Ⓐ	Ⓑ	Ⓒ	Ⓓ
196	Ⓐ	Ⓑ	Ⓒ	Ⓓ
197	Ⓐ	Ⓑ	Ⓒ	Ⓓ
198	Ⓐ	Ⓑ	Ⓒ	Ⓓ
199	Ⓐ	Ⓑ	Ⓒ	Ⓓ
200	Ⓐ	Ⓑ	Ⓒ	Ⓓ

LISTENING SECTION

#	A	B	C	D
1	Ⓐ	Ⓑ	Ⓒ	Ⓓ
2	Ⓐ	Ⓑ	Ⓒ	Ⓓ
3	Ⓐ	Ⓑ	Ⓒ	Ⓓ
4	Ⓐ	Ⓑ	Ⓒ	Ⓓ
5	Ⓐ	Ⓑ	Ⓒ	Ⓓ
6	Ⓐ	Ⓑ	Ⓒ	Ⓓ
7	Ⓐ	Ⓑ	Ⓒ	Ⓓ
8	Ⓐ	Ⓑ	Ⓒ	Ⓓ
9	Ⓐ	Ⓑ	Ⓒ	Ⓓ
10	Ⓐ	Ⓑ	Ⓒ	Ⓓ
11	Ⓐ	Ⓑ	Ⓒ	Ⓓ
12	Ⓐ	Ⓑ	Ⓒ	Ⓓ
13	Ⓐ	Ⓑ	Ⓒ	Ⓓ
14	Ⓐ	Ⓑ	Ⓒ	Ⓓ
15	Ⓐ	Ⓑ	Ⓒ	Ⓓ
16	Ⓐ	Ⓑ	Ⓒ	Ⓓ
17	Ⓐ	Ⓑ	Ⓒ	Ⓓ
18	Ⓐ	Ⓑ	Ⓒ	Ⓓ
19	Ⓐ	Ⓑ	Ⓒ	Ⓓ
20	Ⓐ	Ⓑ	Ⓒ	Ⓓ
21	Ⓐ	Ⓑ	Ⓒ	Ⓓ
22	Ⓐ	Ⓑ	Ⓒ	Ⓓ
23	Ⓐ	Ⓑ	Ⓒ	Ⓓ
24	Ⓐ	Ⓑ	Ⓒ	Ⓓ
25	Ⓐ	Ⓑ	Ⓒ	Ⓓ
26	Ⓐ	Ⓑ	Ⓒ	Ⓓ
27	Ⓐ	Ⓑ	Ⓒ	Ⓓ
28	Ⓐ	Ⓑ	Ⓒ	Ⓓ
29	Ⓐ	Ⓑ	Ⓒ	Ⓓ
30	Ⓐ	Ⓑ	Ⓒ	Ⓓ
31	Ⓐ	Ⓑ	Ⓒ	Ⓓ
32	Ⓐ	Ⓑ	Ⓒ	Ⓓ
33	Ⓐ	Ⓑ	Ⓒ	Ⓓ
34	Ⓐ	Ⓑ	Ⓒ	Ⓓ
35	Ⓐ	Ⓑ	Ⓒ	Ⓓ
36	Ⓐ	Ⓑ	Ⓒ	Ⓓ
37	Ⓐ	Ⓑ	Ⓒ	Ⓓ
38	Ⓐ	Ⓑ	Ⓒ	Ⓓ
39	Ⓐ	Ⓑ	Ⓒ	Ⓓ
40	Ⓐ	Ⓑ	Ⓒ	Ⓓ
41	Ⓐ	Ⓑ	Ⓒ	Ⓓ
42	Ⓐ	Ⓑ	Ⓒ	Ⓓ
43	Ⓐ	Ⓑ	Ⓒ	Ⓓ
44	Ⓐ	Ⓑ	Ⓒ	Ⓓ
45	Ⓐ	Ⓑ	Ⓒ	Ⓓ
46	Ⓐ	Ⓑ	Ⓒ	Ⓓ
47	Ⓐ	Ⓑ	Ⓒ	Ⓓ
48	Ⓐ	Ⓑ	Ⓒ	Ⓓ
49	Ⓐ	Ⓑ	Ⓒ	Ⓓ
50	Ⓐ	Ⓑ	Ⓒ	Ⓓ
51	Ⓐ	Ⓑ	Ⓒ	Ⓓ
52	Ⓐ	Ⓑ	Ⓒ	Ⓓ
53	Ⓐ	Ⓑ	Ⓒ	Ⓓ
54	Ⓐ	Ⓑ	Ⓒ	Ⓓ
55	Ⓐ	Ⓑ	Ⓒ	Ⓓ
56	Ⓐ	Ⓑ	Ⓒ	Ⓓ
57	Ⓐ	Ⓑ	Ⓒ	Ⓓ
58	Ⓐ	Ⓑ	Ⓒ	Ⓓ
59	Ⓐ	Ⓑ	Ⓒ	Ⓓ
60	Ⓐ	Ⓑ	Ⓒ	Ⓓ
61	Ⓐ	Ⓑ	Ⓒ	Ⓓ
62	Ⓐ	Ⓑ	Ⓒ	Ⓓ
63	Ⓐ	Ⓑ	Ⓒ	Ⓓ
64	Ⓐ	Ⓑ	Ⓒ	Ⓓ
65	Ⓐ	Ⓑ	Ⓒ	Ⓓ
66	Ⓐ	Ⓑ	Ⓒ	Ⓓ
67	Ⓐ	Ⓑ	Ⓒ	Ⓓ
68	Ⓐ	Ⓑ	Ⓒ	Ⓓ
69	Ⓐ	Ⓑ	Ⓒ	Ⓓ
70	Ⓐ	Ⓑ	Ⓒ	Ⓓ
71	Ⓐ	Ⓑ	Ⓒ	Ⓓ
72	Ⓐ	Ⓑ	Ⓒ	Ⓓ
73	Ⓐ	Ⓑ	Ⓒ	Ⓓ
74	Ⓐ	Ⓑ	Ⓒ	Ⓓ
75	Ⓐ	Ⓑ	Ⓒ	Ⓓ
76	Ⓐ	Ⓑ	Ⓒ	Ⓓ
77	Ⓐ	Ⓑ	Ⓒ	Ⓓ
78	Ⓐ	Ⓑ	Ⓒ	Ⓓ
79	Ⓐ	Ⓑ	Ⓒ	Ⓓ
80	Ⓐ	Ⓑ	Ⓒ	Ⓓ
81	Ⓐ	Ⓑ	Ⓒ	Ⓓ
82	Ⓐ	Ⓑ	Ⓒ	Ⓓ
83	Ⓐ	Ⓑ	Ⓒ	Ⓓ
84	Ⓐ	Ⓑ	Ⓒ	Ⓓ
85	Ⓐ	Ⓑ	Ⓒ	Ⓓ
86	Ⓐ	Ⓑ	Ⓒ	Ⓓ
87	Ⓐ	Ⓑ	Ⓒ	Ⓓ
88	Ⓐ	Ⓑ	Ⓒ	Ⓓ
89	Ⓐ	Ⓑ	Ⓒ	Ⓓ
90	Ⓐ	Ⓑ	Ⓒ	Ⓓ
91	Ⓐ	Ⓑ	Ⓒ	Ⓓ
92	Ⓐ	Ⓑ	Ⓒ	Ⓓ
93	Ⓐ	Ⓑ	Ⓒ	Ⓓ
94	Ⓐ	Ⓑ	Ⓒ	Ⓓ
95	Ⓐ	Ⓑ	Ⓒ	Ⓓ
96	Ⓐ	Ⓑ	Ⓒ	Ⓓ
97	Ⓐ	Ⓑ	Ⓒ	Ⓓ
98	Ⓐ	Ⓑ	Ⓒ	Ⓓ
99	Ⓐ	Ⓑ	Ⓒ	Ⓓ
100	Ⓐ	Ⓑ	Ⓒ	Ⓓ

Answer Sheet

TOEIC TEST 4

READING SECTION

	101	102	103	104	105	106	107	108	109	110
A	Ⓐ	Ⓐ	Ⓐ	Ⓐ	Ⓐ	Ⓐ	Ⓐ	Ⓐ	Ⓐ	Ⓐ
B	Ⓑ	Ⓑ	Ⓑ	Ⓑ	Ⓑ	Ⓑ	Ⓑ	Ⓑ	Ⓑ	Ⓑ
C	Ⓒ	Ⓒ	Ⓒ	Ⓒ	Ⓒ	Ⓒ	Ⓒ	Ⓒ	Ⓒ	Ⓒ
D	Ⓓ	Ⓓ	Ⓓ	Ⓓ	Ⓓ	Ⓓ	Ⓓ	Ⓓ	Ⓓ	Ⓓ

	111	112	113	114	115	116	117	118	119	120
A	Ⓐ	Ⓐ	Ⓐ	Ⓐ	Ⓐ	Ⓐ	Ⓐ	Ⓐ	Ⓐ	Ⓐ
B	Ⓑ	Ⓑ	Ⓑ	Ⓑ	Ⓑ	Ⓑ	Ⓑ	Ⓑ	Ⓑ	Ⓑ
C	Ⓒ	Ⓒ	Ⓒ	Ⓒ	Ⓒ	Ⓒ	Ⓒ	Ⓒ	Ⓒ	Ⓒ
D	Ⓓ	Ⓓ	Ⓓ	Ⓓ	Ⓓ	Ⓓ	Ⓓ	Ⓓ	Ⓓ	Ⓓ

	121	122	123	124	125	126	127	128	129	130
A	Ⓐ	Ⓐ	Ⓐ	Ⓐ	Ⓐ	Ⓐ	Ⓐ	Ⓐ	Ⓐ	Ⓐ
B	Ⓑ	Ⓑ	Ⓑ	Ⓑ	Ⓑ	Ⓑ	Ⓑ	Ⓑ	Ⓑ	Ⓑ
C	Ⓒ	Ⓒ	Ⓒ	Ⓒ	Ⓒ	Ⓒ	Ⓒ	Ⓒ	Ⓒ	Ⓒ
D	Ⓓ	Ⓓ	Ⓓ	Ⓓ	Ⓓ	Ⓓ	Ⓓ	Ⓓ	Ⓓ	Ⓓ

	131	132	133	134	135	136	137	138	139	140
A	Ⓐ	Ⓐ	Ⓐ	Ⓐ	Ⓐ	Ⓐ	Ⓐ	Ⓐ	Ⓐ	Ⓐ
B	Ⓑ	Ⓑ	Ⓑ	Ⓑ	Ⓑ	Ⓑ	Ⓑ	Ⓑ	Ⓑ	Ⓑ
C	Ⓒ	Ⓒ	Ⓒ	Ⓒ	Ⓒ	Ⓒ	Ⓒ	Ⓒ	Ⓒ	Ⓒ
D	Ⓓ	Ⓓ	Ⓓ	Ⓓ	Ⓓ	Ⓓ	Ⓓ	Ⓓ	Ⓓ	Ⓓ

	141	142	143	144	145	146	147	148	149	150
A	Ⓐ	Ⓐ	Ⓐ	Ⓐ	Ⓐ	Ⓐ	Ⓐ	Ⓐ	Ⓐ	Ⓐ
B	Ⓑ	Ⓑ	Ⓑ	Ⓑ	Ⓑ	Ⓑ	Ⓑ	Ⓑ	Ⓑ	Ⓑ
C	Ⓒ	Ⓒ	Ⓒ	Ⓒ	Ⓒ	Ⓒ	Ⓒ	Ⓒ	Ⓒ	Ⓒ
D	Ⓓ	Ⓓ	Ⓓ	Ⓓ	Ⓓ	Ⓓ	Ⓓ	Ⓓ	Ⓓ	Ⓓ

	151	152	153	154	155	156	157	158	159	160
A	Ⓐ	Ⓐ	Ⓐ	Ⓐ	Ⓐ	Ⓐ	Ⓐ	Ⓐ	Ⓐ	Ⓐ
B	Ⓑ	Ⓑ	Ⓑ	Ⓑ	Ⓑ	Ⓑ	Ⓑ	Ⓑ	Ⓑ	Ⓑ
C	Ⓒ	Ⓒ	Ⓒ	Ⓒ	Ⓒ	Ⓒ	Ⓒ	Ⓒ	Ⓒ	Ⓒ
D	Ⓓ	Ⓓ	Ⓓ	Ⓓ	Ⓓ	Ⓓ	Ⓓ	Ⓓ	Ⓓ	Ⓓ

	161	162	163	164	165	166	167	168	169	170
A	Ⓐ	Ⓐ	Ⓐ	Ⓐ	Ⓐ	Ⓐ	Ⓐ	Ⓐ	Ⓐ	Ⓐ
B	Ⓑ	Ⓑ	Ⓑ	Ⓑ	Ⓑ	Ⓑ	Ⓑ	Ⓑ	Ⓑ	Ⓑ
C	Ⓒ	Ⓒ	Ⓒ	Ⓒ	Ⓒ	Ⓒ	Ⓒ	Ⓒ	Ⓒ	Ⓒ
D	Ⓓ	Ⓓ	Ⓓ	Ⓓ	Ⓓ	Ⓓ	Ⓓ	Ⓓ	Ⓓ	Ⓓ

	171	172	173	174	175	176	177	178	179	180
A	Ⓐ	Ⓐ	Ⓐ	Ⓐ	Ⓐ	Ⓐ	Ⓐ	Ⓐ	Ⓐ	Ⓐ
B	Ⓑ	Ⓑ	Ⓑ	Ⓑ	Ⓑ	Ⓑ	Ⓑ	Ⓑ	Ⓑ	Ⓑ
C	Ⓒ	Ⓒ	Ⓒ	Ⓒ	Ⓒ	Ⓒ	Ⓒ	Ⓒ	Ⓒ	Ⓒ
D	Ⓓ	Ⓓ	Ⓓ	Ⓓ	Ⓓ	Ⓓ	Ⓓ	Ⓓ	Ⓓ	Ⓓ

	181	182	183	184	185	186	187	188	189	190
A	Ⓐ	Ⓐ	Ⓐ	Ⓐ	Ⓐ	Ⓐ	Ⓐ	Ⓐ	Ⓐ	Ⓐ
B	Ⓑ	Ⓑ	Ⓑ	Ⓑ	Ⓑ	Ⓑ	Ⓑ	Ⓑ	Ⓑ	Ⓑ
C	Ⓒ	Ⓒ	Ⓒ	Ⓒ	Ⓒ	Ⓒ	Ⓒ	Ⓒ	Ⓒ	Ⓒ
D	Ⓓ	Ⓓ	Ⓓ	Ⓓ	Ⓓ	Ⓓ	Ⓓ	Ⓓ	Ⓓ	Ⓓ

	191	192	193	194	195	196	197	198	199	200
A	Ⓐ	Ⓐ	Ⓐ	Ⓐ	Ⓐ	Ⓐ	Ⓐ	Ⓐ	Ⓐ	Ⓐ
B	Ⓑ	Ⓑ	Ⓑ	Ⓑ	Ⓑ	Ⓑ	Ⓑ	Ⓑ	Ⓑ	Ⓑ
C	Ⓒ	Ⓒ	Ⓒ	Ⓒ	Ⓒ	Ⓒ	Ⓒ	Ⓒ	Ⓒ	Ⓒ
D	Ⓓ	Ⓓ	Ⓓ	Ⓓ	Ⓓ	Ⓓ	Ⓓ	Ⓓ	Ⓓ	Ⓓ

LISTENING SECTION

	1	2	3	4	5	6	7	8	9	10
A	Ⓐ	Ⓐ	Ⓐ	Ⓐ	Ⓐ	Ⓐ	Ⓐ	Ⓐ	Ⓐ	Ⓐ
B	Ⓑ	Ⓑ	Ⓑ	Ⓑ	Ⓑ	Ⓑ	Ⓑ	Ⓑ	Ⓑ	Ⓑ
C	Ⓒ	Ⓒ	Ⓒ	Ⓒ	Ⓒ	Ⓒ	Ⓒ	Ⓒ	Ⓒ	Ⓒ
D	Ⓓ	Ⓓ	Ⓓ	Ⓓ	Ⓓ	Ⓓ	Ⓓ	Ⓓ	Ⓓ	Ⓓ

	11	12	13	14	15	16	17	18	19	20
A	Ⓐ	Ⓐ	Ⓐ	Ⓐ	Ⓐ	Ⓐ	Ⓐ	Ⓐ	Ⓐ	Ⓐ
B	Ⓑ	Ⓑ	Ⓑ	Ⓑ	Ⓑ	Ⓑ	Ⓑ	Ⓑ	Ⓑ	Ⓑ
C	Ⓒ	Ⓒ	Ⓒ	Ⓒ	Ⓒ	Ⓒ	Ⓒ	Ⓒ	Ⓒ	Ⓒ
D	Ⓓ	Ⓓ	Ⓓ	Ⓓ	Ⓓ	Ⓓ	Ⓓ	Ⓓ	Ⓓ	Ⓓ

	21	22	23	24	25	26	27	28	29	30
A	Ⓐ	Ⓐ	Ⓐ	Ⓐ	Ⓐ	Ⓐ	Ⓐ	Ⓐ	Ⓐ	Ⓐ
B	Ⓑ	Ⓑ	Ⓑ	Ⓑ	Ⓑ	Ⓑ	Ⓑ	Ⓑ	Ⓑ	Ⓑ
C	Ⓒ	Ⓒ	Ⓒ	Ⓒ	Ⓒ	Ⓒ	Ⓒ	Ⓒ	Ⓒ	Ⓒ
D	Ⓓ	Ⓓ	Ⓓ	Ⓓ	Ⓓ	Ⓓ	Ⓓ	Ⓓ	Ⓓ	Ⓓ

	31	32	33	34	35	36	37	38	39	40
A	Ⓐ	Ⓐ	Ⓐ	Ⓐ	Ⓐ	Ⓐ	Ⓐ	Ⓐ	Ⓐ	Ⓐ
B	Ⓑ	Ⓑ	Ⓑ	Ⓑ	Ⓑ	Ⓑ	Ⓑ	Ⓑ	Ⓑ	Ⓑ
C	Ⓒ	Ⓒ	Ⓒ	Ⓒ	Ⓒ	Ⓒ	Ⓒ	Ⓒ	Ⓒ	Ⓒ
D	Ⓓ	Ⓓ	Ⓓ	Ⓓ	Ⓓ	Ⓓ	Ⓓ	Ⓓ	Ⓓ	Ⓓ

	41	42	43	44	45	46	47	48	49	50
A	Ⓐ	Ⓐ	Ⓐ	Ⓐ	Ⓐ	Ⓐ	Ⓐ	Ⓐ	Ⓐ	Ⓐ
B	Ⓑ	Ⓑ	Ⓑ	Ⓑ	Ⓑ	Ⓑ	Ⓑ	Ⓑ	Ⓑ	Ⓑ
C	Ⓒ	Ⓒ	Ⓒ	Ⓒ	Ⓒ	Ⓒ	Ⓒ	Ⓒ	Ⓒ	Ⓒ
D	Ⓓ	Ⓓ	Ⓓ	Ⓓ	Ⓓ	Ⓓ	Ⓓ	Ⓓ	Ⓓ	Ⓓ

	51	52	53	54	55	56	57	58	59	60
A	Ⓐ	Ⓐ	Ⓐ	Ⓐ	Ⓐ	Ⓐ	Ⓐ	Ⓐ	Ⓐ	Ⓐ
B	Ⓑ	Ⓑ	Ⓑ	Ⓑ	Ⓑ	Ⓑ	Ⓑ	Ⓑ	Ⓑ	Ⓑ
C	Ⓒ	Ⓒ	Ⓒ	Ⓒ	Ⓒ	Ⓒ	Ⓒ	Ⓒ	Ⓒ	Ⓒ
D	Ⓓ	Ⓓ	Ⓓ	Ⓓ	Ⓓ	Ⓓ	Ⓓ	Ⓓ	Ⓓ	Ⓓ

	61	62	63	64	65	66	67	68	69	70
A	Ⓐ	Ⓐ	Ⓐ	Ⓐ	Ⓐ	Ⓐ	Ⓐ	Ⓐ	Ⓐ	Ⓐ
B	Ⓑ	Ⓑ	Ⓑ	Ⓑ	Ⓑ	Ⓑ	Ⓑ	Ⓑ	Ⓑ	Ⓑ
C	Ⓒ	Ⓒ	Ⓒ	Ⓒ	Ⓒ	Ⓒ	Ⓒ	Ⓒ	Ⓒ	Ⓒ
D	Ⓓ	Ⓓ	Ⓓ	Ⓓ	Ⓓ	Ⓓ	Ⓓ	Ⓓ	Ⓓ	Ⓓ

	71	72	73	74	75	76	77	78	79	80
A	Ⓐ	Ⓐ	Ⓐ	Ⓐ	Ⓐ	Ⓐ	Ⓐ	Ⓐ	Ⓐ	Ⓐ
B	Ⓑ	Ⓑ	Ⓑ	Ⓑ	Ⓑ	Ⓑ	Ⓑ	Ⓑ	Ⓑ	Ⓑ
C	Ⓒ	Ⓒ	Ⓒ	Ⓒ	Ⓒ	Ⓒ	Ⓒ	Ⓒ	Ⓒ	Ⓒ
D	Ⓓ	Ⓓ	Ⓓ	Ⓓ	Ⓓ	Ⓓ	Ⓓ	Ⓓ	Ⓓ	Ⓓ

	81	82	83	84	85	86	87	88	89	90
A	Ⓐ	Ⓐ	Ⓐ	Ⓐ	Ⓐ	Ⓐ	Ⓐ	Ⓐ	Ⓐ	Ⓐ
B	Ⓑ	Ⓑ	Ⓑ	Ⓑ	Ⓑ	Ⓑ	Ⓑ	Ⓑ	Ⓑ	Ⓑ
C	Ⓒ	Ⓒ	Ⓒ	Ⓒ	Ⓒ	Ⓒ	Ⓒ	Ⓒ	Ⓒ	Ⓒ
D	Ⓓ	Ⓓ	Ⓓ	Ⓓ	Ⓓ	Ⓓ	Ⓓ	Ⓓ	Ⓓ	Ⓓ

	91	92	93	94	95	96	97	98	99	100
A	Ⓐ	Ⓐ	Ⓐ	Ⓐ	Ⓐ	Ⓐ	Ⓐ	Ⓐ	Ⓐ	Ⓐ
B	Ⓑ	Ⓑ	Ⓑ	Ⓑ	Ⓑ	Ⓑ	Ⓑ	Ⓑ	Ⓑ	Ⓑ
C	Ⓒ	Ⓒ	Ⓒ	Ⓒ	Ⓒ	Ⓒ	Ⓒ	Ⓒ	Ⓒ	Ⓒ
D	Ⓓ	Ⓓ	Ⓓ	Ⓓ	Ⓓ	Ⓓ	Ⓓ	Ⓓ	Ⓓ	Ⓓ

Answer Sheet

TOEIC TEST 5

READING SECTION

101	102	103	104	105	106	107	108	109	110
Ⓐ Ⓑ Ⓒ Ⓓ	Ⓐ Ⓑ Ⓒ Ⓓ	Ⓐ Ⓑ Ⓒ Ⓓ	Ⓐ Ⓑ Ⓒ Ⓓ	Ⓐ Ⓑ Ⓒ Ⓓ	Ⓐ Ⓑ Ⓒ Ⓓ	Ⓐ Ⓑ Ⓒ Ⓓ	Ⓐ Ⓑ Ⓒ Ⓓ	Ⓐ Ⓑ Ⓒ Ⓓ	Ⓐ Ⓑ Ⓒ Ⓓ

111	112	113	114	115	116	117	118	119	120
Ⓐ Ⓑ Ⓒ Ⓓ	Ⓐ Ⓑ Ⓒ Ⓓ	Ⓐ Ⓑ Ⓒ Ⓓ	Ⓐ Ⓑ Ⓒ Ⓓ	Ⓐ Ⓑ Ⓒ Ⓓ	Ⓐ Ⓑ Ⓒ Ⓓ	Ⓐ Ⓑ Ⓒ Ⓓ	Ⓐ Ⓑ Ⓒ Ⓓ	Ⓐ Ⓑ Ⓒ Ⓓ	Ⓐ Ⓑ Ⓒ Ⓓ

121	122	123	124	125	126	127	128	129	130
Ⓐ Ⓑ Ⓒ Ⓓ	Ⓐ Ⓑ Ⓒ Ⓓ	Ⓐ Ⓑ Ⓒ Ⓓ	Ⓐ Ⓑ Ⓒ Ⓓ	Ⓐ Ⓑ Ⓒ Ⓓ	Ⓐ Ⓑ Ⓒ Ⓓ	Ⓐ Ⓑ Ⓒ Ⓓ	Ⓐ Ⓑ Ⓒ Ⓓ	Ⓐ Ⓑ Ⓒ Ⓓ	Ⓐ Ⓑ Ⓒ Ⓓ

131	132	133	134	135	136	137	138	139	140
Ⓐ Ⓑ Ⓒ Ⓓ	Ⓐ Ⓑ Ⓒ Ⓓ	Ⓐ Ⓑ Ⓒ Ⓓ	Ⓐ Ⓑ Ⓒ Ⓓ	Ⓐ Ⓑ Ⓒ Ⓓ	Ⓐ Ⓑ Ⓒ Ⓓ	Ⓐ Ⓑ Ⓒ Ⓓ	Ⓐ Ⓑ Ⓒ Ⓓ	Ⓐ Ⓑ Ⓒ Ⓓ	Ⓐ Ⓑ Ⓒ Ⓓ

141	142	143	144	145	146	147	148	149	150
Ⓐ Ⓑ Ⓒ Ⓓ	Ⓐ Ⓑ Ⓒ Ⓓ	Ⓐ Ⓑ Ⓒ Ⓓ	Ⓐ Ⓑ Ⓒ Ⓓ	Ⓐ Ⓑ Ⓒ Ⓓ	Ⓐ Ⓑ Ⓒ Ⓓ	Ⓐ Ⓑ Ⓒ Ⓓ	Ⓐ Ⓑ Ⓒ Ⓓ	Ⓐ Ⓑ Ⓒ Ⓓ	Ⓐ Ⓑ Ⓒ Ⓓ

151	152	153	154	155	156	157	158	159	160
Ⓐ Ⓑ Ⓒ Ⓓ	Ⓐ Ⓑ Ⓒ Ⓓ	Ⓐ Ⓑ Ⓒ Ⓓ	Ⓐ Ⓑ Ⓒ Ⓓ	Ⓐ Ⓑ Ⓒ Ⓓ	Ⓐ Ⓑ Ⓒ Ⓓ	Ⓐ Ⓑ Ⓒ Ⓓ	Ⓐ Ⓑ Ⓒ Ⓓ	Ⓐ Ⓑ Ⓒ Ⓓ	Ⓐ Ⓑ Ⓒ Ⓓ

161	162	163	164	165	166	167	168	169	170
Ⓐ Ⓑ Ⓒ Ⓓ	Ⓐ Ⓑ Ⓒ Ⓓ	Ⓐ Ⓑ Ⓒ Ⓓ	Ⓐ Ⓑ Ⓒ Ⓓ	Ⓐ Ⓑ Ⓒ Ⓓ	Ⓐ Ⓑ Ⓒ Ⓓ	Ⓐ Ⓑ Ⓒ Ⓓ	Ⓐ Ⓑ Ⓒ Ⓓ	Ⓐ Ⓑ Ⓒ Ⓓ	Ⓐ Ⓑ Ⓒ Ⓓ

171	172	173	174	175	176	177	178	179	180
Ⓐ Ⓑ Ⓒ Ⓓ	Ⓐ Ⓑ Ⓒ Ⓓ	Ⓐ Ⓑ Ⓒ Ⓓ	Ⓐ Ⓑ Ⓒ Ⓓ	Ⓐ Ⓑ Ⓒ Ⓓ	Ⓐ Ⓑ Ⓒ Ⓓ	Ⓐ Ⓑ Ⓒ Ⓓ	Ⓐ Ⓑ Ⓒ Ⓓ	Ⓐ Ⓑ Ⓒ Ⓓ	Ⓐ Ⓑ Ⓒ Ⓓ

181	182	183	184	185	186	187	188	189	190
Ⓐ Ⓑ Ⓒ Ⓓ	Ⓐ Ⓑ Ⓒ Ⓓ	Ⓐ Ⓑ Ⓒ Ⓓ	Ⓐ Ⓑ Ⓒ Ⓓ	Ⓐ Ⓑ Ⓒ Ⓓ	Ⓐ Ⓑ Ⓒ Ⓓ	Ⓐ Ⓑ Ⓒ Ⓓ	Ⓐ Ⓑ Ⓒ Ⓓ	Ⓐ Ⓑ Ⓒ Ⓓ	Ⓐ Ⓑ Ⓒ Ⓓ

191	192	193	194	195	196	197	198	199	200
Ⓐ Ⓑ Ⓒ Ⓓ	Ⓐ Ⓑ Ⓒ Ⓓ	Ⓐ Ⓑ Ⓒ Ⓓ	Ⓐ Ⓑ Ⓒ Ⓓ	Ⓐ Ⓑ Ⓒ Ⓓ	Ⓐ Ⓑ Ⓒ Ⓓ	Ⓐ Ⓑ Ⓒ Ⓓ	Ⓐ Ⓑ Ⓒ Ⓓ	Ⓐ Ⓑ Ⓒ Ⓓ	Ⓐ Ⓑ Ⓒ Ⓓ

LISTENING SECTION

1	2	3	4	5	6	7	8	9	10
Ⓐ Ⓑ Ⓒ Ⓓ	Ⓐ Ⓑ Ⓒ Ⓓ	Ⓐ Ⓑ Ⓒ Ⓓ	Ⓐ Ⓑ Ⓒ Ⓓ	Ⓐ Ⓑ Ⓒ Ⓓ	Ⓐ Ⓑ Ⓒ Ⓓ	Ⓐ Ⓑ Ⓒ Ⓓ	Ⓐ Ⓑ Ⓒ Ⓓ	Ⓐ Ⓑ Ⓒ Ⓓ	Ⓐ Ⓑ Ⓒ Ⓓ

11	12	13	14	15	16	17	18	19	20
Ⓐ Ⓑ Ⓒ Ⓓ	Ⓐ Ⓑ Ⓒ Ⓓ	Ⓐ Ⓑ Ⓒ Ⓓ	Ⓐ Ⓑ Ⓒ Ⓓ	Ⓐ Ⓑ Ⓒ Ⓓ	Ⓐ Ⓑ Ⓒ Ⓓ	Ⓐ Ⓑ Ⓒ Ⓓ	Ⓐ Ⓑ Ⓒ Ⓓ	Ⓐ Ⓑ Ⓒ Ⓓ	Ⓐ Ⓑ Ⓒ Ⓓ

21	22	23	24	25	26	27	28	29	30
Ⓐ Ⓑ Ⓒ Ⓓ	Ⓐ Ⓑ Ⓒ Ⓓ	Ⓐ Ⓑ Ⓒ Ⓓ	Ⓐ Ⓑ Ⓒ Ⓓ	Ⓐ Ⓑ Ⓒ Ⓓ	Ⓐ Ⓑ Ⓒ Ⓓ	Ⓐ Ⓑ Ⓒ Ⓓ	Ⓐ Ⓑ Ⓒ Ⓓ	Ⓐ Ⓑ Ⓒ Ⓓ	Ⓐ Ⓑ Ⓒ Ⓓ

31	32	33	34	35	36	37	38	39	40
Ⓐ Ⓑ Ⓒ Ⓓ	Ⓐ Ⓑ Ⓒ Ⓓ	Ⓐ Ⓑ Ⓒ Ⓓ	Ⓐ Ⓑ Ⓒ Ⓓ	Ⓐ Ⓑ Ⓒ Ⓓ	Ⓐ Ⓑ Ⓒ Ⓓ	Ⓐ Ⓑ Ⓒ Ⓓ	Ⓐ Ⓑ Ⓒ Ⓓ	Ⓐ Ⓑ Ⓒ Ⓓ	Ⓐ Ⓑ Ⓒ Ⓓ

41	42	43	44	45	46	47	48	49	50
Ⓐ Ⓑ Ⓒ Ⓓ	Ⓐ Ⓑ Ⓒ Ⓓ	Ⓐ Ⓑ Ⓒ Ⓓ	Ⓐ Ⓑ Ⓒ Ⓓ	Ⓐ Ⓑ Ⓒ Ⓓ	Ⓐ Ⓑ Ⓒ Ⓓ	Ⓐ Ⓑ Ⓒ Ⓓ	Ⓐ Ⓑ Ⓒ Ⓓ	Ⓐ Ⓑ Ⓒ Ⓓ	Ⓐ Ⓑ Ⓒ Ⓓ

51	52	53	54	55	56	57	58	59	60
Ⓐ Ⓑ Ⓒ Ⓓ	Ⓐ Ⓑ Ⓒ Ⓓ	Ⓐ Ⓑ Ⓒ Ⓓ	Ⓐ Ⓑ Ⓒ Ⓓ	Ⓐ Ⓑ Ⓒ Ⓓ	Ⓐ Ⓑ Ⓒ Ⓓ	Ⓐ Ⓑ Ⓒ Ⓓ	Ⓐ Ⓑ Ⓒ Ⓓ	Ⓐ Ⓑ Ⓒ Ⓓ	Ⓐ Ⓑ Ⓒ Ⓓ

61	62	63	64	65	66	67	68	69	70
Ⓐ Ⓑ Ⓒ Ⓓ	Ⓐ Ⓑ Ⓒ Ⓓ	Ⓐ Ⓑ Ⓒ Ⓓ	Ⓐ Ⓑ Ⓒ Ⓓ	Ⓐ Ⓑ Ⓒ Ⓓ	Ⓐ Ⓑ Ⓒ Ⓓ	Ⓐ Ⓑ Ⓒ Ⓓ	Ⓐ Ⓑ Ⓒ Ⓓ	Ⓐ Ⓑ Ⓒ Ⓓ	Ⓐ Ⓑ Ⓒ Ⓓ

71	72	73	74	75	76	77	78	79	80
Ⓐ Ⓑ Ⓒ Ⓓ	Ⓐ Ⓑ Ⓒ Ⓓ	Ⓐ Ⓑ Ⓒ Ⓓ	Ⓐ Ⓑ Ⓒ Ⓓ	Ⓐ Ⓑ Ⓒ Ⓓ	Ⓐ Ⓑ Ⓒ Ⓓ	Ⓐ Ⓑ Ⓒ Ⓓ	Ⓐ Ⓑ Ⓒ Ⓓ	Ⓐ Ⓑ Ⓒ Ⓓ	Ⓐ Ⓑ Ⓒ Ⓓ

81	82	83	84	85	86	87	88	89	90
Ⓐ Ⓑ Ⓒ Ⓓ	Ⓐ Ⓑ Ⓒ Ⓓ	Ⓐ Ⓑ Ⓒ Ⓓ	Ⓐ Ⓑ Ⓒ Ⓓ	Ⓐ Ⓑ Ⓒ Ⓓ	Ⓐ Ⓑ Ⓒ Ⓓ	Ⓐ Ⓑ Ⓒ Ⓓ	Ⓐ Ⓑ Ⓒ Ⓓ	Ⓐ Ⓑ Ⓒ Ⓓ	Ⓐ Ⓑ Ⓒ Ⓓ

91	92	93	94	95	96	97	98	99	100
Ⓐ Ⓑ Ⓒ Ⓓ	Ⓐ Ⓑ Ⓒ Ⓓ	Ⓐ Ⓑ Ⓒ Ⓓ	Ⓐ Ⓑ Ⓒ Ⓓ	Ⓐ Ⓑ Ⓒ Ⓓ	Ⓐ Ⓑ Ⓒ Ⓓ	Ⓐ Ⓑ Ⓒ Ⓓ	Ⓐ Ⓑ Ⓒ Ⓓ	Ⓐ Ⓑ Ⓒ Ⓓ	Ⓐ Ⓑ Ⓒ Ⓓ

Answer Key

Actual Test 1

1 (B)	2 (A)	3 (C)	4 (C)	5 (D)
6 (D)	7 (B)	8 (A)	9 (A)	10 (B)
11 (C)	12 (B)	13 (C)	14 (A)	15 (B)
16 (C)	17 (C)	18 (B)	19 (A)	20 (B)
21 (A)	22 (C)	23 (B)	24 (B)	25 (A)
26 (B)	27 (C)	28 (C)	29 (A)	30 (C)
31 (A)	32 (B)	33 (A)	34 (A)	35 (B)
36 (D)	37 (C)	38 (D)	39 (D)	40 (A)
41 (C)	42 (A)	43 (D)	44 (B)	45 (B)
46 (D)	47 (D)	48 (A)	49 (D)	50 (D)
51 (C)	52 (A)	53 (C)	54 (B)	55 (B)
56 (B)	57 (D)	58 (A)	59 (A)	60 (C)
61 (D)	62 (B)	63 (B)	64 (C)	65 (A)
66 (D)	67 (C)	68 (C)	69 (B)	70 (A)
71 (A)	72 (A)	73 (C)	74 (C)	75 (D)
76 (D)	77 (D)	78 (A)	79 (B)	80 (B)
81 (C)	82 (B)	83 (A)	84 (D)	85 (C)
86 (D)	87 (B)	88 (A)	89 (D)	90 (A)
91 (C)	92 (B)	93 (D)	94 (C)	95 (C)
96 (D)	97 (B)	98 (A)	99 (D)	100 (D)
101 (D)	102 (B)	103 (A)	104 (A)	105 (D)
106 (C)	107 (B)	108 (A)	109 (D)	110 (D)
111 (A)	112 (A)	113 (C)	114 (B)	115 (A)
116 (B)	117 (C)	118 (B)	119 (D)	120 (C)
121 (A)	122 (B)	123 (B)	124 (C)	125 (A)
126 (D)	127 (B)	128 (C)	129 (C)	130 (D)
131 (D)	132 (A)	133 (D)	134 (B)	135 (C)
136 (C)	137 (B)	138 (A)	139 (B)	140 (C)
141 (D)	142 (B)	143 (B)	144 (D)	145 (B)
146 (A)	147 (A)	148 (B)	149 (B)	150 (D)
151 (C)	152 (D)	153 (D)	154 (D)	155 (D)
156 (B)	157 (A)	158 (C)	159 (A)	160 (C)
161 (D)	162 (B)	163 (C)	164 (C)	165 (B)
166 (C)	167 (B)	168 (D)	169 (D)	170 (A)
171 (B)	172 (D)	173 (C)	174 (D)	175 (B)
176 (A)	177 (C)	178 (C)	179 (D)	180 (B)
181 (D)	182 (B)	183 (D)	184 (A)	185 (C)
186 (A)	187 (D)	188 (C)	189 (B)	190 (C)
191 (B)	192 (B)	193 (A)	194 (C)	195 (C)
196 (C)	197 (B)	198 (C)	199 (A)	200 (D)

Actual Test 2

1 (B)	2 (C)	3 (B)	4 (A)	5 (C)
6 (D)	7 (B)	8 (C)	9 (A)	10 (C)
11 (B)	12 (A)	13 (A)	14 (C)	15 (B)
16 (A)	17 (C)	18 (B)	19 (A)	20 (C)
21 (A)	22 (C)	23 (C)	24 (B)	25 (B)
26 (A)	27 (C)	28 (B)	29 (C)	30 (B)
31 (C)	32 (C)	33 (B)	34 (B)	35 (C)
36 (A)	37 (D)	38 (D)	39 (D)	40 (B)
41 (C)	42 (A)	43 (C)	44 (D)	45 (C)
46 (A)	47 (C)	48 (A)	49 (B)	50 (B)
51 (D)	52 (A)	53 (C)	54 (D)	55 (C)
56 (C)	57 (A)	58 (C)	59 (D)	60 (A)
61 (B)	62 (A)	63 (D)	64 (A)	65 (B)
66 (D)	67 (A)	68 (D)	69 (C)	70 (A)
71 (D)	72 (C)	73 (C)	74 (C)	75 (D)
76 (B)	77 (A)	78 (C)	79 (A)	80 (D)
81 (A)	82 (B)	83 (B)	84 (B)	85 (C)
86 (A)	87 (B)	88 (D)	89 (A)	90 (B)
91 (B)	92 (D)	93 (A)	94 (A)	95 (B)
96 (C)	97 (B)	98 (A)	99 (B)	100 (C)
101 (D)	102 (D)	103 (B)	104 (C)	105 (A)
106 (A)	107 (C)	108 (A)	109 (A)	110 (B)
111 (D)	112 (A)	113 (A)	114 (B)	115 (C)
116 (A)	117 (D)	118 (D)	119 (B)	120 (B)
121 (C)	122 (A)	123 (B)	124 (C)	125 (B)
126 (A)	127 (C)	128 (A)	129 (C)	130 (C)
131 (A)	132 (C)	133 (A)	134 (B)	135 (B)
136 (B)	137 (A)	138 (D)	139 (B)	140 (C)
141 (C)	142 (D)	143 (B)	144 (C)	145 (A)
146 (D)	147 (B)	148 (D)	149 (A)	150 (D)
151 (A)	152 (B)	153 (D)	154 (D)	155 (B)
156 (C)	157 (C)	158 (C)	159 (B)	160 (B)
161 (D)	162 (B)	163 (B)	164 (B)	165 (A)
166 (C)	167 (B)	168 (D)	169 (C)	170 (B)
171 (D)	172 (A)	173 (C)	174 (C)	175 (B)
176 (A)	177 (D)	178 (C)	179 (D)	180 (D)
181 (B)	182 (A)	183 (B)	184 (D)	185 (C)
186 (B)	187 (C)	188 (C)	189 (B)	190 (D)
191 (D)	192 (B)	193 (D)	194 (C)	195 (C)
196 (D)	197 (D)	198 (C)	199 (A)	200 (C)

Actual Test 3

01 (A)	02 (B)	03 (C)	04 (C)	05 (B)	101 (C)	102 (D)	103 (A)	104 (D)	105 (A)
06 (D)	07 (B)	08 (C)	09 (A)	10 (B)	106 (D)	107 (B)	108 (A)	109 (A)	110 (C)
11 (B)	12 (B)	13 (A)	14 (C)	15 (B)	111 (D)	112 (C)	113 (D)	114 (B)	115 (C)
16 (A)	17 (B)	18 (A)	19 (C)	20 (A)	116 (B)	117 (C)	118 (B)	119 (A)	120 (C)
21 (C)	22 (B)	23 (C)	24 (A)	25 (B)	121 (B)	122 (B)	123 (C)	124 (D)	125 (D)
26 (A)	27 (B)	28 (B)	29 (A)	30 (C)	126 (C)	127 (A)	128 (A)	129 (C)	130 (B)
31 (C)	32 (B)	33 (C)	34 (D)	35 (C)	131 (B)	132 (C)	133 (C)	134 (A)	135 (D)
36 (B)	37 (A)	38 (C)	39 (A)	40 (B)	136 (A)	137 (C)	138 (A)	139 (D)	140 (B)
41 (A)	42 (B)	43 (A)	44 (A)	45 (D)	141 (A)	142 (C)	143 (D)	144 (C)	145 (D)
46 (A)	47 (C)	48 (A)	49 (B)	50 (A)	146 (C)	147 (B)	148 (C)	149 (A)	150 (C)
51 (A)	52 (B)	53 (D)	54 (D)	55 (B)	151 (A)	152 (B)	153 (C)	154 (A)	155 (B)
56 (B)	57 (C)	58 (A)	59 (B)	60 (D)	156 (C)	157 (B)	158 (A)	159 (D)	160 (C)
61 (C)	62 (B)	63 (B)	64 (C)	65 (A)	161 (A)	162 (A)	163 (B)	164 (D)	165 (B)
66 (C)	67 (B)	68 (B)	69 (D)	70 (C)	166 (B)	167 (C)	168 (A)	169 (B)	170 (B)
71 (B)	72 (A)	73 (D)	74 (C)	75 (C)	171 (D)	172 (B)	173 (A)	174 (C)	175 (B)
76 (B)	77 (A)	78 (C)	79 (A)	80 (A)	176 (B)	177 (A)	178 (B)	179 (B)	180 (C)
81 (B)	82 (B)	83 (A)	84 (B)	85 (A)	181 (C)	182 (A)	183 (B)	184 (A)	185 (D)
86 (A)	87 (A)	88 (B)	89 (D)	90 (A)	186 (C)	187 (B)	188 (C)	189 (C)	190 (D)
91 (A)	92 (C)	93 (A)	94 (D)	95 (C)	191 (B)	192 (D)	193 (B)	194 (B)	195 (A)
96 (D)	97 (D)	98 (A)	99 (C)	100 (C)	196 (C)	197 (C)	198 (D)	199 (A)	200 (A)

Actual Test 4

01 (A)	02 (C)	03 (D)	04 (D)	05 (D)	101 (C)	102 (A)	103 (A)	104 (B)	105 (A)
06 (A)	07 (B)	08 (B)	09 (A)	10 (C)	106 (D)	107 (C)	108 (D)	109 (D)	110 (B)
11 (A)	12 (A)	13 (B)	14 (A)	15 (A)	111 (D)	112 (B)	113 (C)	114 (C)	115 (A)
16 (B)	17 (C)	18 (B)	19 (A)	20 (C)	116 (C)	117 (B)	118 (A)	119 (B)	120 (B)
21 (C)	22 (B)	23 (B)	24 (A)	25 (A)	121 (D)	122 (C)	123 (D)	124 (C)	125 (C)
26 (C)	27 (C)	28 (B)	29 (A)	30 (B)	126 (D)	127 (C)	128 (B)	129 (C)	130 (A)
31 (B)	32 (C)	33 (A)	34 (C)	35 (D)	131 (D)	132 (C)	133 (A)	134 (B)	135 (D)
36 (B)	37 (A)	38 (B)	39 (A)	40 (D)	136 (C)	137 (B)	138 (D)	139 (D)	140 (A)
41 (D)	42 (B)	43 (A)	44 (D)	45 (D)	141 (C)	142 (C)	143 (C)	144 (B)	145 (D)
46 (C)	47 (C)	48 (B)	49 (D)	50 (D)	146 (C)	147 (B)	148 (C)	149 (C)	150 (C)
51 (A)	52 (B)	53 (B)	54 (B)	55 (D)	151 (A)	152 (B)	153 (C)	154 (A)	155 (B)
56 (A)	57 (B)	58 (A)	59 (C)	60 (A)	156 (D)	157 (A)	158 (D)	159 (B)	160 (A)
61 (C)	62 (D)	63 (B)	64 (D)	65 (B)	161 (C)	162 (C)	163 (A)	164 (A)	165 (B)
66 (B)	67 (A)	68 (C)	69 (D)	70 (D)	166 (D)	167 (A)	168 (D)	169 (B)	170 (D)
71 (A)	72 (C)	73 (C)	74 (A)	75 (C)	171 (B)	172 (D)	173 (A)	174 (C)	175 (C)
76 (B)	77 (A)	78 (D)	79 (B)	80 (C)	176 (B)	177 (A)	178 (B)	179 (A)	180 (C)
81 (D)	82 (C)	83 (D)	84 (A)	85 (C)	181 (C)	182 (A)	183 (B)	184 (B)	185 (C)
86 (A)	87 (B)	88 (B)	89 (A)	90 (A)	186 (D)	187 (C)	188 (D)	189 (A)	190 (C)
91 (C)	92 (A)	93 (A)	94 (D)	95 (B)	191 (A)	192 (B)	193 (A)	194 (D)	195 (C)
96 (B)	97 (A)	98 (C)	99 (B)	100 (C)	196 (D)	197 (C)	198 (A)	199 (A)	200 (C)

01	(B)	02	(B)	03	(C)	04	(B)	05	(D)
06	(C)	07	(B)	08	(C)	09	(A)	10	(A)
11	(C)	12	(A)	13	(A)	14	(C)	15	(B)
16	(C)	17	(B)	18	(B)	19	(C)	20	(A)
21	(C)	22	(C)	23	(A)	24	(B)	25	(A)
26	(A)	27	(C)	28	(B)	29	(C)	30	(A)
31	(B)	32	(D)	33	(A)	34	(C)	35	(A)
36	(B)	37	(D)	38	(C)	39	(B)	40	(D)
41	(C)	42	(D)	43	(A)	44	(C)	45	(D)
46	(C)	47	(B)	48	(A)	49	(D)	50	(A)
51	(B)	52	(A)	53	(B)	54	(A)	55	(C)
56	(C)	57	(A)	58	(B)	59	(C)	60	(D)
61	(A)	62	(D)	63	(D)	64	(B)	65	(A)
66	(A)	67	(D)	68	(A)	69	(D)	70	(A)
71	(C)	72	(B)	73	(D)	74	(B)	75	(A)
76	(D)	77	(C)	78	(A)	79	(D)	80	(B)
81	(D)	82	(C)	83	(D)	84	(A)	85	(A)
86	(C)	87	(B)	88	(D)	89	(A)	90	(D)
91	(A)	92	(D)	93	(B)	94	(C)	95	(B)
96	(B)	97	(B)	98	(A)	99	(B)	100	(D)

101	(C)	102	(D)	103	(C)	104	(B)	105	(D)
106	(D)	107	(D)	108	(A)	109	(C)	110	(C)
111	(A)	112	(C)	113	(C)	114	(D)	115	(B)
116	(B)	117	(C)	118	(B)	119	(A)	120	(B)
121	(B)	122	(D)	123	(C)	124	(B)	125	(C)
126	(B)	127	(B)	128	(B)	129	(D)	130	(D)
131	(B)	132	(D)	133	(B)	134	(A)	135	(A)
136	(B)	137	(B)	138	(D)	139	(D)	140	(D)
141	(C)	142	(B)	143	(C)	144	(A)	145	(A)
146	(D)	147	(D)	148	(A)	149	(D)	150	(A)
151	(A)	152	(B)	153	(D)	154	(C)	155	(C)
156	(B)	157	(C)	158	(B)	159	(D)	160	(C)
161	(A)	162	(A)	163	(D)	164	(A)	165	(C)
166	(A)	167	(B)	168	(C)	169	(B)	170	(D)
171	(D)	172	(C)	173	(A)	174	(D)	175	(C)
176	(B)	177	(C)	178	(D)	179	(B)	180	(C)
181	(D)	182	(B)	183	(A)	184	(B)	185	(C)
186	(D)	187	(A)	188	(B)	189	(C)	190	(B)
191	(C)	192	(D)	193	(D)	194	(B)	195	(C)
196	(A)	197	(D)	198	(B)	199	(B)	200	(A)